TOLD UNDER
SPACIOUS SKIES

THE UMBRELLA BOOKS

REGIONAL STORIES
ABOUT AMERICAN CHILDREN

TOLD UNDER
SPACIOUS SKIES

Selected by the Literature Committee of the
Association for Childhood Education International

Illustrated by William Moyers

THE MACMILLAN COMPANY · NEW YORK

To Children Everywhere

with the hope that these stories will
help them to understand the varied
patterns of life that exist in the
United States of America and the
courage and self reliance of its families

Foreword

Supper is ready. The children come running in and take their places. Father sits down and Mother places the food on the table. A short prayer is spoken. Warmth and happiness fill the room, perhaps even tears or laughter.

Dusk falls and the lamp is lighted. A kerosene lamp or a high-powered electric bulb—what does it matter? Outside the windows perhaps deep woods can be seen, or rolling hills, or apartment houses on a crowded street. Outside—the quiet hush of a sleepy countryside, the barking of a neighbor's dog, the roar of wind over a mountain pass, or the mechanical clatter of a noisy city. What does it matter? Within, the room sings with the drama of family life.

The scene varies—perhaps a father is absent; or a child is lost, a mother sick or unworthy of her trust. Perhaps children are thoughtless and unappreciative, parents lacking in understanding. The home is well-furnished or ill, the children have much or little of material things, of food to eat, of clothes to wear, depending on the economic status of the parents and their ability to challenge their environment. Perhaps the children are over-indulged and pampered; they may have just enough, or they may be lacking in the basic necessities for growth and strength. The parents may be away at work all day, or they may lead lives of luxury and leisure.

But the home—underneath all the outer differences—the home is the heart of security for the children. It may not even have a roof—it may be a tent, a trailer, a boat, a quonset hut, a tumble-down shack. American children live in all kinds. They sleep, some on the ground, some on the hard floor, others on resilient springs under the softest eiderdown.

The curtain rises, the lights brighten, the drama begins. A story of American life is told.

Perhaps it is a gay and happy story, perhaps it is sad and thoughtful, or it may be poignant and heart-rending. Through the medium of the printed word, the reader is transported into the lives of others for a short time. He lives with them in their particular setting—on lofty mountain, in crowded city, on farm, ranch, or river, in cotton field or peach orchard. He shares their struggles and their joys, his concern over their fate is actively aroused—he has forgotten himself and his selfish concerns for a while. He has been enriched by the experience of entering the lives of others.

Surely all our children deserve this opportunity, the right to know how others in our own country live.

Through such stories, the child learns not to ridicule or look down upon others because they are different from himself. He learns that the pattern of life is unending in its variety, and need not—in fact, should not—conform to a monotonous similarity. He learns to respect the rights of the individual, though of differing race, creed, culture, or background, in his struggle against conformity in a mass-production, machine-age world. He learns to appreciate people in all walks of life, not only his own. He acquires new respect and reverence for life in all its various manifestations. He begins to look deeper than appearance, deeper than a spoken accent or a surface materialism, deeper than social castes and conventions, to a sounder appreciation of human character. Only as a person is judged in the light of his environment, and the economic and social pressures which it brings on his way of life, can he be understood for his own true worth.

How can children learn to live, if their reading (a vicarious extension of living) does not present honest studies of human beings and their relationships one with another? Why should authors camouflage human character, delete from stories all mention of the tragic and sordid side of life, and present only a glamorized, synthetic picture of life as it never existed? No wonder children become dissatisfied, and turn to other, often spurious, sources of excitement and drama. If the basic essentials of real living are omitted from their reading, books and stories will be automatically cast aside.

Children are honest. They are never satisfied with the spurious. They want the truth, and they are strong enough to take it. They deserve the best—stories of real people as they really live, stories of the experiences which they face in everyday life, of their aspirations and struggles, of their joys and sorrows, and the ultimate rewards of courage facing impossible odds. Such stories will give children faith in the meaning, the purpose and beauty of life; courage in meeting it, and strength to reach beyond the gloom and shadows to the radiant joy of living.

Books are but words, but words are living symbols leaping up from the page, offering a vicarious sharing and enrichment.

In "The Return" by Elizabeth Coatsworth, and in "The Boy Jody" by Marjorie Kinnan Rawlings, the reader senses the dominating power of two different environments, controlling the lives of young Susan and the boy Jody in their families; an island world and a backwoods world, each complete in itself and furnishing drama all its own. Maria Gleit gives us, in "Paul Becomes a Nipper in a Mine," the vivid story of a boy's coming of age in an adult occupation. She lets her readers know how it feels, through Paul, her hero, to enter the shadowy world below ground with all its dangers, a world seldom mentioned in books for children. In "Buttons," Charlie May Simon takes us into river houseboat life and an unusual occupation, mussel-gathering.

Nan Gilbert's "The Meaning of the Word" is a perfect regional story, with all the dramatic give-and-take of farming as an occupation, and vivid true-to-life characters, who show not only their goodness but some of their faults as well, thus becoming unforgettable human beings. "Rosina's Chickens" by Gladys M. Relyea gives us in a satisfying way the real flavor of a region, the inherent drama of what might be a somewhat prosaic occupation, and honestly drawn characters taken from real life.

May these stories help to fill a long-felt need in the lives of our children.

—LOIS LENSKI

January 1, 1952

CONTENTS

xi

TOLD UNDER
SPACIOUS SKIES

The Return

An Island on the Coast of Maine

There were two families of Littles at the Harbor, and everyone distinguished them by calling them the Little Littles and the Big Littles. If it had been the Big Littles whose house the bank was taking over, no one would have been very much surprised; for the Big Littles were happy-go-lucky and rather lazy. Ben Little, the father, clammed or lobstered when he felt like it, and Mrs. Ben and the children knew the insides of the moving-picture house and the five-and-ten-cent store as well as they knew their own kitchen, and maybe better.

But the Little Littles were one of the hardest-working and thriftiest families at the Harbor. There was David, small, weather-beaten, blue-eyed, who would take out his lobster boat in as bad weather as any man on the coast,

"The Return" is from *Thief Island* by Elizabeth Coatsworth; copyright, 1943, by The Macmillan Company; reprinted by permission.

who ran one of the longest strings of gear and was usually the first man out and the last man in, so that the stuttering put-put-put of his motor through the darkness and fog an hour or two before dawn was the alarm clock by which many a man woke, yawning.

Then there was Susan, the image of her father. She wasn't twelve yet, but she ran the house pretty nearly as well as her mother had while she was alive. She looked like a brown Jenny Wren, small, quick, and bright-eyed. But she had plenty of temper and fun in her.

And John—John was a good boy too, smaller than most boys of his age but brown and hard as a little brown nut, upstanding, and taking no nonsense from anyone.

The Little Littles were good neighbors, church-goers, hard workers, and quick to lend a hand to others. It didn't seem right that it should be the Little Littles whom the bank was after. It all came of Dave's trusting what people said.

Harding Jones, who ran the wholesale lobster business at the Harbor, had been after him to put money into his company. He used to come around afternoons while Dave was working at his gear down at his wharf and talk to him, and talk and talk. "Keeping right after Dave, pesky as a deer fly," Aunt Jenny Green said afterward.

In the end he got his way. David Little mortgaged his house and put money in the Eastern Shore and Islands Lobster Company, thinking he was doing his family a good turn.

Now his money had disappeared. Harding said the company had failed, but he seemed as busy as ever working for the Maine Fish and Lobster Company, as it was

now called, and driving around in a new Packard sedan.
"I wouldn't trust that man with a bag of beans," Aunt
Jenny Green said. "Never liked his eye since he was a boy.
He used to copy my geography papers at school."

But it was too late to warn Dave now. The mischief was
done.

"Couldn't you borrow the money from someone, Dad?"
Susan asked, the evening the letter came saying that the
mortgage would be foreclosed.

"I might and I mightn't be able to, Sue," her father
said, looking up from the line he was baiting with pieces
of mackerel outside the shed door. "But I misdoubt I
could ever pay it back, and we've never been beholden
to anyone."

Susan didn't answer at once. She hung out her damp
dishcloth and stood looking for a moment, past the clothes-
line and the little vegetable garden, to the fishhouses and
wharves and the harbor beyond. The water lay so peace-
ful. Ted Barry was sculling in to his wharf and the gulls
were screaming back of the *Donna,* where they must be
gutting fish. The *Donna* had been new-painted and lay
at her mooring above a white reflection.

"Looks as though someone had been painting the gulls
too," Susan said. "They look awfully white tonight."

David Little nodded. His brown calloused hands were
moving expertly in the tangle of line and savage hooks,
tossing the line around and around the inside of the trawl
tub with a circular motion as he had it baited. The smell
of the bait was strong, but he and Susan were used to that.

Susan came and sat on the grass beside him with an old
basket filled with socks to be darned.

After she had worked for a while she said, without looking up, "Where will we go, Dad?"

She did not expect an answer right away, and she did not get one until the last of the three hundred and seventy-five hooks was baited and the line coiled in place.

"There," her father said, carrying the tub into the shed. "Now we're ready for morning. Did you leave the coffee on the back of the stove, Susan? I'm setting the alarm for one."

"Fishing's early work, Dad," Susan said. "Lobstering's not so bad. But if you're getting up at one you'd better go to bed now. I'll make you a couple of corned-beef sandwiches and there are some doughnuts for breakfast. They'll be out on the table, covered."

Her father stood in the door as though not quite certain what to say.

"You asked where we'd live, Sue," he remarked at last. "I don't know as I know. Your Aunt Jenny Green would take us in, I think, but I don't like to be beholden."

Susan looked up at him quietly.

"We'll think up a way, Dad," she said, smiling. "Maybe we could live in the fishhouse."

"I guess the bank takes that with the place," her father answered.

"But the boat?" she asked quickly.

"The boat's clear. Harding wanted me to mortgage it, but I wouldn't."

"Oh, that Harding!" she cried. "When I think of him—"

"Now, don't fret," her father interrupted quickly. "No

good crying over spilled milk. I'm a man grown, and if I take bad advice I must abide the consequences."

Susan sighed and put the socks back into her sewing basket.

"I'd best see about John's going to bed now," she said. "If I don't keep after him he'd read the eyes out of his head. And the light's most gone."

John was inside the house, reading *Swiss Family Robinson,* pressed against the west window.

He faced Susan indignantly above a gray-blue page.

"Of course I can see perfectly well," he insisted. "The light's fine. I've only got a few more pages before the chapter's finished."

"Good night, both," their father called, walking up the bare stairs a little more heavily than usual.

"Come along, John. This isn't like other nights," Susan whispered.

"No, and that's why I want to read—so I can't think about it," John said, lowering his voice too.

"Dad doesn't know where we can live." Try as she would, she couldn't keep a note of terror out of her voice.

John shut the book and put it on the table.

"There'll be a way," he comforted her. "Why, Sue, everyone lives somewhere—they have to."

"Dad won't be beholden."

John stood up. He was two years younger than Susan, and his head scarcely came above her shoulder. But he had almost a man's air of protection as he looked at her.

"I'll think up a way," he promised, and lighted a

candle from the shelf above the sink, and stumped off upstairs after his father.

In the fading light Susan stood alone in the room which was dining room and kitchen all in one. She had her father's breakfast to get ready for his chill arising in the middle of the night. She made three sandwiches and wrapped them in waxed paper with two doughnuts beside them, then set the table with his big cup and his plate. Then she walked quickly about, putting everything to rights on the shelves, pushing the chairs in place, brushing off the salt which had been spilled on the shelf of the stove. She heard a car go by, and a late gull mewing against the sky where the stars were showing.

Everything had been familiar to her since her eyes first opened on life, and yet nothing was now theirs. She took the broom and swept the room neatly and swiftly. Then she put her father's lantern, matches, and flashlight on the end of the oilclothed table where he could find them easily.

Still she was not satisfied. Tonight was a night different from any other. She did not need speech to know that her father lay sleepless overhead, blaming himself for having made them all beggars. He didn't need any speech from her, either, to know that whatever he might do was right in the eyes of his children. But still she went to the screen door and opened it softly. A moth tried to flap by her toward the candle, but she caught it in her quick hand and carried it fluttering between palm and fingers to its freedom.

There was one big yellow rose on the young rosebush by the front door. It was the first rose that the bush had ever had, and Susan had been very proud of it. But now she walked around the house to where it grew and picked it. No other flower but this would do. She put it in a mug beside her father's plate, smiling a little as the perfume reached her nostrils, gave the room a last troubled long look, closed the door, and tiptoed upstairs in her turn.

As she passed the door of John's room he came out like a small owl, his hair standing straight on end.

"Why, whatever!" she began. "You haven't even undressed! John, you look perfectly wild."

"I think better when I rub my head," he explained. "I know where we can live—"

"John Little! You *do*?"

"It's a perfectly grand idea, and it's ours. We can live in Grandmother Snow's old house on Thief Island."

In the candlelight Susan's brown face flashed first with surprise, then relief, and then uncertainty.

Susan stood thinking and thinking. Then she tightened her lips and threw back her head.

"Let's go speak to Dad about it."

David Little had not been asleep. As the children talked, sitting on the end of his bed, his eyes took on a faraway look. When they had finished speaking he nodded

"Wonder I never thought of it before," he said half to himself. "We'll be beholden to no one but ourselves on Thief."

The lobster boat chugged steadily out toward the sea, and the Harbor and green hills behind it dropped slowly from view. There was the house which was no longer theirs, disappearing behind its neighbors; there was the school, a little apart, and there the white church steeple whose bell had called them to church every Sunday morning since they could remember. Those spots of light color, which were beginning to separate now and make their way from the wharves back up the bank to the houses, were the shirts and dresses of their friends who had come to bid them good-by. Now they looked all alike, just pale dots moving away; and their own boat was another pale dot, moving away too . . . out and out over the blue glassy water toward the farther islands.

Father stood up near the bow at the wheel and Susan sat back on the afterdeck, her feet in the cockpit, keeping an eye on all the things stowed there and lashed into place. The water was so slick and shiny, with just enough motion to make it dark blue in some places and light blue in others, that there was little danger that anything would topple overboard. She kept the three hens in a crate beside her, where they would be cooler. Aunt Jenny had brought them as a parting gift.

Dad had opened his mouth to speak, but Aunt Jenny had said quickly, "Now don't you begin, Dave, talking about being beholden, because I've got more hens than I can bother with. Bill's putting in a sack of cracked corn for them; but mostly they'll get along on kitchen scraps, and the children will need an egg now and then. So don't say another word about it."

Susan had kissed Aunt Jenny and quickly carried the hens out of sight. They were big gray-and-black Plymouth Rocks with a sociable way of clucking in an undertone to one another as though they were discussing all that was happening, like three little old women in gray shawls and red bonnets. They would be company on an island.

But the real surprise was Bonny, the dun-colored cow, and Father himself had bought her; for they had never had a cow before.

Abdon Hall lent them his flatboat and there Bonny stood in the middle of it, being towed behind the lobster boat, chewing her cud as though she had gone to sea every day of her life. John had insisted on staying with her to quiet her if she should get excited—and to keep an eye on the dory, which made the tail of the convoy. Now he sat cross-legged, by the cow's head, watching the water near them, all its lights and darks reeling into new forms as they passed. The fumes of the exhaust drifted around John and Bonny, but neither of them seemed to mind it a bit.

"How are you getting on?" Susan shouted back to him.

At first he couldn't hear her through the put-put-put of the engine, but then he grinned and nodded. If he had any regrets at leaving the Harbor he kept them to himself.

Susan sighed. They were passing White Head, now, with the lighthouse, so bright against the blue sky. A cormorant on one of the red harbor buoys stood, with its dark wings spread and motionless, facing what wind there was, and the sun. It was a curious-looking bird, more like a creature than a bird, more like a kind of dragon maybe. Susan didn't know just what, but she did wish it would draw in its wings and look more lucky as they went by. But as long as she could see it, it stayed in the same position. Queer-looking. She hoped the cormorants didn't nest on Thief.

The sea pigeons kept rising from the water, much

smaller than gulls and dark, with round white cheerful spots on their wings. They were pretty birds, and so were the terns—so white with their black caps and swallowtails and the bright red of their beaks and legs. But it was the sea gulls she knew and loved best. She had heard their mewing and crying ever since she was a baby, and from the first day she had been outdoors she had watched them, like wooden toys, stand in a row along the ridgepole of her father's boathouse.

Perhaps some of these flying overhead now were ones she had thrown scraps to at the Harbor. Perhaps on Thief there might be gulls she had known, even if she had no way of recognizing them.

They were passing Pond Island now and the pot buoys were thick. She knew at a glance to whom most of them belonged, by their shapes or the way they were painted, as a range child might read brands on stray cattle. Not that she had often been out with her father; but every man at the Harbor had his buoys piled up by his fishhouse with the new lobster pots in the spring, and the young grass was daubed with the colors the men painted them when the wind promised a spell of fair weather.

Dad's were like a top with a handle or tail, all white with a blue line around them and D. L. burned into the wood.

When they left Pond, there was only Hayton's Island off to the right of the channel buoys; and then four miles beyond lay Thief, the last of the islands not counting Big Gull and Little Gull. But they were just rocks where the gulls nested and the fishing schooners used to anchor to gather barrels of fresh eggs for a long voyage, before the laws protecting the birds were made.

The hens were almost silent now. They had not gone to sleep, for Susan could see their eyes round and fixed, staring at the passing water. She looked behind. There was the flatboat with Bonny, placid as ever, as though she were standing in a meadow; and John still sat at her feet looking at the water, absorbed in his own thoughts.

The hills of the main were all different. She hadn't known they were shaped like that, round, like a row of green elephants kneeling. Small white clouds hung over them, very curly. They were land clouds, not these misty long shapes of the outer waters. She guessed where the Harbor lay. She couldn't see it, not even the spire of the church.

Suddenly Susan was afraid. There was too much space, too much water, too much silence. She passed a rope's end through the crate and tied it firmly in case of an unexpected swell, and crept forward over the litter of things to her father.

He didn't look at her, but he knew she was there.

"Like it, Susan?" he asked, without turning.

She gulped when she tried to answer, and now he did look at her.

"We'll be getting to the island soon," he said. "You'll have a busy day settling. I don't rightly know just how much there will be in the house."

That steadied her—steadied her more than if he had put his hand on her shoulder, or had scolded or soothed her. The house was her domain as the lobster boat and sea were his. Even in this vastness, this lonely waste of waters and lost bits of land, she was to have her place which needed her.

"Nothing was brought ashore after Grandma Snow died, was there?" she asked, her mind turning to practical matters. "But I suppose maybe a lot of things got borrowed and never returned. Not all the families had come to the main yet."

"No," her father said. "And the door was left unlocked a-purpose if anything was needed. Sometimes, too, a man will get stormbound out here; and he's glad of a roof he can get under, I tell you."

Hayton's had fallen astern. There was a swell now—a smooth breathing swell out of which three black porpoises wheeled, keeping them company before they circled southward. Thief Island was taking shape before them—a great cliffhead sloping back—and now they were approaching the fluke of gray shingles which formed the cove, with Bull Island just beyond like a whale calf following its mother.

There were three or four old dilapidated fish sheds built on the usual gray-white piers, and then a stretch of meadow, still white with daisies though they had gone by at the Harbor. As her father swung about and cut off his engine, Susan saw a row of houses sloping up along what must have been a road. They made quite a show, with their barns and sheds and out-buildings. Some even had picket fences. There were apple trees and lilac bushes about them, and vines over their doorways. But not a single wisp of smoke rose from their chimneys; not one door or window stood open to the summer sunlight.

"Hurrah!" shouted John from the flatboat, and Bonny, roused by the smell of meadowland, gave an inquiring moo.

David Little heaved an anchor overboard, let the line run out, and then stood looking shoreward.

"It's a pretty enough place," he said soberly, not to anyone in particular.

"Yes," agreed Susan, speaking low; for even their voices seemed an intrusion in the heavy silence which lay over the island and the deserted houses waiting above them.

Grandmother Snow's house was the oldest on the island, built in the early nineteenth century with two thick chimneys and small panes of glass in the windows. It had been painted red once; but the sea winds had worn its clapboards to a soft mulberry color, and the gray shingles of the roof were curled and here and there broken. Upstairs several panes of glass were out, and Susan, running to explore the rooms, found a big-eared owl staring at her from the footboard of the bed in the south chamber. Downstairs the mice and squirrels had made their nests; and from the musty smell, like old grapes in the air, it seemed as though at some time a fox had got in, hunting them, and perhaps had raised its young here instead of in some cave in the rocks. But mice and squirrels hid from sight at the first turning of the door handle; and at dusk the owl flew away and never returned again, leaving Grandmother Snow's house to the human beings who once more claimed it.

Susan, peering into old mirrors cracked and dusty, running up and down creaking stairs, drawing back curtains which fell to pieces in her hands, felt her heart cold and heavy in her breast. But John seemed delighted with all he saw.

"See, Dad, a stove and cupboards and an iron sink! We can bring in those barrels from the shed for chairs. There's a carpet in the parlor, too—we can put the melodeon over the place where the mice have chewed it. Which room do you want? We've got lots more to start with than the Swiss Family Robinson had!"

There was a loud hollow knock at the front door and Susan jumped. But it was only the unlatched door slamming in a gust of wind. Spiders everywhere, dead flies piled on the window sills, tracks of mice in the dust, little bones and skins in pellets in the owl's room . . . Oh, what a dirty house, she thought.

"We'd better carry up some more things!" she said and ran out into the sunshine.

Suddenly she noticed a number of orange butterflies around some pink milkweed blossoms in what had once been her grandmother's garden. They rose at her passing and settled again like a drift of flowers. "Where did you come from?" she thought. "All the way across the water from the main?"

But she ran on with a little lighter heart, down past Bonny, who looked up at her with dark contented eyes, and on to the crate of hens pulled up above high water-mark.

"Come here, John," she called to her brother, who had followed at her running heels. "Let's get the hens up first thing."

John took one end of the crate and Susan the other,

lugging the heavy hens, which clucked and scolded at every jerk all the way up the hill.

"Let's call them Molly, Polly, and Jolly," John suggested. He always liked to name things.

"I hope they *will* be jolly," Susan answered. "I suppose they'll have to say in here until you and Dad have time to build them a proper yard."

And the children left them peering from the slats of their crate at their new home.

It was an afternoon of very hard work. They found the old well, which fortunately was the best on the island. Dave Little and John carried pail after pail of water into the house, where Susan scrubbed and scrubbed. She couldn't stop till she had scrubbed every floor and chairboard, till she had washed down the windows and swept down the spiders.

"I'll do it all over with hot water and soap," she promised herself, "but now we've just *got* to get the house clean."

As she worked she noticed the floors with their wide smooth boards, and the panes of glass—a very pale lavender and thin with age. When she swept down the spiders in the parlor she saw the molding with suns and stars carved into it with a jackknife by her own great-grandfather probably. The paper was pretty—very old and faded, but there were scrolls of roses on it and bows of ribbons. It must have been a fine room once, for an island. There was a photograph of a lady in an oval frame with her hair smooth over her ears and wide sleeves. She looked like Susan's mother, but of an older day.

"That must be Grandmother Snow," Susan thought,

"but she's very pretty and young-looking. I suppose she wasn't a grandmother then. Maybe she wasn't even a mother."

After she had stared at the picture, the house began to seem different. She imagined her grandmother working beside her, a pretty young woman humming as she worked. Then she thought of her mother as a little girl flying in and out of the house with her brothers and sisters.

As Susan gave first one room and then another its cleaning, her father and John lugged up from the shore the things which were to go into it: the lamps, the pots and pans and dishcloths and dishes for the kitchen, their own beds for the bedrooms, the melodeon for the parlor. The old mouse-nested mattresses in the house were taken down into the shed, and the broken furniture. The curtains were all pulled down and burned back of the kitchen door.

"Time for supper!" Father called at last. "Here, John, you and I will see if we know how to milk Bonny. Susan, I'll fix you up a better kitchen table tomorrow."

It was nearly dark when Susan came downstairs tired in every muscle. There was a light in the kitchen and a fire in the stove, which felt good in the damp salt-smelling island air. Moths came fluttering in though the open door, but it was too late in the summer for many mosquitoes. A pail of fresh clean water stood by the sink ready for her, and there were tins ranged on the shelves and a basket of food, under a napkin, which Aunt Jenny had handed them just as they were getting into the boat. Father had fixed up a rather uneven table of boards across two sawhorses, and covered it with a worn oilcloth table-cover from the Harbor, and there were three barrels drawn up for chairs.

"It will do for now," Susan thought. She heard the small waves against the rocks, and Father's voice speaking to Bonny somewhere outside in the dusk, where the fire-flies were just beginning their sparkling dance.

Dave Little was out at dawn next morning, scouting about in his boat, judging where to put his pots. It would have to be by a trial-and-error method, at first. He could tell as he worked them where he got the best hauls.

But the first few days Father stayed home from lobstering to work at the house. He was a handy man and had brought his tools, of course. While Susan worked indoors, he and John tacked mosquito netting over the windows; made screen doors; mended the roof near the kitchen chimney where it was leaking; built a henhouse and fixed some old wire they found for a chicken run, where Molly, Polly, and Jolly made themselves very much at home. The sawhorses were evened off for the kitchen table, and new shelves were run up for supplies. The kitchen was, of course, the first room in the house to come alive.

Susan had brought all the curtains with her from the Harbor house. She sat at the doorstep with her workbasket, turning new hems, cutting down the cloth for these smaller windows.

John, exploring the loft above the shed, found it un-disturbed from Grandmother Snow's time. The neighbors or stranded fishermen had borrowed a good many things as they needed them from the empty house, but they had never searched the loft. There was a barrel filled with parts of a set of old-fashioned china with a design of wild roses on it. There was a little rosewood sewing table with a broken leg, tied to it by an old piece of rope, which had been put away years ago to be mended, and which Dave Little mended now and put back in its place in the parlor. There was a chair too, with very short rockers, which the parlor claimed, and a picture of a young lady and gentleman, painted on glass, which must have been thought too old-fashioned at some time but which Susan loved. A spinning wheel went back into the loft—"We'd just fall over it," David Little said—but a milking bench came down to stand by the sink for the pail of water. Folded away in a little haircloth trunk they found a few letters, a dress of sprigged muslin, and a sunburst quilt which Father and John insisted must go on Susan's little bed by its dormer window.

"It's as though Grandma were giving us presents," Susan said, standing back to admire the effect.

And it was Susan who must have the green-and-white washbowl and pitcher and mug which were standing in a dusty corner of the loft. Father brought another barrel to hold them, and Susan tacked white oilcloth over the top and hung a towel on a nail beside them.

"When the floor is painted . . ." she thought. "If only I had a little chair!"

She found the little chair herself, not in the loft nor in the shed, but in the barn with various odds and ends of lumber. It was a dark wood with flowers painted on it, and it even had two graceful arms. Nothing was wrong with it except that the cane seating had worn through. Father spent a whole evening whittling down an old board to the right shape for a new seat, and Susan made a cushion for it.

"It ought to go into the parlor," she said. "It's so pretty."

"It's for your room," her father answered. "The parlor looks well enough."

"You're not the only person who can find chairs, Sue," John piped up. "I've found two," and he disappeared, banging the new screen door behind him to return sandwiched between two chairs that seemed as big as he was.

"Now what do you think they were doing in the old pigpen?" he demanded. "But that's where they were."

These chairs needed more done to them than Susan's little armchair. They were mahogany and had had horsehair seats; but the wood was too stained and faded ever to take polish again, and the horsehair was in shreds. But Dave with dark brown paint, and Susan with pieces of flowered carpet cut from the ruined carpet in the hall, made two very good chairs of them, and into the parlor they went.

The three Littles stood surveying the room with a great deal of pride. With the soft rosy paper, the old carpet, the rosewood table, the rocking chair, the two straight-backed chairs, and the melodeon it looked old-fashioned and pretty. They were as excited as birds building a nest. Out of old twigs they were making something to suit them, something of their own for which they were beholden to nobody.

Susan ran out to pick a bouquet for the sugar bowl, and stood it on the melodeon. The windows were open—outside, the sea gulls were crying.

"I declare I'll bake a cake this afternoon," she said, nodding her head.

Susan was at home, in her own world again, with hens by the back door and sea gulls overhead and a house to keep for her family. She drew in a deep breath. "It will do!" she said as she looked around. "It will do fine."

—ELIZABETH COATSWORTH

High Water—High Wind

In the Woods of Vermont

The school bus stopped and the driver looked back over his shoulder. "I can't take you any further, Nate," he said. "The water's running over the bridge and I shouldn't take this heavy bus onto it. You'd better come down the hill with us and spend the night with your Aunt Polly."

"I've got to get home," Nate Wentworth answered. He gathered up his books in their strap and his tin lunch box. "Tomorrow's Saturday and Tom said he needed me. We're doing something important."

He slid down from the bus and stood looking at the

water of the brook, pouring over the floor of the bridge, running so fast that anyone who tried to wade through it would surely be washed away. Sally Owen, sticking her head out of the window, squeaked with terror. "You can't go over, Nate," she said.

"I'll climb along the beams on the side," Nate told her. "I've done it before; Tom and I used to go over that way for a game."

"We—ll," the bus driver agreed doubtfully. He was already backing away from the head of the bridge, for even the road leading up to it might be flooded at any minute. Early spring rain, and melting snow, had filled the brook deep and full; it was coming down the hillside, a roaring white stream full of leaves and sticks and jagged broken branches of trees.

This was a covered bridge, of the sort that has a roof and sides to keep the rain from rotting the wooden floor. It had stood for a hundred years, but before that it had been washed away once and there was always a chance that it might be swept away again by the wild water. Fifty years ago or so, someone had been wise enough to cut openings along the sides so that the high water could run through, instead of piling up and tearing the bridge away.

Nate climbed up on the great beam that braced the wall, halfway to the roof. He edged along it, putting his fingers into the chinks between the boards to hold himself steady. It was true that he and his much older brother Tom had tried this same thing before, but it was in summer, with the soft smell of dust inside the covered space of the bridge, and the brook going smoothly by below. This was different, with the foaming water and the tossing bubbles whirling past. It would be better not to look down, but he could not help hearing how loud and impatient the water sounded. "It's nothing," he kept saying to himself. And when he could not believe that any more, he kept repeating, "I've got to get home. Tom needs me."

He had reached the middle, where the going was hardest. He looked back to where the others were all watching him and saw that a car had slowed up in the road and now was inching its way past the bus. The school driver was making signs to the man to stop. "He's telling him not to go over while I'm climbing down," Nate thought, "for fear the bridge will break down with both of us."

Whatever the advice was, the man in the car paid no attention, even though the bus driver shouted at him. He began to move faster, then came into the bridge at full speed and went shooting through, the water splashing high all around him. The spray went over Nate and blinded him; he slipped and nearly fell. The lunch box, hanging from his arm, slid off and went away down the stream. The floor of the bridge gave a great, terrible creak, but it did not give way. Nate got to the end and jumped down, his clothes all wet and dripping, while the man in the car flashed out of sight up the road. The boy turned to wave to his friends and they sent up a cheer to see that he was safe. He looked up the road after the car. It was not one that he knew and certainly no neighbor would have treated him like that. He must hurry to get home, for already the wind was blowing through his wet coat.

It was good luck that it was not a cold wind, such as blows across the Vermont hills when winter has not yet made up its mind to go. There was snow still left on the higher mountains, but the sky was clear and the late February sun lay longer and warmer on the hillsides. But at any time the clouds could gather again, the water in the ruts of the road could turn to ice, and a storm could come down that might be rain or snow or crackling sleet. But as Nate looked up at the high woods above the house, as he felt the warm wind on his cheek, he knew that this weather meant that the sap was running in the maple trees, that Tom would be going up the hill at daylight to make maple sirup, and that Tom needed him.

Things had not gone very easily on the Wentworth farm that winter. Dad was away at the state capital, at Montpelier, helping to make the laws for Vermont. Nate was proud to tell people that he was in the legislature, but certainly they missed him. While he was gone, Tom, who was seventeen, was in charge of the farm, and Nate, who was seven, was his right hand helper. The weather had been very cold, the cattle and the horses had to be bedded very deep on bitter nights, and Nate knew that Tom was wondering whether the hay and the straw would last. Certainly there was no money to buy more, nor did the neighbors have any to spare. But now it was almost spring and time for sugar making.

Above the house, on the long slope of their mountain, was their "sugar bush," their forest of hard maple trees, delicate red and pink when they budded in the spring, burning with scarlet and gold in the autumn and, at the end of winter, yielding the gallons of sweet sap which was turned into sirup, into sugar, into money. Just at the time when nobody had a single penny to buy coffee or tea or tractor parts or shoes, then would come sugar making. There would be a stretch of cold, a sudden turn to warm winds and sunshine, and just as surely as the birds would begin to twitter and chatter in the branches, the trees would come to life and people would say to each other, "The sap is running."

The kitchen was warm when he came in, with the big oil stove sending out waves of welcoming heat. Mother was kneading bread in the big wooden trough, and Tom was out on the mountain, hanging up the first of the sap buckets. There was light behind the windows still; this was not like mid-winter, when you came home from school in the pitch dark, with your hands and feet nearly frozen. But darkness had come by the time Tom came in and sat down to the table, where bowls of soup were steaming at each place and the thick slices of ham were bubbling and popping on the stove while Mother took fresh rolls out of the oven. Tom and Nate sat opposite each other. Where Nate was short and chubby, Tom was long and lean, but they had the same dark blue eyes and the same square shoulders.

"The water's over the bridge, you tell me," Tom said. "That means that old Bill Oaks, who was going to help us tomorrow, won't get up here after all. We'll have to manage the best way we can, you and Mother and I. I'm glad you made it, Nate, getting across the bridge. Well now, I'm for bed."

Mother was the first one up in the morning, as she usually was, but Nate was the second, and went out by himself to harness the horses. Almost any boy of seven who lives on a farm can harness a horse; in fact, the horses are so well trained that they can almost harness themselves. As he walked across to the barn, the air was clear and the light was gray, that thin light of early morning that does not seem to cast any shadow. Up behind the mountain top was a white clearness that would soon be gold and then sunshine. But inside the stable it was still dark, with the horses pulling at their hay, but they backed obediently when he spoke to them and stooped their heads for the bridles. They were Ben and Betsey, big grays with arching necks and wavy manes. They moved carefully into place in front of the stone boat, so that he could fasten the girths and hook the tugs. A stone boat is a flat wooden sled that slips over ground and mud and snow alike and carries great weight without tipping over. Holding to Ben's bridle, he swung them round and brought them out of the barn.

Someone was standing at the gate of the barnyard, a sturdy, dark-haired girl of ten, their neighbor, Elizabeth Stowe, who lived half a mile up the road. "Mother brought me home from school early yesterday," she said. "So we got over the bridge before the water came up. We wondered how you would get home. Dad said you were going up to the sugar bush today and that Bill Oaks couldn't help you. Dad had to go over the mountain about some cattle, but he said I might be some help and that I might come. He said he wished you and Tom luck."

The warm stream of friendly words gave Nate a little glow of pleasure; they seemed to carry away that hard, cold feeling he had inside him when he thought about the man who had gone splashing by him in the car and had nearly carried them both into the water. Elizabeth trotted alongside, still chattering, as he guided the big horses over to the kitchen door, where Mother and Tom were coming out, turning up the collars of their coats. "It's colder," Mother said, and Tom looked up at the sky.

"I shouldn't wonder if we had snow by the end of the day," he declared. "That's why we will have to hurry, before the sap freezes in the buckets." Mother and Elizabeth got on the stone boat, and Tom and Nate walked beside, Nate holding the horses' reins.

In summer they did the farm work with a tractor, but in winter it was time to use the big horses, for nothing on wheels could clamber up the mountainside and go in and out among the trunks to reach the sugar house, the stout, square building set in a deep hollow with the trees towering high above it. Making maple sirup, though it is hard, cold work, has something of a holiday air about it and is like nothing else that goes forward on a farm. When once the sap is running, a hole is cut in the bark of the tree and a little spout stuck in, with a tin bucket hanging under it. The sap runs out, seeming to come slowly, drip, drip, drip, but the buckets fill up more quickly than a person would think. The stone boat, with two barrels on it, goes through the woods, the buckets are emptied into the barrels, and the load goes bumping and crawling over the rough ground to draw up by the sugar house. Here is the tank to pour the sap into, here is the hot fire to boil it, and the open cupola in the roof to carry away the steam. There is sweet cold air, there are fire-reddened faces and calls back and forth through the woods, and steadily trudging feet going back and forth. No one rests as long as the sap is running.

Among the stumps were some old patches of worn-out snow, which had lain there since the first fall last October. Stamped into the white here and there was a sharp hoof print, where a deer had gone by, and Nate saw one mark of a big, cat-like paw, that might be a bob-cat's or that of a Canada lynx. Mother and Elizabeth set to work to build the fire under the tank while Tom and Nate went here and there emptying the buckets and filling up the barrels with the clear, white liquid. It was getting steadily colder; the sun was gone and the horses' breath went up in steam between the bare trees. The barrels were emptied into the big tank outside the house, from which the sap ran into the shallower one over the fire inside; here it went back and forth in little channels, always dropping lower and lower and getting heavier and heavier as the water in it boiled away. At last it came down to the far end, where Mother tested and tasted until finally she opened a faucet and the warm, gold stream flowed out into the bright tins in which it was closed and sealed. Though all the sounds of the crackling fire, the stamping of the horses outside, and the rustle of dry leaves swept by the wind, ran the stream of Elizabeth's cheerful chatter, always gay even after she had been carrying wood for hours, always full of laughter even though the cold swept in like a jealous enemy whenever the door opened for the boys to come inside.

"We'll change work for a while," Mother said at last. "You boys are cold and Elizabeth and I are stiff in the back from carrying wood."

"I'll go with you. I'm not cold," Nate said. "And I will have to show you where we hung the buckets."

"Don't go too far away," Tom directed. "There's certainly going to be snow, and it might come with a rush. But I really think we won't have it for a good hour yet."

Anyone could tell from the raw feeling of the air that the snow was coming, that it was going to be much colder, and that the sap would soon stop running. Mother led the horses while Elizabeth and Nate ran here and there; they climbed high up the slope of the mountain where Tom had hung the farthest buckets. Nate was pushing through the thick bushes, a full sap bucket in each hand, while Elizabeth climbed higher, to make sure they had got them all. Nate came down toward the horses, passed a cleared space where he could look out northward, and suddenly shouted, "Run."

A huge iron-gray cloud was boiling up from behind the highest ridge, and a breath of icy air went sweeping through the treetops, bending and whipping the branches, though, so far, there was nothing stirring below. Elizabeth came jumping and scrambling down the slope; Nate dumped his sap into the barrel; he took the bridle of one horse and Mother the other. "Get on the stone boat and steady the barrels," she told Elizabeth. Nate smacked big Betsey on the flank and they were off downhill with a rush, the horses choosing their own way, most of the time, but needing a steady hand to hold them back with the stone boat bumping behind their heels.

The wind was roaring through the big trunks now, and the snow was coming, wet and stinging, into their faces whenever they turned to make a wide curve and avoid upsetting their burden of barrels. They needed Tom's shout to guide them, "This way, this way, as quick as you can." Nate swung the horses round to the door of the little storage shed where the wood was kept and where there was a narrow space left just big enough to hold them. He banged the door at their heels; Tom had his arm around Mother and was holding Elizabeth by the hand as they fought their way across the little space to the sugar house. How warm and safe it seemed inside, though the fire veered and fluttered and set up showers of sparks, while the cloud of white steam was torn to tatters as the wind swept it away overhead. After taking a few minutes to get their breath, Tom and Nate went out again, to put blankets on the horses and to empty the barrels into the tank outside. The sap would not freeze at once, there next to the warm house; they would be able to boil the very last of it and would not waste a drop. The wind was beating so furiously against the door, when they came in, that they had to push both together to get it shut and drop the wooden bar that held it.

"Heaven help anyone that's caught out without any shelter near," Tom said. Nate was knocking the snow off his eyebrows and eyelashes so that he could see, and Elizabeth was picking up an armful of wood to add to the fire.

"Isn't it about time we had lunch?" she suggested briskly.

Mother had brought a big basket with thick meat sandwiches and jars of applesauce and beans, and a bowl of biscuits which she set down to warm before the coals. They ate them for dessert, with the hot, new sirup poured over them, tasting like nectar as it came so fresh from the cold woods and the skillful boiling. They sat on boxes and logs, their feet were cold on the bare earth floor, but they laughed and joked as they ate their fill. And when they finished, Elizabeth sang. When neighborhoods gathered to spend a gay evening of games and roasting apples and popping corn, it was always to young Elizabeth Stowe they turned for music at the end of the party. She had a rare voice and they all loved to hear her. The little house now was full of bright, brave music, and they all joined in the last chorus, although Tom, leaning back against the wall, was nodding a trifle. Then they were quiet, and in the stillness Nate, who had the quickest ears, lifted his head to listen. He jumped up, ran to open the door and to let the wind bring in the sound. They all heard it now, a noise that might have been an automobile horn and then, a little after, a faint distant shout. Someone out in the snow was calling for help.

Tom got up and buttoned his jacket. Mother put her hand on his arm, but he shook his head. "No one could live long out there in this snow," he said. "It doesn't sound as though he were a great way off."

"I'm going with you," Nate announced. "You said it isn't far." Tom looked doubtful but nodded reluctantly.

"All right if it isn't too far," he agreed. He told his mother and Elizabeth to open the door now and then so that the fire would shine out. "We can see it at least until we get beyond the shoulder of the hill," he said. "A lantern wouldn't last us a minute in this wind."

The two boys went out into the cold, with the snow in a thick cloud swirling around them. Sometimes it was so thick they could hardly see each other; sometimes the cloud broke and they could look across the dark slope of the mountain. They had sat longer by the fire than they thought, and what little afternoon light there had been was beginning to disappear. They looked back to see the fire shine from the cabin door and they stood to listen. The sound came to them once more, carried down the wind, but their own answering shout was swept backwards the moment it left their lips.

"Didn't you think, at first, you heard a car horn blowing?" Nate said.

"It might be that someone who didn't know very much had tried to drive a car up the old logging road," Tom answered. "Now he's stalled and is trying to get down the mountain on foot." They listened again and Tom spoke slowly. "It's farther off than it was; he's going away from us." He was silent a moment, but Nate knew what he would say when he spoke again. "You'll have to go back," he said gently to his brother. "This is going to be a long tramp until I—until I find that man. And you can't keep up, boy; we both know it. While you can still see the light from the sugar house, you'll have to go, so I won't have to go back with you."

Nate stammered. His spirit was hot within him, but he knew that Tom was right. He turned about, his head drooping. Once he looked back, but Tom had already disappeared into the whirl of white. Nate walked slowly, than suddenly he lifted his head, went faster, ran, and burst in at the door. "Mother, Elizabeth," he cried. "Come quick. I know what we must do."

He ran to the shed where the wood was piled. He gathered his arms full and went stumbling back along the way he and Tom had gone. "We have to build a fire, a big one," he explained to Mother and Elizabeth as they followed him, loaded too. "If it's big enough they can see it all across the valley. Bring all you can. Elizabeth, get a basket and fill it with chips."

They piled the wood higher and higher; they laid in the chips and dry branches for kindling; they brought a burning brand from the sugar house, and thrust it deep into the pile. It smoked, the flame at its end grew smaller and smaller, it was only a pinpoint, it was going out. No, there was still a little glow; then the dry twig near it began to sputter and sparkle and the sharp sweet smell of live smoke came up into their faces. The flame crept, quivered, and suddenly leaped high to shine out through the blackness and the whiteness of the storm. All three went steadily back and forth, trampling the snow as it grew deeper and deeper, feeding the blaze that must not fail.

It might have been nearly an hour later that Tom Wentworth came struggling up the hill, his arm around the half-frozen man he was helping through the snow. Three muffled figures greeted him as he came into the circle of the firelight. "How ever did you think of that?" he asked with stiff lips, holding out his hands to the warmth of the fire.

"It was Nate's idea," Mother said.

"I would never have found you without it," Tom managed to say. "Now let's get this fellow into the house."

Hot drinks and warm food revived the two very quickly. As the stranger drew close to the fire, Nate drew a quick breath. A boy's mind is sharp to remember faces, and this, he knew, was the man who had flashed by him on the bridge. Tom was asking him a question.

"What were you doing, with a car, so far up on the logging road?"

"I was looking at land," the man answered. "I buy land, and sell it again. And I've found that after there's been a hard winter, people at this time of year are apt to sell out cheap." Tom's face looked very grim.

"Not around here, they don't," he said. "They just hold on all the harder. You're wasting your time."

Mother got up and began putting things into the basket. "The wind's dropping," she said. "As soon as you can walk we'd better be getting home."

Nate and Elizabeth went to the door to look out. It was true that the wind was nearly gone by; the snow was coming down thick and steady, making swirls and pockets around the roots of the trees.

Elizabeth said, "The bus will never be able to get up to us on Monday. There will be ice on the bridge and we'll have to go down to school on skis."

—CORNELIA MEIGS

Mountain Born

A New Hampshire Sheep Farm

It was a wild March day and the sky was full of tattered clouds, like a flock of heavy-wooled sheep. The wind was at their heels every moment and never once were they allowed to rest or change their course. On the far side of the mountains there was a pasture that the wind was heading them toward.

The wind was everywhere—banging doors in the house, flapping clothes on the line, whirling dried leaves into the air, searching out winter in all its hiding places and preparing the way for spring. But not all the gustiness of the wind could rise louder than the baaings of sheep in the barn—sounds deep and tender, sounds high and imperative.

The woman in the house plunged her hands into the

soapy water of the tub. It was a day for washing with such a wind for drying. Carrying out her next lot of clean clothes to the line, she set the basket down and ran her hands over the drying things, smiling at their crispness, thinking how good it was to work when nature worked with one. She snapped out a man's shirt, blue and of a tough linen with strong seams, fastening it with pins to the line. Then she snapped out a child's shirt, blue and of the same tough linen with the same strong seams. The wind puffed at the little shirt, filling it prankishly. For a moment it looked as if the little shirt were trying to be the big one, just by puffing itself up. The woman smiled again.

"So like his father in everything," she thought to herself, then turned and went back to the house.

Soon it would be time to start dinner, for the men would be hungry after their work with the lambs. She went toward the stove. The door behind her slammed but she gave it no heed, thinking it was only another one of the wind's tricks. Then, at the sound of a man's heavy footsteps on the floor, she looked around. It was Andrew, carrying something in his arms, something very small and wet.

Martha let out a quick sound and dropped the spoon into the soup she was stirring. She went toward her husband and held out her arms.

"It's the first we've lost today, one of twins and the mother is busy with the other," he said slowly. "Thirty-four fine new lambs and now this little one—" he hesitated —"dead." He moved near the stove and laid it gently in the lambing box. "I'll tend to it presently, the hide is worth saving."

"Are there many more to come?" Martha asked.

"No, not more than three or four. Benj will be in soon for his dinner. I'll come later."

He was gone and the door had closed behind him.

Martha bent over the box and took the lamb into her arms. She felt stunned by the abrupt close of life on this day when life seemed to have such fresh beginnings—the bright sun, the charging winds, the lively sounds from the barn. Stroking the small creature with her fingers, she shook her head over it. Sometimes there was life in these lambs, a tiny spark that could be fanned into flame by tender care; but this one was dead. Andrew had said so. Such a fine lamb, too, a black one. She laid it down again and went back to stirring the soup.

There was a shout of laughter outdoors and the patter of swift feet, then Peter stood in the doorway. His cheeks were tingling and his dark hair had been tousled by the wind. Early that morning he had gone with the calves to their pasture up the hillside so the barn might be free for the sheep.

"Mother, Mother," he began, fresh with all the joyous happenings he had to tell her; then his quick eyes caught the still form in the box by the stove. "Oh," his voice dropped to a whisper, "there is a lamb asleep! I must not wake it, must I?"

Softly he tiptoed across the kitchen and knelt down by the side of the box. His hand reached out and stroked the curly head.

Martha stood beside him. The boy looked up at her. "The lamb is asleep, isn't it?"

"The lamb—" Martha began, reaching vaguely for words, then she dropped to her knees beside the boy and put her arms around him, drawing him close to her. He had not seen death yet. Why should he now when he was only six years old? "The lamb, Peter, is asleep. It will wake soon. Now go and call Benj to his dinner."

Peter went running from the kitchen and Martha bent down again over the stiffening form in the box. Perhaps there was still time to find the spark and coax it into flame.

She took a cloth and dipped it into the tub of clean hot water that stood beside her washtub; then she wrapped the lamb in it. She warmed a few drops of milk on the stove and put them in her palm, pressing her palm to the cold nose and trying to force a drop or two between the tiny tight-clenched teeth. So soon a newborn lamb must have milk or there is no hope for it at all.

She heard the tramp of Benj's feet and the high tones of Peter's voice telling of the lamb asleep by the stove. Good Benj, she thought, he had worked with Andrew on the farm long before she had come to be mistress of the house and he loved the boy. He could be trusted to say nothing that would distress Peter. Martha set the lamb down and hastily poured out two bowls of the thick soup, placing them on the table.

"Father will have his soup in the barn," Peter announced, "and may I take mine to have with him?"

"Yes, of course," Martha nodded, filling another bowl and watching the boy as he went slowly to the barn, carrying the two bowls carefully.

"Is there work for Peter, too?" she asked, turning to Benj.

"There's work for all of us," the old man said. "It's something to keep near forty lambs feeding regularly, for some have sense and some have not, and some of the ewes are good mothers and some are not."

Martha bent over the box to change the cloth for a fresh hot one. Benj stood beside her, giving her help with his silent encouragement and words now and then that came from the slow deep wisdom he had gained through many years of shepherding. The lamb was still stiff and cold, save for the steamy warmth of the hot cloth against its fleece.

"Lifeless, is it?" Benj murmured.

Martha looked up at him. "Andrew said it was dead."

"Andrew does not know as much as God," Benj said. He knelt down and took the lamb in his arms. Pressing his bearded lips close to the black nostrils he blew into them, then he slapped the ribs gently, first one side, then the other.

"Let us have a basin of water as hot as your hand can bear," he said.

Martha hastened to get it.

"And dry cloths, warm dry cloths," Benj went on as he immersed the lamb in the water. He dried it carefully, wrapping it in the cloths Martha brought until only its head showed when he laid it back in the box.

"Keep it warm. Give it milk as soon as it will drink, and then often." In easy gulps Benj downed his bowl of soup and went back to the barn.

Martha worked with the lamb all through the afternoon, keeping the cloths that wrapped its body hot, pressing drops of milk against unwilling lips. She was glad her men folk were so occupied, for she did not want Andrew to chide her for her foolishness nor Peter to be troubled by it.

Sitting down in a low chair by the stove she took the lamb up in her arms and held it close to her, remembering how she had felt when Peter was born and she had held him in her arms for the first time. Once the boy had come safely into the world she realized how her prayers for him had changed. It was not for life and a strong body to hold its treasures she prayed, for he had these; he was a sturdy, shapely baby from the first; it was that he might be kind and useful to the world and that his fellow men might love him. Such a short way could she go with him on that path that was his life, only a few years she would have his hand in hers; then for a few more years he would walk beside her; then he would be a man going his way alone, but if it were a way of kindness, the memory of that first day would always fill her with joy. Recalling it all, she clasped the lamb tightly and for that moment it was the baby Peter and her thoughts for the lamb were the thoughts she had had for her son.

Suddenly there was a convulsive movement in her arms and the lamb's tail quivered as if the wind were at it. Then it became as still and stiff again as it had been since Andrew laid it in the box. But hope had come to Martha's heart, definite and sure. Life was there. It was stirring in the tiny body.

She loosened the warm cloths that the limbs might have more freedom. She poured some milk into the palm of her hand and pressed it to the lamb's mouth. For a moment nothing happened. The next moment there was the faintest sucking sound—scarcely to be heard at all save by one whose ears were straining for it—and there the cupped palm was and no milk in it.

Martha sat back in her chair, half singing, half sobbing with the joy that ran through her. The little tail quivered again and the nose pushed greedily into the empty palm. Martha held the warm body to her, so close that she could feel the sound as it came from way within, the sound that found its way up the small throat and forced open the tight-clenched jaw, the sound of that first querulous ba-a-a.

Taking the cloth off, she set the lamb down on the floor. It wobbled on unsteady legs splayed wide, shook its head, looked up at her, and nuzzled against her skirt. Soon it sucked all the milk she would give it from a nursing bottle and gradually strength came into the shaky legs.

Now twilight came sifting into the room, making pools of shadow. Martha had not thought to light the lamp, so busy was she with the lamb as they made their first acquaintance with each other; but coals glowed red in the stove and their light was a warm friendly one across the floor. The tramping of feet could be heard as the men came from the barn, and the clipped sound of Peter's boots as he ran beside them to keep up with their stride. Voices broke the stillness, a stillness once so fraught with dread and now heavy with bliss. The men were talking of food after the day's work, food to satisfy hunger and give them zest for more work.

The boy's voice rang out: "Perhaps Mother will have a stew for us tonight!"

Martha heard and smiled, catching the lamb in her arms as it ran in little jumps around the room. The door was flung open and light from the lanterns the men were carrying streamed into the darkness.

"What's this?" Andrew exclaimed. "Martha, where are you?"

"Here, Andrew," she answered, and as her voice came to him he threw the beam of his lantern in its direction. "I have no dinner ready but, look you, what I have!"

Andrew stared. "The little dead ewe lamb!"

Old Benj nodded his head slowly and went across the kitchen to light the lamp on the table.

Peter clapped his hands. "It was asleep, Father, and I couldn't play with it before, now I can." His fingers stroked the lamb and then, as if they were old friends, the two began playing together—the lamb with its awkward gamboling gait, the boy with his nimble limbs.

"But, Martha, it was dead when I brought it in here," Andrew insisted, the wonder of what he saw making his face look like a child's.

"It needed warmth," Martha said gaily, so happy now that she could not remember the pain in her heart when he had first laid the lamb in the box by the stove.

"Something more than warmth she gave it," Benj murmured.

"It was Peter who did it," Martha said, as they watched the boy and the lamb at play. "But for hurting him I might have said as easily as you that the lamb was dead. Let it be his cosset to bring up as he will."

"It shall be his cosset," Andrew agreed, "for the lamb still needs more care than its own mother can give it and had best bide with us here in the house for awhile."

Martha smiled in delight.

"Such a fine little ewe lamb it is," Andrew went on, looking proudly at it, "and now we have not lost one of our young ones this year."

—ELIZABETH YATES

Kay's Treasure

A New England Coastal Story

It was one of those perfect days that the people in Rockport, Massachusetts, boast about. Bill and Pete Jenkins were up early and they made so much noise shouting back and forth that their sleepy cousin, Kay, had to get up to join in the excitement.

"What's happening today?" she cried, knowing that each day of her visit brought some new and wonderful adventure. She lived in Wisconsin, far from the little village with the Atlantic ocean almost surrounding it.

Bill replied, "We're going down to Bearskin Neck to

get lobsters for a picnic. Dad has a day off, and we're going over to Thatcher's Island."

"Wait for me," Kay begged. "I'll hurry and eat my breakfast."

So the boys waited and in a jiffy they were walking down the narrow strip of land that reached out into the ocean.

"My!" Kay said. "The smell of the sea makes me feel like bouncing."

Bill nodded. "I know why. It's because the seaweed has been washed up on the rocks and it smells like iodine. Mother says it is a bracing smell."

Soon the children came to the Sandy Bay Lobster Market and went in. "What is in this tank of water?" Kay leaned over. "Look, there are some queer things crawling on the bottom."

"Lobsters, silly," Bill said.

"But I thought lobsters were coral colored." Kay was astonished. "These are a dirty green color."

"They are coral colored after they have been boiled," Pete explained.

Just then the lobster man came to wait on them. "I want ten lobsters, not the large ones," Bill said.

"Yup, I know the size your ma wants. Going on a picnic?" the lobster man asked. "Who's she?" he pointed to Kay.

Pete said, "Kay Carter, our cousin from Wisconsin."

"Here for the summer?" the lobster man grinned at her.

"Yup," said Kay. "I wish I could live here always; I am having such fun." And Kay watched him scoop up the lobsters in a net and weigh them on a scale. He filled two heavy paper bags with the squirming lobsters. "Now don't let them nip you," he warned. "They have powerful pinchers."

Kay backed away from the lobsters in alarm. She let the boys carry them. They stopped at a grocery for potato chips, pickles, buns, hot dogs, and a carton of cokes. When they got home, Mrs. Jenkins had a huge kettle packed with other good things for the picnic.

"Hurry, Dad," Bill called.

Mr. Jenkins was writing his daily column for the Rockport newspaper. "Just finished," he answered, and in a minute they all started for T Wharf, where the dory was tied up. Kay was so excited to be going across the harbor to Thatcher's Island that she could hardly sit still. Bill and his father each pulled on a pair of the oars and the dory set out through the harbor into the open sea. In half an hour they landed on the island where there was a small pier and a bit of beach. The rest of the island was too rocky for landing. The breeze was lively and Kay's red hair was tossed about. She felt wild and free and wanted to yell and jump, but she had so much stuff to lug up the narrow path that she couldn't do anything but puff and stagger.

Thatcher's Island had twin lights at the other end. They rose white and slender against the blue sky. The keeper's house and two others were clustered at their base. At the pier end, the bundles and baskets and kettle were dropped. Everybody sat down to get his breath. Mr. Jenkins stretched out on the crunchy growth of tough grass and creeping vines. He fell asleep at once.

Bill jumped up. "Come on, Pete and Kay; we must gather firewood. I'm hungry already."

Kay laughed, "Me too. And I just had breakfast."

Mrs. Jenkins started to unpack the lunch. Then she yawned and lay back on the ground. "Be careful, children," she mumbled. "Don't crawl on the rocks, don't . . . don't . . ." she too was asleep.

Kay found a dry log to drag back to the picnic place. The boys made many trips until they had a large supply of firewood. Bill rummaged in a basket for something to eat. His father sat up and blinked at him. "Hey, don't start eating. We have to get a kettle of water."

Mrs. Jenkins sat up. "I'm hungry," she announced. "Let's have lunch right away. Pete, you start the fire."

"Is it noon?" Kay asked.

"I don't know. It is probably half past ten or eleven. But on an island, you eat when you are hungry, and you sleep when you are sleepy."

Kay laughed, "Aunt Ellen, you're such fun."

Before long a kettle of sea water was boiling over the fire. Mr. Jenkins dumped the lobsters into the water and let them boil for twenty minutes. In the meantime, Mrs. Jenkins gave a cup of melted butter to each one. Potato chips, pickles, buns and paper napkins were set out. Kay had her first lesson on how to eat a lobster.

"Crack the claws," said Pete, "and cut the body down the middle."

This Kay did and found a long juicy piece of meat.

"A nut pick helps," added Bill. "Here, have one."

Kay caught it and picked tender bits of lobster out of

its claws. All the others were dipping their lobster in the melted butter. Kay followed suit and tasted hers. "Good!" she exclaimed.

There were two lobsters apiece. "I'll never be able to eat again," Kay said.

Bill laughed. "It won't be long before you'll be wanting a hot dog," he remarked. "You'll see," he added.

After clearing up, they started to explore. "Why is the island called 'Thatcher's Island'?" asked Kay.

Mrs. Jenkins answered, "Because once a ship setting sail from Ipswich was wrecked here. They say there were twenty-three people on board and that the ship was broken up on these rocks. Passengers were swept back and forth by huge waves. It was impossible for anyone to hang on to the rocks. Only Mr. Thatcher and his wife were saved. They lost five children. Mr. Thatcher was a minister and he named the island 'Thatcher's Woe.'"

Kay's eyes filled with tears. "Didn't they have anything?" she asked.

"I've heard they saved a coverlet of scarlet cloth. They had two more children after the shipwreck, and they carried each baby to the baptismal font wrapped in the coverlet."

Everybody was still until Mr. Jenkins said cheerfully, "Let's go and visit the lighthouse keeper. I'll race you to the house." They all tore over the ground, yelling like wild Indians.

"How neat and clean the lighthouse is," exclaimed Kay. "White paint everywhere. Can we go up in the tower?"

Just then the keeper of the light came to his door. Mr. Jenkins called, "Hi, Tom, where's the family?"

"They went to the mainland to shop and go to a movie," he said.

"Why didn't you go?" Kay questioned.

"The light is never left without someone on the island," he explained. Then he asked, "Here for the summer?"

"Yes," Kay replied. "I'm visiting my aunt and uncle. I like it here on the island. Did you ever find any treasures buried by pirates?"

"No sirree. Too hard to dig in this island." The lighthouse keeper saw Kay's disappointed face and laughed. "But I find things tossed up on the rocks after a big storm. My oldest girl found a brass candlestick. Probably from a wreck."

Kay was excited. "I want to look right now for a treasure."

"Not now," Bill urged. "We're going to see the light."

The keeper nodded. "That is something to see. You won't find anything on the rocks." He led the way to a door, and they climbed a circular stair up and up until they came to a tiny room at the top.

"How shiny everything is," Kay said. "Do you polish brass every day?"

"Yes sirree," the keeper bragged. "The old style lights that had wicks to be trimmed and kerosene wells to be filled have been replaced by electric lights, but the Government expects everything to be kept spic and span."

Kay stared over the endless waves. "Where would I land if I sailed straight across the ocean from here?" she asked.

Pete cried, "I know! Spain! That is the nearest land to Europe. I wish I could start out right now."

"I don't," Kay said. "I want to stay in Rockport the rest of my life."

They climbed down into the breezy sunny afternoon.

"Good-bye," they called to the keeper, and strolled along the top of the rocky cliffs. There were pools between some of the rocks that were like fairyland. Everything under the water was tiny. The strange growing things moved like trees in a wind. The colors were beautiful. Little marine creatures scuttled back and forth under the moving moss. Kay hung over the pools. She did not want to leave, but Bill was hungry again.

"Come on, Kay," he begged.

"In just a minute. You and Pete go and start up the fire," she said.

Her aunt and uncle were far ahead. "Don't go down on the rocks," Bill warned. "They are slippery with seaweed." Then he and Pete went along, leaving her to follow.

Kay saw a larger pool. She scrambled over a huge rock and dropped down, scratching her bare legs. The edges of the rocks were sharp as knives. She forgot all about the family. She was fascinated with the pools. There was always one more for her to examine.

A deep scratch on her arm was bleeding. Then she remembered that she was supposed to follow Bill. She looked up and saw nothing but rocks above her and rocks at either side. They appeared much larger now than when she had climbed down. There was no sound but the hollow booming of the waves. The tide was coming in, but Kay had not yet learned about tides. An extra large wave threw out its foamy edges and splashed her dress. She made a leap to a higher rock. There was a small cave between the rocks. She poked into all the corners.

"Maybe pirates hid something in here," she talked to herself. But she found nothing. Then she remembered the story of Thatcher's Woe. The waves were coming up higher now. She was frightened. She began to climb the rocks. She did not know where she had come down and she had to find a zigzag way up by rocks she could just about manage to climb. When she reached the top, she didn't see anything she remembered. The two lights stood up tall and far away.

"I don't know which way to go," she said to herself. "But I'm on an island so I can't get lost." She began to call, "Bill, Pete!" But only the gulls screeched back an answer.

Kay began to run. She stumbled in a small hole and came down flat on her face. She skinned her knees, and her chin was covered with gritty sand. She sat up and began to cry. She dashed away the tears and muttered, "I'm not lost." She rubbed her sore chin and whimpered, "I'll find them."

She crouched there waiting for her breath to come back. She stared down into a rocky hollow just below her. She spied a large rusty battered tin can wedged between the rocks.

"I wonder what is in that can," she said to herself, and, forgetting her bruises, she scrambled down and tried to loosen the can. It wouldn't budge. She picked up a small stone and pounded along the edge of the lid. It began to loosen a bit. She worked at it for quite a while. Then the lid came off.

Kay's heart beat fast. The can was stuffed with something that looked like doll's clothes. She held her breath while she pulled them out. There was a doll sitting on top of a pile of doll's quilts. Kay gasped. "It's somebody's doll!"

Tenderly she lifted it out. The doll's eyes opened and looked at Kay. They were blue. Kay smoothed the curly yellow hair and sat the doll on her lap. It was dressed in a Scotch costume.

"You poor lost baby," Kay crooned. "Where did you come from?"

She looked at the other dresses, and she could tell that they had been made by a little girl because the stitches were long and uneven like her own sewing.

Kay piled the doll's clothes into her skirt and held it like a bag. She laid the doll on top and stood up. She had forgotten all about being lost and bruised. She heard her name called.

"Yoo-hoo!" she yelled again and again. Then she saw Bill and Pete running toward her. "Kay, Kay!" Bill cried. "We couldn't find you. We thought you were lost."

Pete began to cry. "We thought you slipped on the seaweed and got drowned."

Then her aunt and uncle came from another direction. "How did you get way over here?" Mr. Jenkins asked.

Her aunt hugged her. "Don't you ever get out of my sight again."

"Come, come," Mr. Jenkins said. "Everything is okay now. Let's hurry back and eat those hot dogs."

"But what have you got in your skirt?" her aunt asked.

Kay held her skirt open and they all cried with astonishment, "Why, it's a doll!"

Kay pointed to the empty can. The boys pried it out of the rocks.

"Look!" Bill said. "There is a name stenciled on it. THE NOVA SCOTIA."

Kay's uncle exclaimed. "That ship went down during the last war. I remember reading about it. The can is the kind they use on ship-board for tea and coffee. The captain's daugher used it for her doll and its clothes."

Kay thought about that little girl and her doll. "Could you find out if she was saved?"

Kay's uncle answered, "I think I could." He knew just how to go about it because he worked on a newspaper. "But, let's get back and eat up those hot dogs."

Kay said, "I am awfully hungry." In a short time they were back at the picnic place where everybody ate as many hot dogs as they could. Then they piled everything in the dory and rowed back to the village. Kay held the doll and wondered about it and the little girl who had lost it.

A week later Kay's uncle came home all excited. "The captain's daughter was saved. Her name is Cathy Campbell. She lives in Nova Scotia and she is going to put in a long distance call and talk to Kay this evening."

Kay didn't know if she was glad or sorry. She loved the doll and all its pretty clothes. When the telephone call came, Kay was almost in tears.

The voice from Nova Scotia was friendly. "Kay," it said. "This is Cathy Campbell. I am twenty years old now, too old for dolls. Will you please give her a good home?"

Kay was delighted. "Oh, yes, I love her dearly. But what is her name?"

"Bonny Jean," was the answer. "My father brought her to me from Scotland."

"The name suits her," Kay said. "No one ever found such a lovely treasure from the sea. I'll keep her all my life. Thank you a million thanks."

"Good-bye," said Cathy.

Kay answered, "Good-bye." Then she turned to the family. "Her name is Bonny Jean, and she is mine to keep."

Her uncle said, "The Rockport newspaper is going to print a picture of you and Bonny Jean, and I am going to write her story. You can send a copy to Cathy in Nova Scotia."

Kay sat and smiled and smiled. Every day of her visit to Rockport was both wonderful and exciting.

—RUTH LANGLAND HOLBERG

Christmas Eve on Beacon Hill

A Story of Boston

Fall comes early in Boston. By the first of November the tall trees that lined the streets of Beacon Hill had been stripped bare of their leaves. Benjy had been very lonely when he first went there to live in the stately house of his Great-aunt Prue. She looked so dignified in her high white pompadour that he was even a little afraid of her.

True, she was kind. She had tried to keep him from being homesick. They had gone on sightseeing trips together, and she had told him so much about the city that

"Christmas Eve on Beacon Hill" is adapted from *Benjy of Boston* by Frances Cavanah; copyright, 1946, by David McKay Company; reprinted by permission of David McKay and Frances Cavanah.

sometimes he was afraid he would burst with information. She never once guessed that what he really wanted was a boy his own age to play with.

Then one day down in the Common, Benjy met Tony. Tony's father had been born in Italy, but now he was an American citizen. Like Benjy's father, he was serving with the Occupation Forces in Germany. That had been the first bond between the two boys. Then it was exciting to hear Tony tell of how he lived in the North End, near the house where Paul Revere once lived. He loved Boston and earned many dimes and quarters showing sightseers around.

At last Benjy had a friend. Soon he and Tony were "in business" together.

All week Benjy worked hard at his lessons with his tutor at home. But on Saturday after lunch, when his aunt was busy with her club, he hurried down to the North End. Being a guide was fun, and business was brisk. Sometimes he earned seventy-five cents in an afternoon, and it was almost more than he could bear not to talk of his success at home. Several times he started to tell Aunt Prue about Tony, but he did not quite dare.

By Thanksgiving, when the first snow blanketed the city, Benjy had earned nearly four dollars, and he had saved every cent of his November allowance. Christmas boxes for men overseas had to be mailed before the first of December, and he felt rich when he went shopping with seven dollars in his pocket. After buying Dad a compass he had enough money left for a box of raisins, several chocolate bars and such gifts as razor blades and soap which the men overseas needed. He wrapped each present in blue paper sprinkled with silver stars and tied it with silver ribbon. Johanna, the Irish housekeeper, added a fruitcake, and after the packages had been placed in a shoebox, she filled in the corners with lumps of sugar.

"Faith, 'tis a lonesome feeling," said Johanna, brushing the back of her hand across her eyes, "not to have your fayther home for Christmas."

Benjy held his chin very firm as he wrapped the shoebox in heavy brown paper. He addressed it to Captain John Lawrence, in care of the Army of Occupation in Germany.

"I guess your fruitcake will taste just as good in German as in English," he said, and tried to grin at his little joke.

Even Aunt Prue smiled. "That is the spirit to have," she said gently. "I am pleased, Benjamin John, to see how wisely you used your November allowance. I don't see how you managed to buy so many gifts. Are you looking forward to your first Christmas Eve on Beacon Hill?"

"Well, you see, Aunt Prue—" Benjy blushed. "There's something I want to tell you—I mean ask you. Are you going to have Open House this year?"

"To be sure. I always have Open House on Christmas Eve."

"Do—do many people come?"

"About twenty-five. The same friends and relatives who have been coming to my Open House for years."

"Don't you ever have anybody new?" asked Benjy in dismay.

Aunt Prue smiled a little at that. "Only you, Benjamin John. And you're not really new, because you are my own grand nephew."

"Oh!" said Benjy flatly.

He had invited Tony to Open House one day, and then regretted the invitation. He was not quite sure that his aunt would approve, and for a while he had hoped that Tony would forget. But Tony had not forgotten. Just last Saturday he had been saying how nice the houses on the Hill looked on Christmas Eve.

The first of the month Aunt Prue gave Benjy his December allowance, and he used part of the money to buy her a dainty little china cat and four even tinier china kittens for her collection of figures on the parlor whatnot. If he could only give them to her now, it might be easier to ask her about Tony. But he couldn't give a Christmas present before Christmas, and Open House was held on Christmas Eve.

As the weather grew colder, few sightseers ventured out into the raw east wind that blew in from the ocean. No one wanted to hire two boys as guides, and they began going down to the Common to play. The elm trees, their branches sheathed in ice, glittered in the winter sunshine. The shouts of the children skating on the Frog Pond sounded high and shrill in the thin, cold air.

"I had a letter from Pop," said Tony the Saturday before Christmas, as the boys sat down on a bench near the pond to put on their skates. "I guess a fellow couldn't have a nicer Christmas gift than that."

"That's right," said Benjy and suddenly felt very lonely. It had been such a long time since he had heard from Dad.

"I had told Pop that—that you—" Tony hesitated—"that you had invited me to Open House. He thought it was just swell. You still want me to come, don't you?"

"Why, of course," said Benjy, more confidently than

he was feeling. To himself he added, "I just *have* to tell Aunt Prue tonight."

But when he reached home there were guests for dinner. The next day Aunt Prue was busy making plans for Open House, and Benjy put off telling her again. The day after that it was the same, until finally it was the afternoon of Christmas Eve.

"Benjamin John," said Aunt Prue. "Will you please help me with these candles?"

Under her careful direction, Benjy placed tall white candles in rows of silver candlesticks on the sills and on the upper sash of every window. Then she sent him down to the florist to buy another wreath of holly. When he came back Johanna had covered the long mahogany table in the dining room with the embroidered cloth that Aunt Prue's seafaring grandfather had brought from China many years before. Aunt Prue was arranging a big bowl of holly as a centerpiece, flanked on either side by red candles in tall, branched candlesticks.

"I am going to my room to lie down," she said, drawing her Paisley shawl a little closer. "I must be refreshed to meet my guests tonight."

"What if—if somebody extra came in?" asked Benjy. "Would there be—enough to eat?"

"Please, Benjamin John!" Aunt Prue was already halfway up the stairs. "Don't bother me with foolish questions. There will be no extra guests tonight."

Benjy's heart seemed to drop down into his shoes.

After dinner, Johanna kindled a taper and Benjy went from window to window lighting the candles. From the third floor to the first he made his rounds, until every window was ablaze with light. In the houses across the street—in nearly every house upon the Hill—soft candle-light shone out upon the snow. The curtains had been parted in many of the windows, so that hundreds of visitors who thronged the sidewalks on Christmas Eve might see the handsome rooms with their fine old furniture and lovely paintings on the walls. In this way the people of Beacon Hill shared their houses with the passers-by.

Shortly after seven the strains of "Holy Night" were borne across the frosty air as the first group of carolers started up the Hill. By half past seven Aunt Prue's parlors were filled with guests. Benjy met aunts and uncles and great-aunts and aunts by marriage and cousins and cousins once removed until he was dizzy trying the remember all their names.

As he passed among the guests with plates of sandwiches and platters heaped high with star-shaped cookies, he kept listening for the knocker on the front door. Time and again it fell with a dull thud and Johanna ushered another guest into the parlor. Perhaps Tony wasn't coming after all.

"Hi-ya, Benjy! Here I am."

Everyone turned to look at Tony, brushed and scrubbed within an inch of his life, standing in the doorway. Benjy set a plate of sandwiches down on a marble-topped table and hurried across the room.

"Hello, Tony." His voice quavered, but he took Tony firmly by elbow and led him over to the divan where Aunt Prue was sitting with a bald-headed gentleman named "Cousin Jonathan."

"Aunt Prue," said Benjy, "this is my friend, Tony Vallento."

Tony held his head high, but Aunt Prue looked into his melting dark eyes and knew that he was frightened. "Welcome, Tony Vallento," she said, holding out her hand. "Johanner, please bring a cup of hot chocolate for our guest."

"Good evening, Miss Lawrence. It was swell—I mean nice—" Tony was choosing his words carefully—"of you to ask me here."

"Have you and Tony known each other long?" she asked.

"We were in business together until it got so cold." Tony seemed surprised that she did not know. "I live near Paul Revere's house and I show sightseers around. I introduced Benjy as the boy whose uncle knew Paul Revere and he recited the poem."

"Benjamin John," said Cousin Jonathan, "if your face gets any redder, it's going to catch on fire."

To Benjy's relief Johanna returned with a cup of chocolate on a silver tray, and Cousin Jonathan gave Tony his place on the divan. For the next ten minutes Tony was very busy with sandwiches and star-shaped cookies, but not too busy to talk.

"Can you beat it—Benjy didn't used to like Boston. He didn't like history, but now he can reel it off like nobody's business. You ought to hear him say 'Paul Revere's Ride.' "

"We'd like very much to hear him, and you, too," said Aunt Prue surprisingly.

"Okay, just as soon as I get through here," said Tony.

Benjy, getting redder every minute, passed the sandwiches again and again. But at last even Tony's appetite was satisfied, and the two boys stood up together near the fireplace while everyone waited expectantly.

"Listen folks," said Tony. "Paul Revere was a great guy. He did a lot of things beside ride a horse. He was a dentist and a silversmith, and he fitted people out with spectacles. Best of all, he joined the Sons of Liberty, and we might never have had a country of our own if it hadn't been for him. Now you're going to hear a poem about how he helped the soldiers get off to a good start, and here beside me stands the great-great-nephew—"

A pained expression flitted across Aunt Prue's thin features, and there was a little gasp from the cousins and the aunts and the great-uncles. Benjy took a deep breath and began:

"Listen, my children, and you shall hear
Of the midnight ride of Paul Revere . . ."

His throat was dry, but as he went on he forgot to be afraid. He remembered that "Paul Revere's Ride" was just a good story, and he told it well. When he had finished even Aunt Prue joined in the applause.

Then she turned to Tony with a curious light in her mild blue eyes. "You like Boston very much, don't you?"

"Sure," said Tony. "Aw, gee, Miss Lawrence, it's beautiful in here. I've always wanted to see the inside of one of these big houses."

"It is one of the oldest houses on the Hill, Tony." Aunt

Prue's voice was edged with pride. "Benjy will be glad to show you some of the other rooms before you leave."

Later that evening when the boys stepped out into the street, it was filled with people. Following in the wake of one group of carolers, Benjy—though he had known that Beacon Hill was beautiful—had never known that it could be so beautiful as this. There was a holly wreath on nearly every door, and the streets were two blazing lines of light.

In Louisburg Square the carolers paused at one end of the little park. The leader struck a note on his tuning fork, and they began to sing: *"O Little Town of Bethlehem."*

The people on the sidewalks listened in silence, and the statue of Columbus seemed to look down benignly from his pedestal.

"I have to go now," said Tony reluctantly. "I had a nice time, Benjy. Your aunt is just swell."

When Benjy reached home, the last guest had gone. "This just came airmail, special delivery," said Aunt Prue, picking up a letter from the marble-topped table.

Benjy tore the letter open. He pored over the pages, as though he could not read them fast enough. "Oh, boy, it's from Dad. Why, he's in London, Aunt Prue. He's on leave. But he got our box just before he left, and he liked everything. Listen, what he says:

> "I've been invited to have Christmas dinner with friends who live in an old London Square that is a dead ringer for Louisburg Square."

Benjy turned a page, and there was a catch in his voice as he went on reading:

"I hope you like Boston better than you did, Benjy. Some wise man once said that Boston was more than a city, that it was a way of feeling. I think Boston is a way of feeling about our country. Probably this is because it has done so much to make the history of our country."

Benjy laid the letter down. "I do like Boston now. I sort of feel that it belongs to me—just the way Tony does."

Aunt Prue looked at her nephew with an odd smile. "Tony seems to have done what I failed to do. He's made you a good Bostonian. He—he's a fine boy."

"Oh, he likes you, too, Aunt Prue," said Benjy earnestly. "He thinks you're swell—and I do, too."

Aunt Prue grew pink and then crimson. But all she said was, "Thank you, Benjy. A gentleman hasn't paid me a compliment like that in years."

He looked at her in astonishment. She had never called him anything but Benjamin John before.

Together they walked over to the window. A group of carolers had gathered on the sidewalk. The candlelight fell softly on their upturned faces as they sang:

"Silent night, holy night,
All is calm, all is bright."

Benjy felt his father's letter in his pocket. Then he slipped his free hand into Aunt Prue's.

—FRANCES CAVANAH

Dot for Short

Living Next an "El" in a Large City

It was a cold, sunless day in January, and although she wore a sweater under her coat, Dot shivered. She and her older sister, Fluff, who was twelve, were walking homeward along Third Avenue in New York. As usual Fluff was talking, and Dot was listening with one half of her mind and dreaming with the other half.

Very often Fluff's voice, and all the street noises, too, would be swallowed by the roar of the Third Avenue El trains directly overhead. Then, after a second, the roar would gradually disappear and Dot could hear all the street noises again—the tinkling bell of the trolley, the tooting of taxi horns, the deep rumble of big trucks, the screeching of brakes, the shouting of children.

The noise did not bother Dot and Fluff. They were so used to it that they did not notice it at all. They had always lived on Third Avenue facing the El tracks, and on a rainy day, when they could not go out, it was fun to watch the trains rush past. Once a train had stopped before it reached the station. Dot looked into the car and there, looking back at Dot, was a girl her own age. The girl smiled and showed Dot, through the window, the book she was reading. Then the train started again and the girl disappeared forever.

A taxi horn tooted when Dot and Fluff stopped for a red light. They did not notice it until the toot was repeated three times—short, firm little blasts. Then the girls realized that someone was trying to get their attention. They looked up and there was Daddy in his taxi. They waved to him and he grinned and waved back. Then he said something to the lady passenger. She stared hard at Dot. The red light turned green and the taxi sped away.

Dot thought she knew why the lady had stared at her. She was probably wondering how Fluff, who was so pretty and golden-haired, happened to have such a short, dark, plain sister.

They passed the "boarded-up" house. No one lived in it. The Board of Health said that it was not a good enough building for people to live in, so the door and all the windows were covered with boards. Two boys were playing ball against the building. Their ball made a loud, smacking noise as it hit the wood. Both boys stopped when the girls came near. They looked at Fluff admiringly. One of the boys called "Hi, Gorgeous!" and the other chimed in with "Hello, Beautiful!" Fluff tossed her head and tried to look as if she hadn't heard.

Then the boys looked at Dot. "Hi, Shorty!" shouted one of them and the other greeted her with "Hello, Peanut!"

Dot began to walk very quickly. She turned her head so Fluff would not notice that her cheeks had turned very red and her lips were trembling.

"Slow down, Silly," said Fluff. "Act as if you didn't hear them."

It was good to get into the warm hallway. A radiator made a sizzling, bubbling sound. Dot and Fluff started to climb the two flights that led to their apartment. On the first floor Fluff sniffed.

"Mrs. Adams is having cabbage tonight," she whispered and giggled. "I wonder what we're having."

In summer, when the doors were open, you knew what every family would have for dinner. In winter, though, it was only strong smells like cabbage or coffee that escaped through the doors into the hall.

Just as Dot and Fluff were about to ring their own doorbell, the door suddenly opened from the inside—so suddenly that Dot almost fell in. "Boo!" shouted a small boy with bright red hair and red freckles. He was Mike, who was eight years old, two years younger than Dot, who was two years younger than Fluff, who was two years younger than Peg, who was now fourteen and went to high school.

"It's Friday!" Mike yelled. "We don't have to do any homework. We can stay up and have dinner with Daddy. Golly, I wish I had a dog!"

He turned a somersault in the narrow hall and his feet hit the wall.

Mommy was in the living room and in her lap was a hill of stockings that needed darning. The girls kissed her and Dot thought again how pretty she was. She had always wanted to be pretty and tall like her mother and sisters. Nothing exciting would ever happen to anyone as small and dark as she was!

"Come in and say hello to me," said a cheerful voice from the kitchen. Dot went in to see Grandma, leaving Fluff to tell Mommy about school and their meeting with Daddy. Grandma Fleming had plump cheeks that were pink and white like a fat baby's. She had short, curly silver hair and the curls jumped merrily when she shook her head. She had merry brown eyes, too. They just looked at you and knew what you were thinking. Now they looked straight at Dot and Grandma said, "What's bothering you, Dorothea Ann?"

That was one of the things that Dot loved about Grandma. Everyone else called her Dot because they said that Dorothea Ann was too big a name for such a little girl. Whenever Grandma called her by her full name, Dot straightened up and felt tall and important.

"A boy called me Shorty and another one called me Peanut," she explained.

Grandma looked at Dot and pressed her lips together. She shook her head and Dot knew that she was not going to be given any sympathy at all.

"How often, Dorothea Ann Fleming, have I told you it's the size of the mind and the kindness of the heart that count? You're such a foolish girl that I can't believe you're my grandchild. Now help me put the chocolate frosting on the cake and you can lick the spoon and half the bowl. Leave one side of the bowl for Mike."

Dot loved to be in the kitchen on Friday. It was filled with such wonderful smells—the appetizing smell of meat cooking in its own juices; the delicious bakery smell of cake baking in the oven; the candy smell of chocolate in a bowl, waiting to decorate the cake. Dot was sure that no kitchen in the whole world smelled as good as the Fleming kitchen did on Friday, when the whole family waited for Daddy and all had dinner together in the living room.

For a few minutes, while Dot worked, she forgot about the boys and the names they had called her. Grandma had taught her how to decorate a cake when she was a little girl and she loved doing it. She dipped the big tablespoon into the bowl of delicious-looking, dark chocolate. Then she tilted the spoon over the middle of the cake. The chocolate was just right for frosting, not too thin and not too thick. It began to spread from the center in all directions. Some of it ran down the sides of the cake.

Dot dipped the spoon into the bowl again, and again she let the chocolate flow over the cake and down the sides. Some of it fell into the plate that held the cake. Dot wanted very much to take it up with her finger and then lick her finger the way she used to when she was small. Instead she scooped it up with a knife and patted it onto the sides of the cake wherever a place wasn't thickly covered. Then she smoothed the top and sides with her knife until the chocolate was smooth and even, without a single lump. Dot stepped back and looked at the cake. It looked as pretty as a chocolate cake in a bakery window, she thought.

Grandma seemed to agree with her. "I couldn't have done as well myself," she said, shaking her head so that her curls danced merrily.

Now that her work was done, Dot's thoughts went back to her walk home from school. "Grandma," she said, "if you could have one wish, what would you wish?"

"I'd wish," said Grandma, without hesitating one second, "that we Flemings would always stay the same happy, healthy family that we are today."

"What a funny wish!" thought Dot. Whenever she and her sisters and Mike wished, it was for something real, like ten dollars or something to wear or a dog. Dot always had another wish that she never told the others, but now she found herself telling it to Grandma.

"I'd wish that after vacation is over next summer, I'd go back to school and the teacher would tell us to form a line according to our size. I'd take first place the way I always do because I'm the shortest one in the class. Teacher would say, 'Dorothea, you've grown during the summer. Get further back.' I'd measure myself with all the other girls, and I'd be taller than anyone except the very last girl."

"And why not taller than the very last girl?" Grandma asked.

"Because everyone notices you and says things if you're the tallest, same as if you're the smallest."

"That's a rhyme," said Grandma. "The tallest—the

smallest. Well, Dorothea, your wish strikes me as being very silly. Some day you'll be glad you're small, see if you're not."

"I can't imagine when," Dot answered.

Now it was time to help the others pull the table into the middle of the room and put two boards into it to make it bigger. Usually the family ate in the kitchen, Mike, Dot, and Fluff eating first. Now that Peg was in high school, she ate with the grown-ups.

It was exciting to have dinner with Daddy. He always had such wonderful stories to tell about the people who rode in his taxi—how they looked and what they said. Sometimes they were important people whose names appeared in the newspaper. How exciting it must be, Dot thought, to have your name in the paper!

When Daddy came home, you could hear his voice above the noise of the El trains. He looked just the way Mike would look some day, with red hair, freckles, and jolly blue eyes. As he opened the door, he yelled, "I'm hungry enough to eat the first person I see. Get out of my way!" Dot noticed that he was carrying a package.

"If it's something for me," shouted Mike, "I'd rather have a dog."

"I hope it's a dress for me. I need one," said Peg, who had come in a little earlier. She was just as pretty as Fluff, but her hair, like Mommy's, was redder and her eyes were violet color. She was tall and slim.

"No looking till after dinner," said Daddy, giving Mommy a kiss. He put the package on a chair where they could all see it while they ate their dinner. All during dinner everyone around the table, except Daddy, kept looking at the package and wondering which lucky person it was for.

When dinner was over, Mike rushed for the package and was about to open it.

"Oh, no," said Daddy, taking it from him. "I'll do the opening."

He did, and he held up a girl's coat—a lovely plaid coat with lots of red in it and with a pretty beaver collar. Mike's face fell. "Anyway, I knew it wasn't a dog, so I didn't care," he mumbled. "But if it's ever a dog, I get it."

"It's for the one it fits best," said Daddy. "Everyone gets a chance to try it on—that is, everyone but Mike and me." He winked at Mike and Mike grinned. "The oldest first. Come on, Grandma."

Grandma put the coat over one shoulder and they all laughed because she looked so funny. Mommy tried it next but she could not even get her arm into the sleeve. Peg looked very hopeful and excited when her turn came. She tried her best to get into the coat, but she had to admit that it was too tight.

Dot's heart began to beat faster. Fluff was really as plump as Peg though she wasn't as tall. If the coat did not fit Peg, then maybe . . . It was too good to be true! A beautiful plaid coat that had not belonged first to Peg, then to Fluff, and then to her! No, nothing that wonderful could ever happen.

"You, Dot," said Daddy, like a teacher calling one pupil after another. Dot's cheeks were very red and her eyes were bright.

An El train thundered by and swallowed the shouts that came from all of them when Dot buttoned the coat. Even

Mike was jumping with joy. Daddy turned Dot around slowly so that they could all see how perfectly the coat fitted.

"Look at yourself in the mirror," said Mommy, and they all went into the little bedroom that Dot shared with Peg. They filled every inch of it. Dot, looking at herself in the mirror over her dresser, could hardly believe her eyes. The coat fitted as if it had been made just for her. Red was her favorite color, too. She stroked the beaver collar lovingly.

"She's really very pretty," said Grandma so low that only Mommy was supposed to hear. But Dot heard, too, and almost burst with happiness. Everyone was always so busy telling how pretty Peg and Fluff were that they didn't even notice her.

"Now, Jim, where did the coat come from?" Mommy asked, and suddenly Dot wished that Daddy would never tell and that it would always be a mystery.

"Well," said Daddy, "I guess the girls told you I met them on Third Avenue. The woman who was in the cab thought Dot was one of the cutest kids she had ever seen. She asked how old she was and she sure was surprised when I said ten. She thought she was lots younger."

There it was! Dot's happiness began to fade a little. She looked at herself in the mirror again and touched the beaver collar.

"The lady's name is Mrs. Roberts. She said her kid is ten, too, but much bigger. She said that her girl is getting so fat that she outgrows her clothes before she even wears them. Said she had a beautiful winter coat from last year that the girl can't even get into. I feel sorry for her kid.

She's got everything, but she's so plump that her friends make fun of her. Well, anyway, the lady wanted to know if I'd like to stop and get the coat and give it to Dot. That's the whole story."

Everyone looked at Dot with admiration. Dot could read Grandma's mind just as clearly as if she were reading a printed page. Grandma's eyes said, "See? Didn't I tell you that lots of exciting things are going to happen to you, Dorothea Ann Fleming?"

Mommy smiled at Dot lovingly and said, "I think this is going to be a lucky year for you, Dot. It's starting that way, isn't it?"

—FRIEDA FRIEDMAN

Saturday Five

Life in the City of New York

After a while, very slowly, it began to be spring. There were rust-colored buds on the ailanthus trees, and one day Mona heard a blue jay in the backyard sounding countrified and out of place. Pretty soon it would be time to go to the valley; back to the rambling old wooden house that the Melendys rented every summer. Mona was homesick thinking about it, and got all her summer clothes out of their boxes to see if she had outgrown them (which she had, and Randy was glad because now they would descend to her) and forgot to put them away again until Cuffy got after her. Rush took his baseball bat to school, and Randy wrote a poem. Oliver spent hours in the back yard digging fortifications in the mud. The seats and knees of his overalls were a constant source of despair for Cuffy.

The Independent Saturday Afternoon Adventure Club had so far been entirely successful. Randy had spent her second Saturday at the Ballet Theatre and was now able to walk on her toes quite easily, and had made a ballet skirt out of five pairs of muslin curtains that couldn't be darned any more. Rush had gone to hear Rudolph Serkin play the piano, and had been practicing furiously ever since in the hours that were not occupied by school or baseball. Mona had seen Katharine Cornell in a play and was very hard to live with as a result. She now moved queenlike and distant through a world of her own.

But this particular Saturday was Oliver's, and they had agreed to stay home. Not that he could go out by himself, of course, as they could; but in order to make him feel like a proper member of the I.S.A.A.C., they respected his Saturday and stayed at home. Also, besides giving him back the three dimes he had lent them, each added a dime of his own. "That'll be almost half what we have to spend on our Saturdays, and it will look like a million dollars to him," Rush said; it was his idea.

The day passed pleasantly enough. There was lemon pie for dessert at lunch, and afterwards Rush and Randy gave Isaac a bath in the basement washtub. He was philosophical about this ordeal by now and stood passive, though loathing every minute of it. When he was dry, they took him for a walk to show him off. Mona didn't want to go because she had borrowed some of Cuffy's big steel hairpins and was doing her hair in a pompadour just for an experiment.

The walk was a great success, and so was Isaac. People stopped them frequently to admire and pat him; and every time they asked what kind of dog he was, Rush gave them a different answer in a polite, serious voice. A Bronx beagle, he might say, or a Central Park setter, or an Interborough Rapid Transit retriever. Randy almost died.

When they came back to their own block, they could see Mona hanging out of the second-story window of their house.

"Where's Oliver?" she called, when they drew near.

Rush and Randy looked at her blankly.

"I don't know. Where is he?" shouted Rush.

"Isn't he home?" cried Randy.

"We can't find him *any* place," answered Mona, withdrawing her head and closing the window with a bang.

They ran up the steps and into the house. Cuffy looked pale and distracted. "Rush, you go down the street to the Potters' and see if by any chance he's gone to play with Petey, though goodness knows he's *never* done such a thing before. Randy, you run round the block. Maybe he's trying out his roller skates again."

"Maybe he's just hiding," suggested Randy.

"His coat and cap are gone," Mona told her. "And anyway I've looked everywhere. In all the closets and underneath the beds. Even in the trunks in the basement."

"Where's Father?"

"Gone to Philadelphia to lecture. He won't be back till five and we don't know where to get him. Hurry up, Randy, run along."

At that moment the object of all this concern was seated comfortably at Madison Square Garden. His knees were crossed, he was leaning back with a bottle of pop in one hand, and watching a lady in spangles hanging by her teeth to a rope fifty feet above the ground.

It had all been very simple, but it was also a well-thought-out campaign. Four weeks ago Oliver had received seven dimes which he had prudently concealed in one of his last summer's sandals. Today he had received seven more, which together with the sandal money made fourteen dimes. Untold wealth, but he did not let it go to his head. Everything proceeded according to plan.

Today when he was supposed to be resting he had got up, put on his coat and cap, and walked, faintly jingling, right out of the house. There was no trouble of any kind. When he got to Fifth Avenue he went up to a policeman and said, "Where is the circus, please?"

And the policeman said, "Madison Square Garden. Aren't you kinda young to be out alone?"

Oliver simply said, "No, I don't think so," and went his way. When he came to another policeman some blocks farther on he went up to him and said, "Where is Madison Square Garden, please?"

"Going to the circus, eh?" said the policeman. "It's at Fiftieth Street and Eighth Avenue. You all alone?"

Oliver simply said, "Yes, I am," and proceeded on his way, leaving the policeman with his hands full of traffic.

At Fiftieth Street he went up to another policeman and said, "Which way is Eighth Avenue, please?"

"That way," said the policeman, jerking a white cotton thumb westward. " 'Bout three blocks over. Ain't nobody with you?"

Oliver simply said, "No, nobody," and crossed the street with the red light.

It was easy when he got there, too. He just stood in a long line of grownups and children and held tight to his dimes and listened to what the people in front of him said when they got to the window. So when he got there he was able to say, "One, please. The kind that costs one dollar," and count out ten dimes slowly and carefully. The man behind the window had to peer down in order to see him at all. Then holding his ticket tightly he followed close behind a large family and tried hard to look like one of them.

"Like to hold your own ticket, eh, sonny?" said the ticket man.

"Yes, I do," replied Oliver, and entered the magic portals. It was wonderful. It smelled of elephants the minute you got in, even before you came to the real circus part. Breathing the smell deeply, Oliver climbed some steps that a uniformed man told him to, and then walked along a corridor that another uniformed man told him to. He thought he heard a lion roar some place, and his feet crunched on peanut shells. It was very exciting. Finally he came to the right door, entered it, and found himself in another world. It was a vast world, carpeted with blue sawdust and walled with thousands of faces. A complicated web of cables and rope ladders and nets rose from the huge arena to misty regions high overhead. On the blue sawdust at the bottom there were three large caged rings, and in each of these rings the most extraordinary things were happening.

"This way, Bud," said the usher, steering the bedazzled Oliver to a seat. Oliver sat down without knowing that he did so. After a long time he removed his coat and cap blindly, never taking his eyes off the ring nearest him. In it three lions, two bears, and a black leopard were climbing ladders, while on high gold stools seven other lions sat and snarled and battled with their paws at their trainer who was the bravest man in the world and wore a red coat. He could make those animals do anything. Before he was through, one of the bears was pushing the other in a huge baby carriage while all the lions, on a bridge overhead, sat up on their hind legs and begged. Oliver sighed deeply; it was almost too much. His only regret was that he was too busy watching his ring to pay attention to the others. The air rang with the crack of whips and the sharp commands of the trainers.

As the cages were dismantled and the animals taken away, Oliver began to notice the men who were going up and down the aisles selling things: jeweled canes, and clown hats, and things to eat. They called their wares hoarsely like a lot of crows. "Hot dogs, hot dogs!" cried one, and "*Get*cha roasted peanuts here," cried another, and "*Ice*cole pop," still another. But the one Oliver was most interested in was the man who kept saying "Cotton candy, Cotton c-a-a-a-n-dy," as he went by with what looked like a lot of pink birds' nests on sticks. Oliver finally bought one. It was interesting; you bit into a cloud of pink spun sugar and it instantly became nothing in your mouth. He ate it lingeringly, to make it last. All the time fascinating things were going on in the huge arena before him. Clowns came out and did their stunts, a man jumped over three elephants, ladies in spangles rode standing up on the backs of broad white horses, and dozens of tiny taffy-colored ponies, with plumes on their foreheads like the frills on lamb chops, pranced delicately about the rings and performed the most astonishing tricks. Oliver bit into his pink cloud and stared dreamily.

"I want some of that candy," said a sharp little voice at his side. Oliver turned a startled glance on the occupant of the next seat. He had forgotten there was anyone else in the world besides himself and the circus people.

"Don't bother the little boy, Marleen," said the little girl's mother in the kind of weak, uncertain way that no self-respecting child pays any attention to.

"I *want* some," repeated Marleen through her nose. She meant business. She was a very little girl and she had a pointed chin, dark eyes, black curls as stiff as cigars, a blue hair ribbon, a gold ring, and pink stuff on her tiny fingernails. Oliver detested her. He looked coldly away and went on eating his candy.

"Now, Marleen," said her mother.

"I want some. I *want* some of that boy's candy!"

"I'll get you some when the man comes by. Now you be a good girl and look at the pretty horsies."

"I want some of his. You give me that candy, boy!"

Oliver swallowed the last of it at a gulp and Marleen uttered a piercing scream of frustration. Heads in the row turned and looked at them. "Now, Marleen, now Marleen," said her mother helplessly. But Marleen continued to scream like a steam whistle until her mother had consoled her by buying her a cotton-candy stick of her own, and a fancy cane besides. Even then she stared unblinkingly at Oliver. She could not be persuaded to look at the arena, and after a while the consciousness of that baleful scrutiny spoiled even Oliver's enjoyment. He couldn't pay the proper attention to the jugglers. A few rows away, on the aisle, he noticed a vacant seat and after some deliberation made his way to it without a backward glance at Marleen.

After this unpleasant episode the performance progressed blissfully without a flaw. The procession was magnificent beyond description; from zebra-drawn coaches to elephants wearing tasseled capes and jeweled howdahs. Oliver watched it raptly while eating a hot dog with mustard. He surveyed the acrobats (whose muscles seemed to stretch like garters) while eating another hot dog, this time with sauerkraut. It was forbidden Paradise. Cuffy didn't believe in hot dogs or mustard or sauerkraut, but Oliver believed in them all. By the time the aerial artists had come along he was quenching a violent thirst with a bottle of pop. (It was at this moment that his entire family was in an uproar about his disappearance.) The act was so exciting that he couldn't finish the pop till it was over, because it made his stomach feel so queer when one of the glittering creatures high overhead leaped from her fragile swing and arched through the air like a bird to the next glittering creature. The climax came when one of the creatures stood on her head on a trapeze without holding on and swung to and fro, shimmering like a dragonfly, far above the arena. It was breath-taking.

Oliver felt so weak after watching her that he quickly finished his pop and purchased a bag of peanuts to fortify himself.

What a circus it was! One continual blaze of glory from beginning to end; from the flashing, bounding acrobats to the trained seals clapping their flippers; from the daring tightrope walkers to the fat clown who kept finding live ducklings in his pockets. Oliver did not want to believe it was over and sat for quite a while with people climbing over him and pushing past him, in the hope that they were all mistaken and something new was about to begin in the arena.

"Whatcha waitin' for, Bud?" said the usher, coming up to him. "Don'tcha know you'll get swept up with the trash and fed to the elephants if you wait *too* long?"

Probably he doesn't mean it, Oliver thought, but he got up hastily. At first he couldn't find his coat or cap, but then he remembered he had left them in the seat from which Marleen had driven him. There they still were luckily, though littered with peanut shells and a piece of chewing gum, doubtless the work of the vindictive Marleen. Oliver cleaned them off as well as he could, put them on, and after quite a lot of blundering about in the wrong direction (owing to the fact that he didn't understand the meaning of the word "exit") he found himself out on the street. Already it was dusk, and he began to hurry. For the first time the probable consequences of his adventure began to trouble him. It made him especially uncomfortable to think of Cuffy, for some reason.

And now the streets kept turning out the wrong way, and he found himself on Tenth Avenue instead of Fifth.

The place looked strange; full of high, dark buildings, and big noisy boys who went bowling by him on roller skates, and shouted at him hoarsely to get out of the way. As if that weren't enough, he began to have a terrible stomach-ache. Though he was a calm and resourceful person, Oliver was only six years old after all. So the next move seemed to be to cry. He stumbled and banged along the street, sobbing quietly and wiping his nose on his sleeve, wishing with all his heart that he was at home with Cuffy, and that he had never heard of hot dogs or cotton candy. Dimly he was aware of a clopping of hoofs on pavement but he was too miserable to look up until he heard a voice say:

"Whatsa matter, sonny?"

Oliver saw a big square policeman seated on a big square horse, magnificent as anything at the circus. All his buttons and two gold teeth glittered richly in the light of the street lamp.

"What's eatin' you?" repeated the policeman kindly.

"I'm lost!" wept Oliver. "And I'm sick at my stomach, and I want to go *home*!"

"What's your name?"

"Oliver M-Melendy."

"Know where you live?"

Oliver told him.

"Okay. You quit crying now," said the policeman. "You and me will take a little ride to your house. Think you can hold out?"

"I guess so," replied Oliver dubiously. His stomach felt awfully unreliable. The policeman got off his horse and hoisted Oliver up on it as if he had been a kitten.

Then he got on himself, behind Oliver, clucked at the horse and away they went. Oliver thought gloomily that it was probably the only time in his whole life that he was ever going to ride with a mounted policeman and he felt so sick he couldn't appreciate it.

"I guess I'm going to get a scolding when I go home," Oliver told the policeman. "Maybe I'll get a spanking too." All the shine was gone off the day.

"Why, what did you do?"

"Will you promise not to arrest me?" said Oliver cautiously.

"I doubt if it will be necessary," said the policeman, so Oliver told him.

"Well, I'll let your family take care of the penalty," the policeman decided. "It's a very serious offense all right, but it seems to me you've been punished almost enough as it is."

The traffic cop at Fifth Avenue looked at the mounted policeman and Oliver and said, "You've run in another big-time gang leader, I see."

"You'd be surprised," replied Oliver's policeman, and gave Oliver a pat on the shoulder.

At the Melendy house all was confusion. Randy was in tears. Father (who had returned from Philadelphia) and Rush were still out searching, and Cuffy was saying into the telephone, "Six years old. He has blue eyes, blond hair, and he weighs—" when the doorbell rang, and she dropped the receiver.

"Oh, Oliver darling, where *were* you?" cried Mona's voice, and Cuffy arrived to see her on her knees beside Oliver, who looked smaller and paler than ever before.

Behind him stood the largest, most solid policeman she had ever seen in her life.

Aching with relief, Cuffy hugged Oliver, then she looked up at the policeman and said, "That's the quickest response I ever got from anything. I hadn't no more than just finishing describing him to the police this minute—"

"The police force is never at a loss, ma'am," replied the officer with a wink.

Cuffy held Oliver away from her:

"Where in the world have you been?"

"To the circus," replied Oliver wanly.

"To the circus! Alone?" Cuffy was horrified.

"I wouldn't be too hard on him, ma'am," advised the officer.

"Go ahead and spank me if you want to," Oliver said, and was sick on the doormat.

Long, long afterwards, when all the thunder and lightning in his stomach had subsided, and the danger of a spanking was past, Oliver lay in the small bed with his hand in Father's.

"Why did you go without telling us, though?" asked Father. "You could have gone to the circus. Rush or Cuffy would have been glad to take you. I would have taken you myself if I could have stolen the time."

Oliver sighed. "I did ask Cuffy about it once, but she said oh no there's too much measles around. And everybody else was going out alone on their Saturdays, so I just thought I'd go alone, too. I did want to see the circus so badly."

"Didn't you know we'd worry?"

"I guess I didn't think about it till afterwards," Oliver admitted.

"Well, you'll never give us a scare like that again, will you?"

"No, I never will, if I can help it," promised Oliver.

"All right then. That's that. Now suppose you tell me what you liked best at the circus."

"Oh, everything was wonderful. I liked the man on the one-wheel bicycle, and the elephants, and that automobile with all the clowns and the donkey in it, and the lady who stood on her head on the swing, and I liked all the things I was eating, while I was eating them. But the thing I liked *best* of all wasn't in the circus."

"What was that?" said Father.

"It was when the policeman brought me home on the horse," replied Oliver.

For now, no longer overshadowed by stomach-aches or unhappy apprehensions, the memory of that ride had become a radiant thing. He remembered the horse's two pointed ears that could move independently of each other, and its brawny, arching neck with the tidy black mane; and its strong, healthy smell. It was sort of like riding on a boat, only better because it felt alive, and you were higher up. And behind, immense and gorgeous in his uniform, rode the officer of the law who had befriended him. Oliver remembered how he held the reins in white gloved hands the size of baseball mitts. The splendor of that ride would never die.

—ELIZABETH ENRIGHT

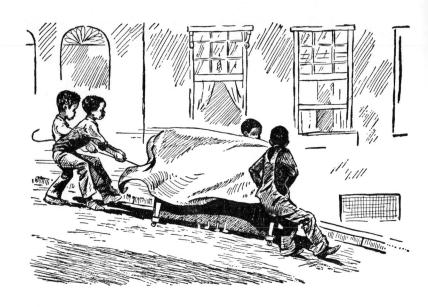

Mary Ellis Has a Birthday Party

Harlem

On Tuesday, Steppin went back to school and resumed his dancing classes and kitchen police duties at Dad Kirby's. The dancing classes were held in the afternoon now, and each class met only three times a week. Still, it was the busiest fall and winter Steppin had ever known.

Although he had been promoted to Dad's advanced class before his vacation, he attended nearly every session of the beginners' class. Two afternoons a week he stayed after class to clean the studio. What with the homework he had to do for school and helping High Pockets with the janitor work, it seemed to Steppin he almost never had a minute to call his own. At night he was so tired he seldom teased his mother to let him go out and play under the street lights.

Friday evenings, Pete usually had supper with the Stebbins family and as likely as not Roy and Snakey would drop in later. Usually Virginia Day came to spend the evening with Mary Ellis. As soon as the supper dishes were done Pete would get out his guitar and Mary Ellis would settle down at the organ. Then, until the clock struck ten, the five of them would make the house ring as they played and sang and danced. And sometime during the evening the boys always put on their stunt just as they had done it at Camp Oneishta.

Often Pete would play the organ. He declared that pumping the floor boards and working the hand valves was much more fun than playing a piano. But Mary Ellis still yearned for a real piano with all the keys working.

"My, I'd admire to play like you do," she confided to Pete one evening. "I reckon taking lessons costs a heap of money," she added wistfully.

"My mother taught me music for my first four years," Pete explained. "Now I go to a teacher way down on West Fifty-seventh Street. I think he does charge quite a lot."

Mary Ellis shook her head. "I guess I'll just haf to keep in patience until Steppin becomes a famous dancer before I can ever take lessons. But I surely do pine to do so," she sighed.

Just then Mrs. Stebbins and Virginia Day came in with a plate of hot fudge. When they had eaten every crumb of it and were ready to leave, Mary Ellis invited all of them to her birthday supper on Saturday of the following week.

"It isn't my true birthday until Tuesday, a week," she confessed. "But Mom always has us celebrate on a Saturday whether it's the right day or not."

All the way home, Pete kept thinking about Mary Ellis and how she longed to take music lessons. His mother was alone when he came in and it suddenly occurred to Pete that she might give Mary Ellis lessons just as she had given them to him.

On the following Friday he was idly glancing over the weekly Amsterdam News when he saw an item that made his eyes bulge with excitement.

"Will give upright piano to any reliable person who will call for same," he read. "If interested, apply in person to L. G. Carter, 290 St. Nicholas Terrace."

It seemed almost too good to be true. Pete's fingers trembled as he tore out the notice. Without a word to anyone he skipped out of the house and hurried to Dad Kirby's to consult with Steppin. Steppin, too, was overjoyed at the prospect of getting a free piano for Mary Ellis.

"We'll get them to deliver it tomorrow," he told Pete. "Boy, oh, boy, what a birthday gift that's going to be!"

"Do you know where St. Nicholas Terrace is?" Pete asked.

"Sure I do. It's up on Sugar Hill. I know right about where that number is, too. I've delivered plenty of laundry up there. We better go right off now before they give it to someone else."

"I wonder why they call this 'Sugar Hill'?" Pete asked as they trudged along.

"That's easy. It's because the Negro folks who live here are so rich they don't have to eat anything but sugar unless they want to," Steppin explained.

"I should think they'd call it *Candy Hill* instead of *Sugar Hill*," Pete protested. "Candy is a heap better than sugar."

"That's right, too. How-so-ever, they both eats good—here we are," Steppin interrupted himself. "It's a right nice place, too," he approved as they peered through a huge iron gate at a modern apartment house built around a garden courtyard like a medieval monastery. "The Cloisters" was written in bronze letters over the gate.

"Some people think these churchy-looking places are even more toney than Striver's Row," Steppin told Pete as they studied the list of tenants' names. "But not me! To my mind they're not a patch on having a whole house to yourself and a brass plate with only your own name on it."

He pressed the button marked "L. G. Carter." When the lock clicked, Pete turned the big knob on the gate and they stepped inside. The gate had hardly closed behind them when the bright blue door of Apartment 3 opened and a pleasant-looking dark-skinned man in a red moire dressing gown looked out.

Pete snatched off his cap.

"Is this where Mr. Carter lives?" he asked, politely.

"That's right," the man replied, taking a puff on the pipe he was holding. "I'm Carter."

"My name is Manuel Pierre Bergeret," Pete introduced himself. "And this is my friend, Steppin A. Stebbins."

"Bergeret?" Mr. Carter took his pipe out of his mouth. "Any relation to Mannie Bergeret, the boxer?"

"Yes, sir, he's my dad," Pete told him.

"Well, now, isn't that something," Mr. Carter smiled. "And what can I do for you?"

"We've come about the piano you are giving away," Pete told him.

"We thought, like as not, there was some mistake," Steppin spoke up. "It doesn't make sense that any one would up and give a piano away free. But Pete, here—I mean, Pierre and I figured it wouldn't do a mite of harm to find out about it."

"No, there is no mistake. My wife's mother is giving her a baby grand and she would rather give away the one she has than sell it for next to nothing. But what puzzles me is why you boys want a piano. Come on in and tell me about it."

Mr. Carter led them into a beautifully furnished living room.

"It's like this, sir," Pete explained. "Steppin's little sister, Mary Ellis, wants to study piano playing the worst kind of way. I've got it all fixed up that my mother will give her lessons if we can get a piano for her to practice on."

"So when we saw by the paper how you were giving away a piano, we came right on up," Steppin put in eagerly.

"You see," Pete finished, "tomorrow is Mary Ellis' birthday and we want the piano for a big surprise at her party."

"Well, that sounds all right," Mr. Carter announced

after he had asked them a few questions about Mary Ellis and the Stebbins family.

He nodded toward a small cottage-size piano standing against the wall behind them. "There it is, boys, and it's all yours."

"Boy, isn't that neat!" Steppin exclaimed.

They got up and went over to admire the piano more closely.

"She's got a shine that puts the noon day sun to shame," Steppin beamed. "I bet Mary Ellis' eyes will bug right out of her head when she casts them on this baby."

"She certainly is just about perfect and we sure are in your favor for letting us have her," Pete said earnestly.

"Oh, that's all right," Mr. Carter assured them. "The next question is have you boys enough money to pay for having the piano moved?"

"Money to pay for having the piano moved!" For a minute, the boys were speechless. They had just taken it for granted that the Carters would deliver the piano for them.

"About how much does it cost to move a piano?" Steppin tried not to sound as dismayed as he felt.

"What floor do you live on?" Mr. Carter asked.

"Basement," Steppin told him.

"Well, that's good. What with only a few steps at that end and none at all here, it shouldn't cost more than ten or fifteen at the most."

"Ten or fifteen dollars!" Steppin turned away to hide his disappointment.

After a long pause, Pete spoke up.

"Oh, we can manage that easy enough. Will it be all

right if we send some one for it the first thing in the morning?"

"Sure, the sooner the better," Mr. Carter nodded. "I won't be here, but the maid will let them in. By the way, what is your dad doing now?"

Pete told Mr. Carter about his father's boxing school, and then after thanking him again for the piano, the boys left.

"Only ten or fifteen dollars," Steppin groaned as soon as they were out on the street. "Gosh, Pete, wouldn't you know there would have to be a catch like that somewhere? I'm right glad you pretended that we would send some one for it, though. I'd hate to have Mr. Carter know that we were dumb enough to think he'd pay for moving it."

"Listen, Steppin, I wasn't just pretending or at least not all together. When he first let out about our paying to have it moved, I was so flabbergasted I didn't know what to say. Then I got to thinking—it isn't a very big piano—Steppin," Pete broke off. "You don't suppose we could move it ourselves, do you?"

"Hot diggity, that's an idea!" Steppin stared admiringly at Pete. "Maybe we could get it over to my house, Pete, but how ever would we carry it down our basement stairs?"

"Well," Pete explained, "I figured if we got it that far, maybe some one would help us."

"There's something in that, too. Harmon's Moving and Express business is just three doors down from our house," Steppin remembered. "But old Harmon just naturally hates everybody and especially kids," he added gloomily. "But like you say, there surely ought to be *some* one who would lend us a hand."

"Roy is awfully big for his age," Pete was thinking out loud. "We could get him to dress up in some of his father's clothes and go with us. The Carters' maid wouldn't know but what he was a sure enough moving man."

"And we can get Snakey to come along and help us," said Steppin. "You know, Pete, I wouldn't wonder if by tomorrow night that little old piano would be shining away right in my own parlor."

Early the next forenoon, a strange procession trudged up to Mr. Carter's apartment on Sugar Hill. It was headed by Roy, wearing his father's overalls and a faded blue shirt. He had a square of burlap tied around his waist as an apron, and he carried an old khaki blanket over one arm. Next came tall, lanky Snakey who, too, was wearing overalls and a burlap apron. He carried a coiled clothes line. To make himself look more grown up, Snakey had glued a tiny black moustache over his upper lip.

"Gosh, Snakey, your own father wouldn't know you," Steppin declared.

It was quite true that Snakey's appearance was changed. However, instead of making him appear older, the dab of black on his light-brown face was so out of keeping with his childish features that he looked rather stupid. Pete and Steppin wore long pants but did not try to disguise their age. Their cue was to keep out of sight until Roy and Snakey had the piano safely out of the Carters' apartment.

The iron gate of The Cloisters was open and a moving van was backed up to the curb.

"What luck," Steppin exclaimed. "Now the maid will think we belong with the van."

After a whispered last-minute rehearsal, Roy and Snakey swaggered up to Apartment 3 and rang the bell.

"We've come to get de pianer for Mr. Stebbins," Roy growled in the deep bass voice he had practiced.

Outside the gate, Pete and Steppin held their breath until they heard the maid answer, "Right this way." Then they waited anxiously, watching the open door of Number 3.

"What if they can't budge it?" Steppin fretted. "Oh, boy, I wish they would come."

After what seemed a very long time, they heard a heavy rumbling and squeaking and presently the blanket-covered piano moved into sight. As soon as Roy and Snakey had pushed it into the court, Pete and Steppin came to their aid. The maid followed them to the door and stood watching them as they slowly shoved the piano across the courtyard. The moving van which was still backed up to the curb seemed to dispel any misgivings she had, for to their relief, they heard her slam the door just as they started through the gateway.

Two huge men came out of another apartment, carrying a davenport, and had to wait until the boys had shoved the piano out to the sidewalk. They stopped grumbling and looked puzzled when the boys turned the piano about and started to push it down the street. A few passersby stopped and stared at them. But the boys were so relieved to have the piano in their possession and so occupied with the business of moving it that they were unaware of everything else.

"If we can get it down off the sidewalk at the crossing,

we'll be all right," Roy puffed. "After that, we can run it on the street all the way home."

Sliding the piano off the curb to the street was not nearly as difficult as they had anticipated. Their next problem was to steer it down the steep hill from St. Nicholas Terrace to Eighth Avenue. Snakey tied his rope around it and then Roy gave them their directions.

"Now, Steppin, you and Pete keep behind and pull back on the rope with all your might and main. Snakey and I will keep in front and do likewise. Get all set and on the next green light, we will let her go."

They turned the piano so that one end was headed toward the foot of the hill. When the traffic light changed to green Steppin and Pete braced themselves and clutched the rope while Roy and Snakey gave it a gentle shove. The piano started rolling.

"All right, let's go," Roy sang out.

"Hold back, hold back!" he shouted as the piano began rolling faster and faster.

The four of them were pulling back with all their strength but still they had to run to keep up with the piano. Steppin was sure his arms would be pulled off any minute and the rope was burning his hands so badly that he could scarcely keep them clenched. Pete, too, was having a bad time. But even so their task was easier than that of Roy and Snakey who were almost in front of the piano. Faster and faster they went toward the intersection at the foot of the hill. They crossed the intersection just as the light changed. Half way down the next block the piano began moving more and more slowly and finally it stopped. The boys eased it close to the curb and sat down to get their breath and rest their aching arms before starting on the last lap of their journey. From now on they had only the heavy Eighth Avenue traffic to trouble them, and in a few minutes they had the piano parked at the curb in front of Steppin's basement home.

Dozens of children gathered around them, besieging them with questions. All up and down the block grown-ups leaned out of windows to watch them. Mr. Harmon took his feet down from the iron courtyard railing of his Moving and Express office and whirled around in his swivel chair to see what was going on. Charley Kee came hurrying out of the laundry, wiping his steamy glasses to get a better look at the strange sight.

"What you up to, Steppin?" he scolded.

Briefly, Steppin explained. "Are Mom and Mary Ellis still out?" he asked. Mr. Kee nodded.

"I think they come home pretty quick now," he told Steppin.

"Gosh, I wish we could get it in the parlor before they get back," Steppin said. "Here comes old Harmon, but it's no use asking *him* to give us a hand."

Mr. Harmon strolled slowly toward the group of chattering children and stood with his arms folded, scowling down at the four boys. Mr. Kee pattered over and stood beside him.

"These so foolish youths think they try to carry the little piano down the steps," he confided sadly.

"I'll say they are fools!" Mr. Harmon agreed scornfully.

"That's what I try to tell them," Charley sighed. "I say to them that it would need ten men even of the great strength of you to do this feat."

"Ten men to carry that little music box?" Mr. Harmon spat contemptuously. "Give me one more good man and I could carry it to the top of the Statue of Liberty."

Mr. Kee's little almond eyes became almost round with amazement. He looked over the crowd and sighted Buck Norman, a strapping young fellow who helped his father in his ice and coal business.

"You say you and one other strong man such as Buck could do this feat?" he asked incredulously. Buck shoved his way through the crowd.

"Sure, we could, couldn't we, Harmon?" he bragged.

Mr. Kee looked so doubtful that the crowd of boys and girls became impressed by the difficulty of the task.

"Sure they could move it. I bet anything they could," some of them began saying.

"I bet you three to one they couldn't," others protested.

Mr. Kee spread his small hands helplessly and shook his head.

"I take your word, Mr. Harmon. I do not wish you or our young Buck to be hurt to prove that you can do this feat."

Buck threw out his chest and swaggered up to the piano.

"Oh, come on, Harmon, let's show the Chinaman what a couple of real he-men can do."

"Okay," Harmon laughed.

The crowd of children became silent, watching intently

as the two men lifted the piano over the sidewalk and slowly maneuvered it down the steep narrow steps.

"What did I tell you? I knew they could do it! Hurrah for Buck and Harmon," they chattered and shouted as the men set the piano down in the areaway.

"Well, what do you think of that, Charley?" Buck chaffed the little laundry man.

Mr. Kee folded his arms in his sleeves and bowed low to hide the twinkle in his eyes.

"I have seen a miracle," he declared solemnly.

The boys had just time to install the piano in the parlor and move the organ out to the caboose before Mrs. Stebbins and Mary Ellis returned. Steppin met them at the door.

"Mom, we boys have the parlor all set for a little surprise we cooked up for the party," he explained. "So will you and Mary Ellis keep out of there until after supper?"

"I only hope you haven't made a mess in the parlor," Mrs. Stebbins told Steppin when he came in for lunch.

Steppin slid into his place at the table and stretched his legs wearily.

"I'd sure hate to work as hard as I have this morning just making a mess," he grinned.

When the time to reveal their wonderful surprise drew near, the boys could hardly wait. They kept whispering to each other and exchanging mysterious remarks until Mary Ellis became so curious she declared she must see what was in the parlor before she could ever cut her birthday cake. As all of them had taken the edge off their appetites with several hot dogs each, potato salad, doughnuts, sweet potato pie and quantities of sweet cider, they decided this would be a very good plan. But, first of all, they insisted that she must open the packages beside her plate.

The boys watched impatiently while Mary Ellis exclaimed over a little bottle of perfume which Virginia had brought her, and a manicure set which her mother had given her. But when she picked up a large white envelope and opened it, they were all attention.

Mary Ellis' pretty brown face shone with pleasure as she read the letter enclosed.

"Mom, oh, Mom, listen to this: 'Dear Mary Ellis,' " she read, " 'Pierre tells me that you wish very much to study piano music. This little note is to wish you a happy birthday and to tell you I shall be most happy to give you lessons. Would you like to commence Monday after school?

" 'Sincerely yours,
Pierre's mother
Gregoire Bergeret.'

"Oh, Pete, you teased your mother to give me music lessons, I know you did! So it's really a birthday gift from you. I just couldn't ever have had a gift I wanted more. I'm going to practice my head off even if the old organ gets so bad not one of the keys play. You see if I don't, Mom!"

"I know you will do your very best, honey," Mrs. Stebbins smiled, "and we hardly know how to thank you and your mother, Pete," she told him warmly.

"You still have another letter to look at, Mary Ellis,"

Snakey urged. Mary Ellis opened the second envelope.

"We have hidden a little gift in the parlor. Find it and it's yours. Signed, 'The Oneishta Four.'"

"You all come with me," Mary Ellis begged when she finished reading their mysterious note. "And while I'm searching, you boys have to tell me if I'm hot or cold."

"No, mam!" they declared as they solemnly trailed after her, "you've got to find it your own self even if it takes you all night."

"Oh, dear, I'm so poor at finding things like that," she protested as she led them into the dark parlor, "sometimes when we play Hide the Thimble, I can't see it even when it's right under my nose."

"Like as not, you'll be a great grandma before you find this thimble," Roy assured her, and all of them roared with laughter.

"Goodness, I can't even find the light," Mary Ellis declared as she swept her arm over her head, trying to locate the bulb. She finally found it and turned on the light.

"As soon as my eyes stop blinking, I'm going to start hunting in this corner and go right smack around the room—" Just then Mary Ellis saw the piano. "Oh!" She caught her breath.

For a whole minute she stood twisting her brown fingers and staring at the piano. Then she turned to her mother who was clutching the door knob and looking as if her knees were about to collapse under her.

"Mom, Mom," Mary Ellis ran to her mother and, hiding her face in her apron, began to sob.

"There, there, honey, don't cry." Mrs. Stebbins sank

weakly into an arm chair and gathered Mary Ellis to her breast. Virginia Day, round-eyed, watched cautiously from the adjoining room as if she feared the piano might charge at her any minute.

After the first shock of Mary Ellis' unaccountable behavior, Roy, Pete and Snakey looked to Steppin for an explanation.

"Mom, doesn't she even like it?" Steppin demanded.

"Like it! Of course she likes it. But she is overcome, and so am I," Mrs. Stebbins added.

Mary Ellis turned her tear-stained face toward Steppin.

"I love it," she sobbed.

It took considerable reassurance from Mrs. Stebbins and Mary Ellis before the crestfallen boys could be made to believe that Mary Ellis' tears were really an expression of perfect happiness.

"And now, if you don't mind, I'd be pleased to know how this piano got here," Mrs. Stebbins suggested when tranquility was restored.

Mrs. Stebbins, Mary Ellis and Virginia listened with flattering attention while the boys, all talking at once, gave them the piano's history from the moment Pete had seen the notice in the newspaper.

"Except for Pete, we would never have known about it," Steppin said.

"Yes, but if it hadn't been for Roy and Snakey helping us, we never could have moved it," Pete put in.

"And if it hadn't been for Charley Kee, Mary Ellis would have had to sit right out on the street to practice her scales," Roy reminded them.

As it was growing late, Mrs. Stebbins suggested it was time to cut the birthday cake.

"I'm going to cut it right in here so I can look at my piano while I'm eating," Mary Ellis insisted. "And, Mom, will you and Virginia please get things ready and light the candles? I'm going to invite Mr. Kee to my party," she declared.

Mrs. Stebbins and Virginia covered the parlor center table with a white napkin and brought in the cake. When Mary Ellis came back with Mr. Kee, the pink candles were lighted and the room light was turned out.

"Before I blow out the candles, I'm going to make a wish that every one of you will always be as happy as I am tonight," Mary Ellis told them. "And if I blow them all out with one puff, it will come true for sure."

She took a big breath and blew as hard as she could, and every candle light went out.

—HOPE NEWELL

Paul Becomes a Nipper in a Mine

A Pennsylvania Coal Mine

It was October in Ashburn, and the middle of
the week. There was a glaring sun on the breaker when
one looked at it from the outside. Paul swallowed hard.
His mouth set. Money was needed more than ever before
in the Tiber family. He couldn't go home without it when
payday came. His mother counted on it. His college fund
waited, hungrily, for the weekly rate. He couldn't let
himself be fired without getting another job immediately.
And there was only one place where a man could get work
these days.

"Paul Becomes a Nipper in a Mine" is from *Paul Tiber: Forester* by Maria
Gleit; copyright, 1949, by Maria Gleit; reprinted by permission of Charles
Scribner's Sons, publishers.

Toeing in a little and swinging from the hips as if he were walking through heavy underbrush, Paul Tiber strode down Jones and across to the office of the Candanoah Coal Company. "Sorry, old man," he said to someone who seemed to be walking with him, arguing, but couldn't be seen. "But there isn't an alternative."

He climbed the steps up to the office.

"I've been fired in the breaker," he said to the man at the employment desk. "Can I apply for work in the mine?"

They accepted him immediately. "Indeed you can," the man answered. "What is your name?"

The name was Paul Tiber, and the job the young man was supposed to start on the following morning was that of a nipper—same thing Father had started with as a kid of ten.

At home that night he didn't dare drop as much as a hint of what had happened. Knowing too well how his mother would feel about it and that it would be something like the world's end for Father, he kept the news carefully to himself. "Once you have started in the mine, you'll never get out. You are like the mules . . ." That's what Father would say. Why did Father have to be so stubborn? With him, Paul, it would be different, couldn't Father see that? Couldn't he see that Paul had to wait just a little longer to make the jump and leave the mine behind forever?

Because he needed it so, he started dreaming again. Next spring perhaps he would already be on the payroll of the state. Firefighting. Protecting, in this way, his beloved forests until he got around to being a full-fledged forester himself.

Father would refuse to believe him, if he told him so. All the other miners would. They'd laugh at him; ridicule him. "Once you start in the mine you are lost to the world, son." He knew it too well. And he couldn't help remembering that story about Father's first day down below as a nipper.

Good old Dad. Things were different now. The Company wasn't omnipotent any more. Conditions weren't quite as bad as they had been.

A slight apprehension of mishap began to cloud over Paul Tiber's dreams. Father had survived not only this accident but others as well. It was true, however, that he had made every possible effort to get out of the mines. He had even moved his big family, from one state to the other; but the mines had not let him go. Or was it the hills? Or both?

Uneasily, Paul tossed. Next morning, he woke up much earlier than usual. Not to arouse his mother's suspicions, he stayed in bed till the very last moment, trying to sound and behave as if nothing out of the ordinary had happened. Quietly, he slipped out of the house. Father was on night shift, heaven be thanked. Thoughtfully, Paul marched up to the shaft; friendly, he greeted the men who changed to their work clothes; determinedly, he put on the miner's helmet; firmly his fingers closed around the miner's lamp. His mouth was tightly drawn. His eyes were hard. But underneath them burnt excitement. He'd pry into the secret of the mine, finally.

He crossed the tracks. There was the entrance to the mine. Nothing spectacular, just a wooden door leading to the cage, crowded already with miners. "By gosh, if this isn't the oldest Tiber boy," one said. He squinted at Paul. "An' Frank havin' always boasted no son of his—"

"Know the entrance, don't you, Greenie," they'd asked him at the shaft. "Driver McKellan be waitin' for you."

"Are you McKellan?" he asked now, "Mule driver McKellan?"

The man was. "Git goin'," he said. "An' just imagining that the old cuss has always bragged—"

"Don't tell my father, please don't."

Mule driver McKellan found that a capital joke. "Don't you worry, he'll know soon enough."

Open on all sides, the cage rumbled down. It stopped a few times to dispose of some of the men who worked on higher planes.

"They tell you at the shaft what part of the business is your share?" McKellan wanted to know. He was a big, fleshy man known for his irate temper as well as his innate antipathy against any kind of a razor blade.

"They said you would."

"Okay. Better for you an' me I break you in. Now you listen," he said as, at the last stop, they ambled out of the cage. "There's them mules. Only thing you can do is curse'm an' kick'm and try to get some work out of'm. Thing you have to do is open them gangway doors for them gol'derned critters and bolt the doors when they're through. Then you run ahead again and open the next door before they reach it. An' don't you dawdle or you'll be sorry fer it, unnerstand?"

They had to stoop as they half crawled through one of the subterranean corridors but now Charlie McKellan straightened up. They entered another door and there three impatiently snorting animals were waiting for them —Fox, Mike and Daisy mule. Charlie McKellan opened the amenities with a not too good-natured kick. "Okay, you beasts, git goin', Pete ahoi!"

Freely distributing as many curses and kicks as he thought necessary, Charlie managed to get his three-head of mules harnessed and out of the place where the poor wretches had spent the night.

"What you waiting fer, boy? Git goin', Pete ahoi!"

There was the angry snorting and stamping of the mules, and the rattling of the empty cars they pulled. There was Charlie with the stubbly chin and the mean little eyes; there were endless gangways of rock and doors opening into darkness. There was the glowworm light of the miners' caps, the hammering and picking and crashing of coal. There were pillars holding up the roof of the place the men were working at—props that once had been trees—there were other corridors, and openings into blackness. There was coal.

For the first time, Paul Tiber saw the broad black silver streak pressed in between the rock and slate—the coal vein running through the body of the earth like an artery through the body of man.

He ran and opened a door. He waited for the darkly looming forms of the mules to pass. He bent down and bolted the door shut so that the air current in the mine would not be disturbed. And while starting to run again, it came to him with a pang that this silvery black layer compressed between dustblack slate and gray brown dripping rock had also once been trees! And while his driver was cursing him indiscriminately, a sense of wonder began to fill Paul Tiber's heart—wonder at the miracle that was a tree. He ran and opened the door. He waited and bolted it shut. Where there were trees, he thought, there was life, even down here. Where there were trees, there was growth, and usefulness. Trees improved the soil, controlled floods, regulated rivers. Where there were no trees on the mountain, rains would beat heavily upon the ground, form tiny rivulets which in their turn would carry away small grains of fertile top soil. Where there were no trees, the rivulets would join others, and before long raging mountain torrents would rush into the streams and lakes, filling them with silt and debris.

Where there were trees, there was hope. There were houses. There was furniture. There were newspapers and books.

And where there had been trees, hundreds of thousands of years ago—there now was coal! And if Paul Tiber had until this moment admired trees for their beauty and the mystery of their growth, he now began to marvel at the place they had assumed in the service of man.

"Git goin', ye fools, Pete ahoi!" Charlie McKellan cursed. The mules kicked their hoofs; the miners wanted more empty cars and wanted them faster; the laden cars had to be pulled back, more doors had to be opened, more doors closed.

At the end of the shift, Paul Tiber felt as if a year of his life had passed, or his life itself, and he had never done anything but opened the closed gangway doors; never hoped anything but not to be trampled under by the mules or squeezed against the wall; never eaten his lunch anywhere but in the mine; never heard anything but Charlie McKellan's vile cursing. And above all; that he'd never before seen the light of day.

The men in the cage that brought him up scowled at him.

"Liked it down there, uh?"

Again, he began to plead. "Don't tell my Dad, not yet."

They shrugged, too tired to care. He did not know whether he could trust them. But they kept mum. For nearly two weeks neither his father nor his mother had the faintest idea that their son was working in the mine. On the day he received his first pay envelope, however, there was no way to keep the knowledge back from them any longer.

His mother heaved a weary sigh. Father took it sitting down. Paul had expected him to raise the roof. Relieved as he felt for a moment that Father wasn't launching into rhetorics, he didn't know what to make of this sudden, complete surrender. Pa's arms were hanging between his knees, his hands seemed limp, with the blue scratches strangely in evidence. His eyes were tired.

"Now, listen, Pa. It's only for a short time."

Father said nothing. His shoulders sagged.

"Don't take it too hard, man," Mother began. "He'll sure get out of the mine, Paul will."

"No," said Father like one who knew better, "he won't. Once you start in the mine . . ."

"Not Paul," said Mother. "He's different. I've always told you that boy's different. From the day he sewed his first button on his coat I told you so. And if he tells you he'll quit the mine he'll do just that."

"Don't lie in your throat, Ma," Father said in a very gentle and very hopeless tone. "The mine has got him and will keep him, no matter what. It has got him," he went on in that desperate gentleness, "and it will get Dave. And after Dave, when his time comes, it will get little Pete."

Paul stood up. This was intolerable. "It won't get Dave, Pa," he said. Dave, who was lolling on the kitchen sofa, turned his head. He said nothing.

"And what else do you think Dave could do?"

"Dave will go to college."

"What?" cried Dave sitting up.

"You'll go to Forestry School and study forestry, that's what you will do."

"I?" cried Dave. His eyes burned. His mouth stood a little open.

"Haven't you always liked to work with trees?" It was like a cross examination. "Have you, or not?"

"Trees!" cried Dave, his voice shaking. "You know it isn't that I don't like trees—"

"I know," said Paul. "I know it's a matter of money. And don't you worry about it, Dave. As truly as I'm sitting here, we'll put you through Forestry School."

"But Paul—"

"You shut up," Paul said, "and listen. I'll turn over to you what I have saved, but don't you think that you'll get it for nothing or that it's a present. I'll go on earning

and saving and you do the studying meanwhile. The time's
short, Dave. We can't afford to lose much more. You'll
study all the books you have to in order to get your degree
—but God help you if you don't teach me every blessed
thing you learn. You'll send me the books and you'll write
me about assignments. In a little while I'll try to get into
practical work—yes, practical forest work, fighting forest
fires, and doing I don't know what—but in order to succeed I'll have to have the theoretical knowledge, too. And
this you'll furnish me with, Dave, and don't you get any
wrong ideas—"

Dave's voice was full of brotherly adoration. "I'll never
forget it, Paul, never—"

"Skip it," Paul said. "It won't be all fun. You'll have
to work for it, kid. It's a matter of pure expediency, you
know."

But it wasn't. Not quite. It was just that he hadn't been
able to see Father look the way he had. It was just that
he had suddenly realized that he had forgotten all about
Dave. In former years, he had thought about him. Dave
will have to get an education. Things like that. Afterwards, he had started to think of himself alone. It was a
bad habit. He had been wrapped up in his own dream,
day and night, pondering about ways and means of making it come true. Meanwhile, for all he had cared and
known, Dave might have had to start in the coalbreaker
as a dust sweeper, gradually working up his way to a
picker of slate and a jig tender. Like Whitey he might
have slipped and fallen. He might— But he wouldn't.
Not now.

With some effort, Father scrambled to his feet. "You

are a good boy, Paul," he said. "But you can't do it. It'll be too much. Much too much. Though we all could help and pitch in and scrimp and pinch—"

"I won't have it," cried Dave. "I don't want a sacrifice, and I don't want to be a burden!"

Paul only laughed. "Burden? Sacrifice? You crazy, kid?"

"It would be my fault if you never got out of the mine," Dave said, "and I won't have it."

Paul's face took on a serious expression. "Listen, Dave, if I don't get out of that mine, it'll be *my* fault and nobody else's. Is that understood?"

Dave said, yes, it was, though he was not quite certain about it; and Mother smiled and sighed and Father shook his head and rubbed his hands and stuck out his chin in a tentative kind of way.

Paul sat down again. "Get me paper and pen, Dave," he said. "We'll go right at it and ask if we can enter you at State University coming term." And while he was waiting for his brother to bring him the writing materials, the world of the mine flashed past his mind's eyes for one endless moment—a world of shadows populated by four-legged demons otherwise called mules, and silent, wary slaves usually called men.

—Maria Gleit

The Isle of Que

A Tale of a Pennsylvania Flood

The Isle of Que was really a peninsula, and a
Frenchman, exploring southward from Canada and rec-
ognizing its resemblance to a tail, named it the Isle of
Queue, which was soon simplified to Que.

On the mainland close by lay the borough of Selinsgrove; here, crossing a bridge, the residents of the Isle of
Que voted, went to church and to motion pictures, sent
their children to school and did their shopping.

The Lutheran Church in Selinsgrove faced on Main
Street, and there, at eleven o'clock on Sunday morning,
Tim sat in the Yoder pew. Once the family had filled two

pews, or even three, and that was still the case in summer when Yoders came for their vacations. They did not all come to Mother's house, the older boys had begun to acquire houses of their own, all facing the river. Now, for only Mother, Tim and Rosemary, one pew more than sufficed. Tim sat next the side aisle, then Mother, then Rosy. Sometimes Rosy leaned forward to catch Tim's eye, but he looked straight ahead, frowning, his attention fixed not on what he could see in the church but what he could hear from without.

In summer, sitting where he sat now, he could hear or shut out from his mind as he chose, the careless horns of pleasure-seeking motorists, or the steady roar of a long line of trucks, traveling impatiently behind a church-going family in an ancient car. Perhaps, so limited was the supply of gasoline, the obstacle to speed might be an aged phaeton or surrey. Sometimes he could hear above other sounds, the long lonely whistle of a freight.

This morning he could not have heard cars or trucks if any had passed. There was no through traffic; to north and south all vehicles were stalled—buses and army lorries, tanks carrying oil or milk, heavy trucks and light, loaded with stone or timber. Machinery, crated for foreign shipment, halted far from ships or airplanes. Those who depended on "Aunt Sally's" bread would go hungry. Some drivers, misjudging the depth of water over the road, or taking a chance, lost their cargoes and saved their own lives with difficulty. On the highway where the river was out of its proper bounds, and on the river, past the Yoders, floated boxes and bales, tin containers, crates of bread. Already, boated sheep, cows and even horses revolved in the swift current. Sometimes large trees sailed along, waving desperate arms.

No engine whistles punctuated other noises. Trains loaded with ore from Lake Superior halted in long lines. Travelers looked anxiously out the windows of day coaches, parlor cars and sleeping cars, and seeing little but pouring rain and a brimming river, complained irritably because they were delayed.

Tim did not miss the horns of the truck drivers or pleasure seekers. He did not realize that he had said good morning to friends when he entered the church or that he had risen to chant the *Gloria Patria* or the *Kyrie,* or in more or less of a croak, had petitioned the Lord for a pure heart. The small choir had bravely sung an anthem, the minister had begun to preach—Tim was deaf to singing and preaching.

He was not, however, deaf to everything—he heard one loud, continuous sound. Reverberating on the sloping roof of the church, gurgling loudly down drainpipes, dripping directly from roof to earth because the pipes could not carry half that fell, poured the rain. Striking smartly the north wall, near which he sat, the bouncing drops descended upon unmelted ice.

He knew how, beside and over highways and railroad beds, flood waters were rising. Foundation, trestles and bridges were weakening, down hillsides water was cascading, into stations and telegraph offices water was seeping. Cars loaded with timber, slag and stone were being shifted toward sections of greatest danger; in railroad yards, impatient engines belched smoke. Engines pushed enormous cranes from whose long arms were suspended steel rails which could be lowered to crush buildings carried against bridge piers or threatening to block openings between piers. A barn or house might lay the foundation of a huge dam.

Remembering Charlie's stories, hearing last night's warning broadcasts, Tim listened intently for a sound louder than the rain. It was queer how nothing at hand seemed real. The gray light, darkened and faintly colored by stained glass, suggested the dim twilight in which divers and pearl-fishers ply their trade. A green shade ringed the familiar faces of the few choir members, they looked to Tim for an instant as though they were dead.

Why, Tim asked himself, did the congregation sit here stupidly? What were they waiting for? It was true, as Mother reminded him, the river was wide and every minute excess water was pouring into Chesapeake Bay.

"We're still a foot above water," she had said this morning, stepping into Old Pybus. "Think of the millions of gallons required to raise a river three quarters of a mile wide another foot! Especially when all the time millions of gallons are running off."

In spite of what Mother said, Tim listened with growing alarm. His hands clenched as they rested on his knees, his cheeks pricked. Suddenly he heard what he waited for—the sound described by Old Charlie—a rough, deep roar, unbroken like the pour of the rain, but different and strange. He glanced at Mother, it was clear from the placid expression of her blue eyes that she did not hear what he heard. He rose and went down the aisle, though the minister was talking now about the flood. The church, he said, would be open all day and night. There would be food for refugees and a place to sleep, if any needed shelter. Tim did not hear the minister, he heard only Charlie.

"When she really comes, you'll know it. You'll hear her, never fear, boy! When she comes all the rocks is covered, an' the banks is soft so she don't make too much noise when she strikes against 'em. She flows fairly quiet round the islands. But the railroad bridge makes her beller like kingdom come. You can't believe it, boy! You can't believe how soft water can make such a uproar. It's hell let loose, Tim! I told you how I went to Niagara for three dollars, an' how—"

Tim ran down the church steps to the Sunday school, his boots thumping, and snatched his cap and raincoat from a chair. It was cold enough for snow on the Buffalo Branch, but he wouldn't be cold with all he had on. He ran to Pine Street and down to the bridge. The water was almost to the roof of *Little Norway*. Higher on the bank, it lapped the threshold of Fred's shed.

Toward the bridge from the Isle of Que approached a procession. No matter where you lived on the Isle of Que, you could reach Selinsgrove proper only by a boat or the bridge. Islanders were leaving *en masse;* only the Yoder house and one other were not abandoned. Most of the houses were in the same state, their first stories empty of furniture, except pieces too heavy to be carried, their second stories packed to the ceilings.

The travelers shouted warnings and questions.

"You hear her, Tim?"

"Yes, I do."

"You Yoders'll take one chance too many! Where's your Mother?"

"In church. Where would she be?"

"Is she coming back to the island?"

"Sure she's coming back to the island!"

This, determined Tim, was his final reply. He had business more important than chattering. He ran round a baby carriage and leaped across a wheelbarrow. He tore over the bridge and flung back the door of Fred's shed. One shove and the motor-boat would be launched. He gave the necessary shove and leaped in. A snap, and the engine was coughing. The watchers on the bridge screamed and shouted.

"Don't risk your life for Old Charlie! He had a chance to leave and he wouldn't take it. You'll never get back!"

A tall slouching boy cupped his hands into a trumpet. "Did your mother say her little boy could go?"

Tim answered grimly to himself, "No, she said I couldn't go." He recalled with sinking sensations in his stomach a defiant question shouted to the quiet river long ago on a summer day. "Am I man or mouse?"

"I hope I'm a man," he yelled, not now to a quiet river but to a raging flood.

Instantly the past was wiped out, he ceased to think of any moment of time but this. The boat was moving slowly, and protesting against the current, but gaining speed. In the slack water next the Isle of Que, it traveled more rapidly than he expected.

He had not been mistaken about the roar under the span on which the railroad crossed the river. Ahead and to his right, the thunder grew each second more horrifying. Surely Niagara itself could be no louder! Under the span over the creek, the current was swift but smooth, and the water was still, he guessed, more than two feet below the ties. The river had not yet broken across the island; when that happened, the opening beneath the span now directly before him would close.

Was it possible that he could see the water rising? His heart leaped in his side, he threw himself forward, his head low, and passed safely under.

"When we come down," he said, over and over. "When we come down—"

He pushed the motor to the limit of its power; with loud splashing, fountains rising on each side, he sped through the broad lake at the bend of the stream, up to Charlie's cabin. Jumping out on the stone step, the mooring rope in his hand, he pushed and kicked open the door. Its crash against the wall roused Charlie in his chair before the stove. The fire was out, the kitchen was saturated with moisture, in one corner, where the boards sagged, lay a pool. Was it possible that the house trembled?

"Come on, Charlie!" he yelled. "Come on, quick! We gotta beat it, Charlie! Quick!"

Charlie shook his head.

"Take you for a ride, Charlie!"

"A ride?" Charlie staggered to his feet. "A ride?"

"Yes, a ride! Come on!" If he could coax Charlie into the boat without having to moor and cross the room and fetch him, that much time would be saved. It might mean that their lives would be saved.

Weak, hampered by many layers of clothing, Charlie tottered forward. In the doorway he looked about dumbfounded. "Why, she's over everything!" he said thickly. "An' I can't stand! My legs is give' out!"

"Don't try to stand. Kneel down and creep into the boat."

"I never seen nothing like this!"

Tim reached out his hand. "Get a move on!"

Charlie lowered himself into the boat with the aid of Tim's arm and lay on his face.

"Now stay there. Don't move, Charlie! I'll be only a few minutes."—Tim was now shouting at himself—"You said it! I betcha it'll be only a few minutes!" He managed to drag shut the door and pull off his raincoat. He spread the coat on Charlie and lay down beside him. Perhaps they couldn't get under the bridge even lying face down! In rain which almost blinded him, he steered to the center of the creek.

"It's not so bad, Charlie!" he shouted unheard. "Lie still, Charlie! Be sure to lie still, that's all you need think of!"

Caught by the full current, the boat shot forward. The upper streets of Selinsgrove would by now be canals. If he could only run into one of them, he would be safe. But to cross the creek might be fatal, even on a wide slant.

Two feet of space remained open under the bridge, but no more, and as he stared, the two feet appeared to shrink to one. He held the tiller rope in his teeth and the rudder with both hands. *Little Norway* was no more than thirty yards away when he realized that he had shot through the shallow space and the span was behind him. He had intended to proceed down the creek beyond Pine Street—

at Walnut he was sure he could enter the old canal bed and come to a stop on the lot. Alas, the Pine Street bridge seemed to lie on the water. He could never pass beneath it—it was *Little Norway* or nothing.

As fast as he dared, he reversed the engine, and slowly, with grunts and sputtering, the engine obeyed. His heart, too, seemed to grunt and sputter. For a moment in the shallow water before Fred's shed he lay still. He nudged Charlie with his elbow.

"Can you get up, Charlie?" he yelled.

Charlie responded by opening one eye and struggling to get from under the rubber coat. Tim did not need his mother to tell him that he and Charlie should be dry and warm as quickly as possible. Lifting himself on both hands, he saw that his return, like his departure, had an audience. On the bridge, his wheels in a few inches of water, stood Old Pybus; on the running board poised Mother and Rosy. Along the rail stood half a dozen men in hip boots. They splashed off the bridge and down the slippery bank.

"Don't tell me you've got him!" shrieked Rosy, above the noise of the water and the engine.

"There he is!"

The men helped Charlie up to the street and into Old Pybus. Water sloshed in his boots and ran from him in streams. Having moored Fred's boat, Tim followed.

"You look all in," wailed Rosy.

"Nonsense!" Tim looked at Mother. Only the paleness of her cheeks showed her disturbance of mind. She said two words, "Why, Tim!"

Rosy drove close to the kitchen door and Tim and his helpers got Charlie into the kitchen. Rosy mounted the car on the tricky rack and ran up the walk.

"I have two gallons of vegetable soup, hot on the stove," Mother was saying. "That's the best food for Charlie. I'll get him dry clothes and then he can eat."

Mother ran upstairs and then down, her arms filled with old clothing and towels. She handed them to Tim and stepped into the living room where Rosy stood looking out the window.

"Don't cry now, Rosy!" said she. "He's all right."

"You're crying," sobbed Rosy.

Tim flung open the door. "We're dry," said he in a loud voice. "Now let's eat. I can eat something more solid than soup. We'll probably get enough soup."

"I have a pot roast," said Mother. "And a ham."

Sitting in the kitchen, his feet in Herb's knitted socks, Charlie blinked at the boots turned up against a chair beside him. "I got all the levels marked now on this pair."

"Don't put them on again till they're dry," warned Mother.

"Uppermost is still '89," said Charlie. "We ain't goin' above that."

Tim looked past Mother and out the kitchen window to where, conspicuous against the white wall, hung coils of black rubber hose. "You're ready to wash up, I see?"

Mother opened the oven of the electric stove; from within issued an odor of baking ham, maddening to a starving man.

"Rosy and I brought up the hose," said she. "Last time we forgot, and then we couldn't get it till the water was pumped out. This time we're ahead of the game."

Suddenly Rosy ceased to ladle soup into a plate, Mother laid down the large fork with which she was about to lift out the roast. Tim ceased to chew the bread Rosy had buttered. The little radio on the cupboard shelf was sputtering a confused message. In a flash it became clear.

"We've had word from Selinsgrove that a few moments ago, the cabin of old Charlie Saunders, the riverman, was washed away. Yesterday a rescue squad sent there by his son, who is ill, tried to get Charlie to leave, but he refused to abandon the house where he had survived so much high water. His house was, we are told, more than seventy years old; it is an indication of the unprecedented volume and power of this flood that it should—"

Into the minds of all Yoders came the same thought. Tim raced to the dorm. A few treetops showed the location of Fisher's Island and Berratora and Cherry. Of smaller islands to the south nothing was to be seen. A huge old white oak sped downstream; the current did not carry it on the surface of the water, it pushed it, and the surface was now high in the center like a barrel.

Tim put on his ear phones and began to shout, "My number is—"

From the foot of the stairs, Rose prompted shrilly, "W9DEC."

"W9DEC, Isle of Que. Calling Sunbury! Calling Sunbury!"

Contact was prompt. "You don't need a number, Isle of Que; today belongs to all hams, licensed or not. What's your name?"

Tim didn't think much of Tim as a name for a man. Besides when the boys went into the army, they had to give their first names and make their middle names merely initials. Herb was not J. Herbert, he was John H.

"I'm Martin T. Yoder. I want to tell you that Charlie Saunders was not in his cabin and was not washed away. He's here in our house."

"How did he get there?"

"I fetched him."

"When?"

"A few moments ago."

"In what?"

"In Fred Finch's motorboat. I couldn't get ours over to the creek."

"How did you get under the railroad bridge?"

"Lying down. Now listen, ham! I need food, and food's all ready to eat. I'll call you. I'll call you at two o'clock. O. K. over to you!"

"Ask them—" Mother was calling and running upstairs at the same time. "Tim, do ask them to find out about poor Cousin Mamie."

"O. K." Tim signaled again. "Find out if Miss Mamie Sampson is on the mainland. Call you at two."

Tim leaped downstairs—rather, weak from hunger, he fell down. The kitchen was filled with the odor of Charlie, his boots, his lighted pipe. He sat at the table, before him a deep bowl of vegetable soup, thick slices of bread and butter spread with applebutter, a cup and saucer and a coffeepot.

"Oh, my!" sighed Rosy. "What a horrible morning!"

"His house is gone," signaled Tim from behind old Charlie's back. "How'll we tell him?"

"Perhaps he'll be glad now to stay with his son," said Mother. "Remember, everybody, not to drink any water, or brush your teeth with any water except what is boiled. I've boiled six gallons."

"I'm breaking in two!"

Rosy held out a piece of buttered bread. "Eat."

"Now in this house we stay," said Mother. "No more excursions till—" Mother interrupted herself, her blue eyes widening, her lower jaw dropping. She said no more. Charlie, whose back was turned, said nothing. Only Rosy spoke.

"For Pete's sake!" said Rosy. "See who's here!"

It was Miss Mamie Sampson!

—Elsie Singmaster

Pony Penning Day

An Annual Event in Virginia

Pony Penning Day always comes on the last Thursday in July. For weeks before, every member of the Volunteer Fire Department is busy getting the grounds in readiness, and the boys are allowed to help.

"I'll do your chores at home, Paul," offered Maureen, "so's you can see that the pony pens are good and stout."

Paul spent long days at the pony penning grounds. Yet he could not have told how or by whom the tents were rigged up. He hardly noticed when the chutes for the bronco busting were built. He did not know who pounded the race track into condition. All he knew was that the pens for the wild ponies must be made fast. Once the Phantom was captured, she must not escape. Nothing else mattered.

The night before the roundup, he and Maureen made last-minute plans in Phantom's stall. "First thing in the morning," Paul told Maureen, "you lay a clean bed of dried sea grass. Then fill the manger with plenty of marsh grass to make Phantom feel at home."

"Oh, I will, Paul. And I've got some ear corn and some 'lasses to coax her appetite, and Grandma gave me a bunch of tiny new carrots and some rutabagas, and I've been saving up sugar until I have a little sackful."

In the midst of their talk, Grandpa, looking as if he had a surprise, joined them.

"I hain't rode on a roundup to Assateague for two years," he smiled, hiding one hand behind his back, "but I recommember we allus had a chaw and a goody after the ponies was rounded up and afore we swimmed 'em across the channel. Here, Paul," he said, with a strange huskiness, "here's a choclit bar fer ye to take along." And he pressed the slightly squashed candy into Paul's hand.

It was dark and still when Paul awoke the next morning. He lay quiet a moment, trying to gather his wits. Suddenly he shot out of bed.

Today was Pony Penning Day!

His clothes lay on the chair beside his bed. Hurriedly he pulled on his shirt and pants and thudded barefoot down to the kitchen where Grandma stood over the stove, frying ham and making coffee for him as if he were man-grown!

He flung out his chest, sniffing the rich smells, bursting with excitement.

Grandma glanced around proudly. "I picked the first ripe figs of the year fer ye," she exclaimed. "They're chuckful of goodness. Now sit down, Paul, and eat a breakfast fit for a roundup man!"

Paul sat on the edge of his chair. With one eye on the clock he tried to eat the delicious figs and ham, but the food seemed to lump in his throat. Luckily Grandpa and Maureen came downstairs just then and helped clean his plate when Grandma was busy testing her cornbread in the oven with a long wisp of straw.

"I got to go now," Paul swallowed, as he ran out the door. He mounted Watch Eyes, a dependable pony that Grandpa had never been able to sell because of his white eyes. Locking his bare feet around the pony's sides, he jogged out of the yard.

Maureen came running to see him off.

"Whatever happens," Paul called back over his shoulder, "you be at Old Dominion Point at ten o'clock on a fresh pony."

"I'll be there, Paul!"

"And you, Paul!" yelled Grandpa. "Obey yer leader. No matter what!"

Day was breaking. A light golden mist came up out of the sea. It touched the prim white houses and the white picket fences with an unearthly light. Paul loped along slowly to save his mount's strength. He studied each house with a new interest. Here lived the woman who paid Maureen three dollars for hoeing her potato patch. There lived Kim Horsepepper, the clamdigger they had worked for. Mr. Horsepepper was riding out of his lane now, catching up with Paul. Along the road, men were turning out of their gates.

"Where do you reckon you'll do most good, Bub?" taunted a lean sapling of a man who, on other days, was an oysterman. He guffawed loudly, then winked at the rest of the group.

Paul's hand tightened on the reins. "Reckon I'll do most good where the leader tells me to go," he said, blushing hotly.

The day promised to be sultry. The marsh grass that usually billowed and waved stood motionless. The water of Assateague Channel glared like quicksilver.

Now the cavalcade was thundering over a small bridge that linked Chincoteague Island to little Piney Island. At the far end of the bridge a scow with a rail fence around it stood at anchor.

In spite of light talk, the faces of the men were drawn tight with excitement as they led their mounts onto the scow. The horses felt the excitement, too. Their nostrils quivered, and their ears swiveled this way and that, listening to the throb of the motor. Now the scow began to nose its way across the narrow channel. Paul watched the White Hills of Assateague loom near. He watched the old lighthouse grow sharp and sharper against the sky. In a few minutes the ride was over. The gangway was being lowered. The horses were clattering down, each man taking his own.

All eyes were on Wyle Maddox, the leader.

"Split in three bunches," Wyle clipped out the directions loud and sharp. "North, south, and east. Me and

Kim and the Beebe boy will head east, Wimbrow and Quillen goes north, and Harvey and Rodgers south. We'll all meet at Tom's Point."

At the first sound of Wyle's steam-whistle voice, the sea birds rose with a wild clatter.

"They're like scouts," Paul said to himself. "They're going to warn the wild ponies that the enemy has landed."

"Gee-up!" shouted Wyle as he whirled his horse and motioned Kim and Paul to follow.

Paul touched his bare heels into Watch Eye's side. *They were off!* The boy's eyes were fastened on Wyle Maddox. He and Kim Horsepepper were following their leader like the wake of a ship.

As they rode on, Paul could feel the soft sand give way to hard meadowland, then to pine-laden trails. There were no paths to follow, only openings to skin through—openings that led to water holes or to grazing grounds. The three horses thrashed through underbrush, jumped fallen trees, waded brackish pools and narrow, winding streams.

Suddenly Paul saw Wyle Maddox' horse rear into the air. He heard him neigh loudly as a band of wild ponies darted into an open grazing stretch some twenty yards ahead, then vanished among the black tree trunks.

The woods came alive with thundering hooves and frantic horse calls. Through bush and brier and bog and hard marshland the wild ponies flew. Behind them galloped the three riders, whooping at the top of their lungs. For whole seconds at a time the wild band would be swallowed up by the forest gloom. Then it would reappear far ahead—nothing but a flash of flying tails and manes.

Suddenly Wyle Maddox was waving Paul to ride close. "A straggler!" he shouted, pointing off to the left. "He went that-a-way! Git him!" And with a burst of speed Wyle Maddox and Kim Horsepepper were after the band.

Paul was alone. His face reddened with anger. They wanted to be rid of him. That's what they wanted. Sent after a straggler! He was not interested in rounding up a straggler that couldn't even keep up with the herd! He wanted the Phantom. Then Grandpa's words flashed across his mind. "Obey yer leader. No matter what!"

He wheeled his pony and headed blindly in the direction Wyle had indicated. He rode deeper into the pine thicket, trying to avoid snapping twigs, yet watching ahead for the slightest motion of leaf or brush. He'd show the men, if it took him all day! His thin shirt clung to him damply and his body was wet with sweat. A cobweb veiled itself across his face. With one hand he tried to wipe it off, but suddenly he was almost unseated. Watch Eyes was dancing on his hind legs, his nose high in the air. Paul stared into the sun-dappled forest until his eyes burned in his head. At last, far away and deep in the shadow of the pines, he saw a blur of motion. With the distance that lay between them, it might have been anything. A deer. Or even a squirrel. Whatever it was, he was after it!

Watch Eyes plunged on. There was a kind of glory in pursuit that made Paul and the horse one. They were trailing nothing but swaying bushes. They were giving chase to a mirage. Always it moved on and on, showing itself only in quivering leaves or moving shadows.

What was that? In the clump of myrtle bushes just ahead? Paul reined in. He could scarcely breathe for the wild beating of his heart. There it was again! A silver flash. It looked like the mist with the sun on it. And just beyond the mist, he caught sight of a long tail of mingled copper and silver.

He gazed awestruck. "It could be the Phantom's tail," he breathed. "It is! It is! It is! And the silver flash—it's not mist at all, but a brand-new colt, too little to keep up with the band."

The blood pounded in his ears. No wonder the Phantom was a straggler! No wonder she let herself be caught. "She's got a baby colt!" he murmured.

He glanced about him helplessly. If only he could think! How could he drive the Phantom and her colt to Tom's Point?

Warily he approached the myrtle thicket, then stopped as a hot wave of guilt swept over him. Phantom and her colt did not want to be rounded up by men. He could set them free. No one had brought the Phantom in before. No one need ever know.

Just then the colt let out a high, frightened whinny. In that little second Paul knew that he wanted more than anything in the world to keep the mother and the colt together. Shivers of joy raced up and down his spine. His breath came faster. He made a firm resolution. "I'll buy you both!" he promised.

But how far had he come? Was it ten miles to Tom's Point or two? Would it be best to drive them down the beach? Or through the woods? As if in answer a loud bugle rang through the woods. It was the Pied Piper!

And unmistakably his voice came from the direction of Tom's Point.

The Phantom pricked her ears. She wheeled around and almost collided with Watch Eyes in her haste to find the band. She wanted the Pied Piper for protection. Behind her trotted the foal, all shining and clean with its newness.

Paul laughed weakly. *He* was not driving the Phantom after all! She and her colt were leading him. They were leading him to Tom's Point!

—MARGUERITE HENRY

The Boy Jody

In and Around a Florida Clearing

A column of smoke rose thin and straight from the cabin chimney. The smoke was blue where it left the red of the clay. It trailed into the blue of the April sky and was no longer blue but gray. The boy Jody watched it, speculating. The fire on the kitchen hearth was dying down. His mother was hanging up pots and pans after the noon dinner. The day was Friday. She would sweep the floor with a broom of ti-ti and after that, if he were lucky, she would scrub it with the corn shucks scrub. If she scrubbed the floor she would not miss him until he had reached the Glen. He stood a minute, balancing the hoe on his shoulder.

The clearing itself was pleasant if the unweeded rows of young shafts of corn were not before him. The wild bees had found the chinaberry tree by the front gate. They burrowed into the fragile clusters of lavender bloom as greedily as though there were no other flowers in the scrub; as though they had forgotten the yellow jessamine of March; the sweet bay and the magnolias ahead of them in May. It occurred to him that he might follow the swift line of flight of the black and gold bodies, and so find a bee-tree, full of amber honey. The winter's cane syrup was gone and most of the jellies. Finding a bee-tree was nobler work than hoeing, and the corn could wait another day. The afternoon was alive with a soft stirring. It bored into him as the bees bored into the chinaberry blossoms, so that he must be gone across the clearing, through the pines and down the road to the running branch. The bee-tree might be near the water.

He stood his hoe against the split-rail fence. He walked down the cornfield until he was out of sight of the cabin. He swung himself over the fence on his two hands. Old Julia the hound had followed his father in the wagon to Grahamsville, but Rip the bull-dog and Perk the new feice saw the form clear the fence and ran toward him. Rip barked deeply but the voice of the small mongrel was high and shrill. They wagged deprecatory short tails when they recognized him. He sent them back to the yard. They watched after him indifferently. They were a sorry pair, he thought, good for nothing but the chase, the catch and the kill. They had no interest in him except

when he brought them their plates of table scraps night
and morning. Old Julia was a gentle thing with humans,
but her worn-toothed devotion was only for his father,
Penny Baxter. Jody had tried to make up to Julia, but
she would have none of him.

"You was pups together," his father told him, "ten
year gone, when you was two year old and her a baby.
You hurted the leetle thing, not meanin' no harm. She
cain't bring herself to trust you. Hounds is often that-a-
way."

He made a circle around the sheds and corn-crib and
cut south through the black-jack. He wished he had a
dog like Grandma Hutto's. It was white and curly-haired
and did tricks. When Grandma Hutto laughed and shook
and could not stop, the dog jumped into her lap and licked
her face, wagging its plumed tail as though it laughed
with her. He would like anything that was his own; that
licked his face and followed him as old Julia followed
his father. He cut into the sand road and began to run
east. It was two miles to the Glen, but it seemed to Jody
that he could run forever. There was no ache in his legs,
as when he hoed the corn. He slowed down to make the
road last longer. He had passed the big pines and left
them behind. Where he walked now, the scrub had closed
in, walling in the road with dense sand pines, each one so
thin it seemed to the boy it might make kindling by itself.
The road went up an incline. At the top he stopped. The
April sky was framed by the tawny sand and the pines.
It was as blue as his homespun shirt, dyed with Grandma
Hutto's indigo. Small clouds were stationary, like bolls

of cotton. As he watched, the sunlight left the sky a moment and the clouds were gray.

"There'll come a little old drizzly rain before nightfall," he thought.

The down grade tempted him to a lope. He reached the thick-bedded sand of the Silver Glen road. The tarflower was in bloom, and fetter-bush and sparkleberry. He slowed to a walk, so that he might pass the changing vegetation tree by tree, bush by bush, each one unique and familiar. He reached the magnolia tree where he had carved the wildcat's face. The growth was a sign that there was water nearby. It seemed a strange thing to him, when earth was earth and rain was rain, that scrawny pines should grow in the scrub, while by every branch and lake and river there grew magnolias. Dogs were the same everywhere, and oxen and mules and horses. But trees were different in different places.

"Reckon it's because they can't move none," he decided. They took what food was in the soil under them.

The east bank of the road shelved suddenly. It dropped below him twenty feet to a spring. The bank was dense with magnolia and loblolly bay, sweet gum and graybarked ash. He went down to the spring in the cool darkness of their shadows. A sharp pleasure came over him. This was a secret and a lovely place.

A spring as clear as well water bubbled up from nowhere in the sand. It was as though the banks cupped green leafy hands to hold it. There was a whirlpool where the water rose from the earth. Grains of sand boiled in it. Beyond the bank, the parent spring bubbled up at a higher level, cut itself a channel through white limestone and began to run rapidly down-hill to make a creek. The creek joined Lake George, Lake George was a part of the St. John's River, the great river flowed northward and into the sea. It excited Jody to watch the beginning of the ocean. There were other beginnings, true, but this one was his own. He liked to think that no one came here but himself and the wild animals and the thirsty birds.

He was warm from his jaunt. The dusky glen laid cool hands on him. He rolled up the hems of his blue denim breeches and stepped with bare dirty feet into the shallow spring. His toes sank into the sand. It oozed softly between them and over his bony ankles. The water was so cold that for a moment it burned his skin. Then it made a rippling sound, flowing past his pipe-stem legs, and was entirely delicious. He walked up and down, digging his big toe experimentally under smooth rocks he encountered. A school of minnows flashed ahead of him down the growing branch. He chased them through the shallows. They were suddenly out of sight as though they had never existed. He crouched under a bared and over-hanging live-oak root where a pool was deep, thinking they might reappear, but only a spring frog wriggled from under the mud, stared at him, and dove under the tree root in a spasmodic terror. He laughed.

"I ain't no 'coon. I'd not ketch you," he called after it.

A breeze parted the canopied limbs over him. The sun dropped through and lay on his head and shoulders. It was good to be warm at his head while his hard calloused feet were cold. The breeze died away, the sun no longer reached him. He waded across to the opposite bank where the growth was more open. A low palmetto brushed him. It reminded him that his knife was snug in his pocket; that he had planned as long ago as Christmas, to make himself a flutter-mill.

He had never built one alone. Grandma Hutto's son Oliver had always made one for him whenever he was home from sea. He went to work intently, frowning as he tried to recall the exact angle necessary to make the mill-wheel turn smoothly. He cut two forked twigs and trimmed them into two Y's of the same size. Oliver had been very particular to have the cross-bar round and smooth, he remembered. A wild cherry grew half-way up the bank. He climbed it and cut a twig as even as a polished pencil. He selected a palm frond and cut two strips of the tough fiber, an inch wide and four inches long. He cut a slit lengthwise in the center of each of them, wide enough to insert the cherry twig. The strips of palm frond must be at angles, like the arms of a windmill. He adjusted them carefully. He separated the Y-shaped twigs by nearly the length of the cherry cross-bar and pushed them deep into the sand of the branch bed a few yards below the spring.

The water was only a few inches deep but it ran strongly, with a firm current. The palm-frond mill-wheel must just brush the water's surface. He experimented with depth until he was satisfied, then laid the cherry bar between the twigs. It hung motionless. He twisted it a moment, anxiously, helping it to fit itself into its forked grooves. The bar began to rotate. The current caught the flexible tip of one bit of palm frond. By the time it lifted clear, the rotation of the bar brought the angled tip of the second into contact with the stream. The small leafy paddles swung over and over, up and down. The little wheel was turning. The flutter-mill was at work. It turned with the easy rhythm of the great water-mill at Lynne that ground corn into meal.

Jody drew a deep breath. He threw himself on the weedy sand close to the water and abandoned himself to the magic of motion. Up, over, down, up, over, down— the flutter-mill was enchanting. The bubbling spring would rise forever from the earth, the thin current was endless. The spring was the beginning of waters sliding to the sea. Unless leaves fell, or squirrels cut sweet bay twigs to drop and block the fragile wheel, the flutter-mill might turn forever. When he was an old man, as old as his father, there seemed no reason why this rippling movement might not continue as he had begun it.

He moved a stone that was matching its corners against his sharp ribs and burrowed a little, hollowing himself a nest for his hips and shoulders. He stretched out one arm and laid his head on it. A shaft of sunlight, warm and thin like a light patchwork quilt, lay across his body. He watched the flutter-mill indolently, sunk in the sand and sunlight. The movement was hypnotic. His eyelids fluttered with the palmleaf paddles. Drops of silver slipping from the wheel blurred together like the tail of a shooting star. The water made a sound like kittens lapping. A rain frog sang a moment and then was still. There was an instant when the boy hung at the edge of a high bank made of the soft fluff of broom-sage, and the rain frog and the starry dripping of the flutter-mill hung with him. Instead of falling over the edge, he sank into the softness. The blue, white-tufted sky closed over him. He slept.

When he awakened, he thought he was in a place other than the branch bed. He was in another world, so that for an instant he thought he might still be dreaming. The sun was gone, and all the light and shadow. There were no black boles of live oaks, no glossy green of magnolia leaves, no pattern of gold lace where the sun had sifted through the branches of the wild cherry. The world was all a gentle gray, and he lay in a mist as fine as spray from a waterfall. The mist tickled his skin. It was scarcely wet. It was at once warm and cool. He rolled over on his back and it was as though he looked up into the soft gray breast of a mourning dove.

He lay, absorbing the fine-dropped rain like a young plant. When his face was damp at last and his shirt was moist to the touch, he left his nest. He stopped short. A deer had come to the spring while he was sleeping. The fresh tracks came down the east bank and stopped at the water's edge. They were sharp and pointed, the tracks of a doe. They sank deeply into the sand, so that he knew the doe was an old one and a large. Perhaps she was heavy with fawn. She had come down and drunk deeply from the spring not seeing him where he slept. Then she had scented him. There was a scuffled confusion in the sand where she had wheeled in fright. The tracks up the opposite bank had long harried streaks behind them. Perhaps she had not drunk, after all, before she scented him, and turned and ran with that swift, sand-throwing flight. He hoped she was not now thirsty, wide-eyed in the scrub.

He looked about for other tracks. The squirrels had raced up and down the banks, but they were bold, always. A raccoon had been that way, with his feet like sharp-nailed hands, but he could not be sure how recently. Only his father could tell for certain the hour when any wild things had passed by. Only the doe had surely come and had been frightened. He turned back again to the flutter-mill. It was turning as steadily as though it had always been there. The palm-leaf paddles were frail but they made a brave show of strength, rippling against the shallow water. They were glistening from the slow rain.

Jody looked at the sky. He could not tell the time of day in the grayness, nor how long he may have slept. He bounded up the west bank, where open gallberry flats spread without obstructions. As he stood, hesitant whether to go or stay, the rain ended as gently as it had begun. A light breeze stirred from the southwest. The sun came out. The clouds rolled together into great white billowing feather bolsters, and across the east a rainbow arched, so lovely and so various that Jody thought he would burst with looking at it. The earth was pale green, the air itself was all but visible, golden with the rain-washed sunlight, and all the trees and grass and bushes glittered, varnished with the rain-drops.

A spring of delight boiled up within him as irresistibly as the spring of the branch. He lifted his arms and held them straight from his shoulders like a water-turkey's wings. He began to whirl around in his tracks. He whirled faster and faster until his ecstasy was a whirlpool, and when he thought he would explode with it, he became dizzy and closed his eyes and dropped to the ground and lay flat in the broomsage. The earth whirled under him and with him. He opened his eyes and the blue April sky and the cotton clouds whirled over him. Boy and earth and trees and sky spun together. The whirling stopped, his head cleared and he got to his feet. He was light-headed and giddy, but something in him was relieved, and the April day could be borne again, like any ordinary day.

He turned and galloped toward home. He drew deep breaths of the pines, aromatic with wetness. The loose sand that had pulled at his feet was firmed by the rain. The return was comfortable going. The sun was not far from its setting when the long-leaf pines around the Baxter clearing came into sight. They stood tall and dark against the red-gold west. He heard the chickens clucking and quarreling and knew they had just been fed. He turned into the clearing. The weathered gray of the split-rail fence was luminous in the rich spring light. Smoke curled thickly from the stick-and-clay chimney. Supper would be ready on the hearth and hot bread baking in the Dutch oven. He hoped his father had not returned from Grahamsville. It came to him for the first time that perhaps he should not have left the place while his father was away. If his mother had needed wood, she would be angry. Even his father would shake his head and say, "Son—" He heard old Caesar snort and knew his father was ahead of him.

The clearing was in a pleasant clatter. The horse whinnied at the gate, the calf bleated in its stall and the milch cow answered, the chickens scratched and cackled and the dogs barked with the coming of food and evening. It was good to be hungry and to be fed and the stock was eager with an expectant certainty. The end of winter had been meager; corn short, and hay, and dried cow-peas. But now in April the pastures were green and succulent and even the chickens savored the sprouts of young grass. The dogs had found a nest of young rabbits that evening, and after such tid-bits the scraps from the Baxter supper table were a matter of some indifference. Jody saw old Julia lying under the wagon, worn out from her miles of trotting. He swung open the front paling gate and went to find his father.

Penny Baxter was at the wood-pile. He still wore the coat of the broadcloth suit that he had been married in, that he now wore as badge of his gentility when he went to church, or off trading. The sleeves were too short, not because Penny had grown, but because the years of hanging through the summer dampness and being pressed with the smoothing iron and pressed again, had somehow shrunk the fabric. Jody saw his father's hands, big for the rest of him, close around a bundle of wood. He was doing Jody's work, and in his good coat. Jody ran to him.

"I'll git it, Pa."

He hoped his willingness, now, would cover his delinquency. His father straightened his back.

"I near about give you out, son," he said.

"I went to the Glen."

"Hit were a mighty purty day to go," Penny said. "Or to go anywhere. How come you to take out such a fur piece?"

It was as hard to remember why he had gone as though it had been a year ago. He had to think back to the moment when he had laid down his hoe.

"Oh." He had it now. "I aimed to foller the honey-bees and find a bee-tree."

"You find it?"

Jody stared blankly.

"Dogged if I ain't forgot 'til now to look for it."

He felt as foolish as a bird-dog caught chasing field mice. He looked at his father sheepishly. His father's pale blue eyes were twinkling.

"Tell the truth, Jody," he said, "and shame the devil. Wa'n't the bee-tree a fine excuse to go a-ramblin'?"

Jody grinned.

"The notion takened me," he admitted, "afore I studied on the bee-tree."

"That's what I figgered. How come me to know, was when I was drivin' along to Grahamsville, I said to my-self, 'There's Jody now, and the hoein' ain't goin' to take him too long. What would I do this fine spring day, was I a boy?' And then I thought, 'I'd go a-ramblin'.' Most anywhere, long as it kivered the ground."

A warmth filled the boy that was not the low golden sun. He nodded.

"That's the way I figgered," he said.

"But your Ma, now," Penny jerked his head toward the house, "don't hold with ramblin'. Most women-folks cain't see for their lives, how a man loves so to ramble. I never let on you wasn't here. She said, 'Where's Jody?' and I said, 'Oh, I reckon he's around some'eres.' "

He winked one eye and Jody winked back.

"Men-folks has got to stick together in the name o' peace. You carry your Ma a good bait o' wood now."

Jody filled his arms and hurried to the house. His

mother was kneeling at the hearth. The spiced smells that came to his nose made him weak with hunger.

"That ain't sweet 'tater pone, is it, Ma?"

"Hit's sweet 'tater pone, and don't you fellers be too long a time now, piddlin' around and visitin'. Supper's done and ready."

He dumped the wood in the box and scurried to the lot. His father was milking Trixie.

"Ma says to git done and come on," he reported. "Must I feed old Caesar?"

"I don'e fed him, son, sich as I had to give the pore feller." He stood up from the three-legged milking stool. "Carry in the milk and don't trip and waste it outen the gourd like you done yestiddy. Easy, Trixie—"

He moved aside from the cow and went to the stall in the shed, where her calf was tethered.

"Here, Trixie. Soo, gal—"

The cow lowed and came to her calf.

"Easy, there. You greedy as Jody."

He stroked the pair and followed the boy to the house. They washed in turn at the water-shelf and dried their hands and faces on the roller towel hanging outside the kitchen door. Ma Baxter sat at the table waiting for them, helping their plates. Her bulky frame filled the end of the long narrow table. Jody and his father sat down on either side of her. It seemed natural to both of them that she should preside.

"You-all hongry tonight?" she asked.

"I kin hold a barrel o' meat and a bushel o' biscuit," Jody said.

"That's what you say. Your eyes is bigger'n your belly."

"I'd about say the same," Penny said, "if I hadn't learned better. Goin' to Grahamsville allus do make me hongry."

"You git a snort o' 'shine there, is the reason," she said.

"A mighty small one today. Jim Turnbuckle treated."

"Then you shore didn't git enough to hurt you."

Jody heard nothing; saw nothing but his plate. He had never been so hungry in his life, and after a lean winter and slow spring, with food not much more plentiful for the Baxters than for their stock, his mother had cooked a supper good enough for the preacher. There were poke-greens with bits of white bacon buried in them; sand-buggers made of potato and onion and the cooter he had found crawling yesterday; sour orange biscuits and at his mother's elbow the sweet potato pone. He was torn between his desire for more biscuits and another sand-bugger and the knowledge born of painful experience, that if he ate them, he would suddenly have no room for pone. The choice was plain.

"Ma," he said, "kin I have my pone right now?"

She was at a pause in the feeding of her own large frame. She cut him, dexterously, a generous portion. He plunged into its spiced and savory goodness.

"The time it takened me," she complained, "to make that pone—and you destroyin' it before I git my breath—"

"I'm eatin' it quick," he admitted, "but I'll remember it a long time."

Supper was done with. Jody was replete. Even his father, who usually ate like a sparrow had taken a second helping.

"I'm full, thank the Lord," he said.

Ma Baxter sighed.

"If a feller'd light me a candle," she said, "I'd git shut o' the dishwashin' and mebbe have time to set and enjoy myself."

Jody left his seat and lit a tallow candle. As the yellow flame wavered, he looked out of the east window. The full moon was rising.

"A pity to waste light. ain't it," his father said, "and the full moon shinin'."

He came to the window and they watched it together.

"Son, what do it put in your head? Do you mind what we said we'd do, full moon in April?"

"I dis-remember."

Somehow, the seasons always took him unawares. It must be necessary to be as old as his father to keep them in the mind and memory, to remember moon-time from one year's end to another.

"You ain't forgot what I told you? I'll swear, Jody. Why, boy, the bears comes outen their winter beds on the full moon in April."

"Old Slewfoot! You said we'd lay for him when he come out!"

"That's it."

"You said we'd go where we seed his tracks comin' and goin' and criss-crossin', and likely find his bed, and him, too, comin' out in April."

"And fat. Fat and lazy. The meat so sweet, from him layin' up."

"And him mebbe easier to ketch, not woke up good."

"That's it."

"When kin we go, Pa?"

"Soon as we git the hoein' done. And see bear-sign."

"Which-a-way will we begin huntin' him?"

"We'd best to go by the Glen springs and see has he come out and watered there."

"A big ol' doe watered there today," Jody said. "Whilst I was asleep. I built me a flutter-mill, Pa. It run fine."

Ma Baxter stopped the clatter of her pots and pans.

"You sly scaper," she said. "That's the first I knowed you been off. You gittin' slick as a clay road in the rain."

He shouted with laughter.

"I fooled you, Ma. Say it, Ma, I got to fool you oncet."

"You fooled me. And me standin' over the fire makin' potato pone—"

She was not truly angry.

"Now, Ma," he cajoled her, "suppose I was a varmint and didn't eat nothin' but roots and grass."

"I'd not have nothin' then to rile me," she said.

At the same time he saw her mouth twist. She tried to straighten it and could not.

"Ma's a-laughin'! Ma's a-laughin'! You ain't riled when you laugh!"

He darted behind her and untied her apron strings. The apron slipped to the floor. She turned her bulk quickly and boxed his ears, but the blows were feather-light and playful. The same delirium came over him again that he had felt in the afternoon. He began to whirl around and around as he had done in the broomsage.

"You knock them plates offen the table," she said, "and you'll see who's riled."

"I cain't he'p it. I'm dizzy."

"You're addled," she said. "Jest plain addled."

It was true. He was addled with April. He was dizzy with spring. He was drunk as Lem Forrester on a Saturday night. His head was swimming with the strong brew made up of the sun and the air and the thin gray rain. The flutter-mill had made him drunk, and the doe's coming, and his father's hiding his absence, and his mother's making him a pone and laughin' at him. He was stabbed with the candlelight inside the safe comfort of the cabin; with the moonlight around it. He pictured old Slewfoot, the great black outlaw bear with one toe missing, rearing up in his winter bed and tasting the soft air and smelling the moonlight, as he, Jody, smelled and tasted them. He went to bed in a fever and could not sleep. A mark was on him from the day's delight, so that all his life, when April was a thin green and the flavor of rain was on his tongue, an old wound would throb and a nostalgia would fill him for something he could not quite remember. A whip-poor-will called across the bright night, and suddenly he was asleep.

—Marjorie Kinnan Rawlings

Johnny's Experiment
The T.V.A.

Everyone around Burning Branch knew about Johnny's experiment with concentrated fertilizer. Often now the neighbors reined in as they went past the slopes on the Heiskell farm. The news even traveled as far as Doc Pedigo's store, where the farmers nodded.

"Yep, I know the family. Kinda no-count folks. Usta be back up there on Cat Creek a-ways. Tom Heiskell had to get him a job on the dam to keep 'em from starving. I doubt if the boy'll ever do anything with that new place they got there."

The distrust was general. It didn't help Johnny in these critical days. He was upset by his father's departure, worried suddenly to find himself with the whole farm to handle. Yet give up that experiment he would not. Now more than ever he was determined to see it through, despite the disbelief of his neighbors.

"You jest wait, son; you jest wait and see. Moment you start puttin' that dust on the land like you're doin', land'll belong to the gov'ment. Gov'ment'll come in and take away yer property."

He knew it was absurd. Such talk made no sense. Yet you could not get around the fact that the government *had* stepped in. TVA *had* taken property for the dam site. Sometimes at night, with the responsibility for the place weighing on him, Johnny had doubts, wondering just how far the government could go. Then, looking over his cultivated field the next morning, he would laugh. Nevertheless he felt alone. This made things difficult those warm spring days, when so much hung on what happened to that field along the slopes above the house.

Grandpappy was the first to come around. The old man had never been favorable to the ideas of the county agent, but now he realized the heavy burden Johnny was carrying and was impressed with his determination to save the land. As a good farmer, Grandpappy loved the soil. He became first sympathetic, then interested, then aroused, and finally anxious to help and see things through. While Johnny was in school the old fellow worked his head off. Much of the time he spent on what the family jokingly referred to as "Grandpappy's project."

All his life Grandpappy Heiskell had loved the woods.

"Mister, I'd shoot my own brother effen I caught him firin' the woods," he used to say with emphasis. You felt he meant what he said. Always he had looked forward to the time at Cat Creek when he would replant the depleted timber after the loggers had cleaned out the hills. Johnny himself could recall his father and his grandfather standing on the porch of the old home, the older man looking with narrowed eyes at the slopes, saying: "I usta think I'd be able some day to get out on them hills, but it's hard to do much when you ain't got nothin', never had nothin', never hope to have nothin'."

The stand of timber at Burning Branch, inferior though it was, overjoyed the old man. For he went back to a time before the hills of the region had felt the hand and ax of the lumbermen swarming over the countryside. He knew how to protect and take care of the forests. Day after day he dragged up the back slopes with his ancient ax, often assisted by Uncle Herve Rice, whose line ran through the wood lot in the rear. The two men worked hard on both sides of the boundary, clearing out the small growth, piling up the brush, and burning it on wet days when there was no danger. They cut down the weed trees and the old, rotten ones which kept light and moisture from the young growth. Uncle Herve even persuaded his friend to forget his dislike of the government long enough to set out some black walnut saplings which, thanks to the help of the county agent, were provided by the Forestry Department of TVA and deposited one day by a truck at the farm.

Soon there were more trees to be planted. The county agent also arranged for a soil conservation crew to come and help for a few days. They rolled up with tractors, and

under the admiring eyes of Johnny, who stayed home
from school while they were there, built small check dams
over the worst washes on the hillsides. He learned a lot
from their work—how to plow up the small gullies, how
to construct brush dams across the larger ones, how to
plant saplings to hold the collected earth. To some of the
neighbors the rattle and roar of the tractors on the farm
was blasphemy. To Johnny Heiskell it was music.

Although the load of increased work had fallen mostly
on the boy and his grandfather, the blow of her father's
departure hit Martha hardest of all. She missed him, and
she shared his distrust of the new experiment, wondering
how her brother could succeed where older men had
failed.

Somehow, someway, Johnny realized, she must be made
a part of the farm. One evening he was working by the
lamp over his green 4-H record book, filling up the pages
as he had been told to show exactly what he was doing
and how he used the fertilizer in his soil conservation
activities. He looked at Martha as he finished.

"Say, sister, you oughta have a 4-H project too."

She was bored. "Don't want none."

"Now, Martha," said her mother. She was worried
about Johnny and the load he carried. True, the weekly
money order from their father, working on the dam,
which had begun to arrive regularly, was a help. It was
a steady sum they had never before been able to count
upon. But the whole burden of the farm was on the boy.
It disturbed his mother.

Johnny, as usual, persisted. "Look, Martha, you could

even have a regular project of your own, effen you wanted."

"I don't want one. I'd hafta have sewing or canning or some such."

"No, you don't hafta. You could have animals."

Martha was interested. "Oh, I kin. Kin I have a calf?"

"A calf? Where on earth would I get a calf?" Then Johnny stopped, for he knew her love of animals. Was this a way to bring her into the work of the farm and secure her help, which would be badly needed in the months ahead?

He replied cautiously. "Who said anything about a calf? What for you want a calf? You're too young, you're not old enough yet."

"Yes-I-am," she answered quickly. Johnny was astonished. "Mary Sue Lane in our 4-H Club has a heifer. She's no older'n me. Mr. Sam got it for her. He might get one for me effen you was to ask him. He likes you."

Johnny glanced at her. She was growing fast. She seemed taller now than she had been a few weeks before, when Pa left to go to work on the dam. Something had changed her, too, since then.

He leaned over and put his arm on her shoulder. "Why, now, Martha, I dunno but what you *are* old enough. Only this would be your project. No one here has any time to help. For instance, suppose you did get a heifer, you'd have to water and feed it every day, see it was clean and all that."

Ma Heiskell spoke up. "Martha'd do whatever, Johnny."

"Yes, shore. Only, Martha, you could help Ma on the chickens. You could go halvers with her on the hens."

"No, she wants a calf. I'll tend to the chickens myself."

That was the start, the start of the project which began when the county agent finally secured for Martha a small Black Angus heifer all her own from the Agricultural College. So now the whole family was working. Johnny rose before the rest to get things done. He worked late evenings with Grandpappy. There was no time Saturdays or Sundays for fishing lazy mud cats or fat perch from the creek, his favorite sport, with a couple of sandwiches in his pocket and Rover at his side. No time for anything but trying to keep up with the work on the farm.

The rains came, the spring rains, heavy and then heavier still, so intense that Grandpappy shook his head, hoping with Johnny that the seed planted on the newly prepared slope would not be washed away to make the whole experiment a failure. The rains continued, became a deluge. Finally the sun broke through; the Smokies in the distance really smoked.

Then they turned their attention to other pressing problems, the old man and the boy—to the gullies on the slopes, to repairing the check dams where the spring torrents had broken through, to planting more seedlings in the washes to hold the earth. Warm, sunny weather came within a few days, lasted a week, a fortnight. A faint green began to show in the field on the slope. It meant the seed had taken hold.

The warm weather persisted, the sun shone. Early one morning Johnny came out on the porch and stopped, suddenly dazzled. Overnight the pasture had become lush

and green, a fertile field where only a few weeks before
the earth had been gray and dull with broom sedge. He
could hardly believe his eyes. It was a miracle. He looked
and looked away and looked back again, and still there
it was before his eyes. The cows, he noticed, knew it before
he did. Already they were up against the fence, trying to
poke their noses through to get at the new growth.

There was a stranger sight at the far end of the field.
Old Man Treadway and his boy Zeke were leaning on
the fence. Their mouths were open. Amazement and not
amusement was on their faces.

Johnny turned to the room inside. "Grandpappy."

Despite himself, excitement crept into his tone. What
would the old man make of *this*? Laugh it off as a freak,
as a stroke of luck, most likely. "Grandpappy! C'mon out
here and see this pasture."

The old man stepped onto the porch. Before him was
the field on the slope, radiant in the light of early morning. He shaded his eyes with one hand, dazzled as Johnny
had been by the transformation of the soil. For a long time
he said nothing. At last he shook his head.

"Son . . . I see it . . . I see it . . . but I can't be
lieve it."

—JOHN R. TUNIS

The Ones That Count

Tennessee's Oak Ridge

After the music teacher's party, when the others strolled down the road with their arms around each other and boasted about their valentines, one little girl hid hers inside her coat and said it was a secret how many she had. She walked ahead by herself, faster and faster, her brown curls swinging in the wind, her grey eyes full of tears.

"What you scooting off so fast for, Carrie?" asked Myrtle Cash. "You're going away from your street. I reckon you don't know where you live yet."

"Maybe I don't," the other girl called back, blinking hard. "All these flat tops look just alike."

"They do not," cried Myrtle indignantly. "Every other house is a different color, and I don't know why they call them flat tops. The roofs slant so the rain can run off, and they're real pretty. Everybody's house is as nice and new as the others. Where I came from back in the mountains some houses hadn't even any paint on them."

"What's the matter, Carrie, you mad about something?" Myrtle's brother Tom called.

"I bet her best friend didn't send her a valentine," joked Ruby.

"Shut up," Myrtle whispered, but Carrie heard it. "She got only a few."

Carrie swallowed hard and turned away. Tomorrow's party at the school would be even worse than this.

"You're liable to get wet if you go play on the hill, Carrie," called Myrtle. "It's clabbering up to rain."

"In New York a grey sky like this would never rain a drop," said Carrie resentfully.

"Well, in Miller's Falls, Massachusetts, where Ruby used to live, the sun shines so little in winter it hurts your eyes," said Myrtle giving Ruby a little shove.

Carrie ran away from them off up the hill. She plumped down in the thick grass all by herself and stared out over Oak Ridge, listening to the sad sweet call of a white-throated sparrow. The bright-colored one-story houses, with their hilly yards where playpens and baby carriages were out despite the rain clouds, formed a protective wall around the factories in the valley. With no tall buildings anywhere, the streets lay like garden paths among the grey-green winter yards, with the soft pastel colors of houses for garden flowers.

It was a pleasant, spring-like day for February thirteenth, but Carrie wished she were sitting in the Automat in New York, even with dirty snow outside and the rumble of taxis and buses. She and Grandma would sip their hot chocolate and afterwards ride to the Museum of Natural History. Her father had promised to take her to the Museum here in Oak Ridge. He said there was nothing like it in the whole world. Well, there wasn't any Grandma here. She hadn't seen a single grandma in Oak Ridge. All the grown-ups were young, and had so many babies the town looked like a nursery. She was probably the only girl around with no sisters or brothers for company.

Carrie pulled out her valentines, but the little hearts blurred and wiggled through a mist of tears. Only three valentines, and the others had handfuls. One was from Ruby and one from Myrtle and the last, either from the teacher, or from Sue Smith. Sue was the friendliest girl Carrie had ever met, but everybody was friendly here, friendlier than anywhere else her father had worked. And still, three valentines were all she had. Well, I don't care, she told herself, getting up and starting down the hill toward her street. But the moment her mother opened the door and looked at her, Carrie broke down and cried.

"Why Carrie!" said her mother. "Why Carrie!"

"I wish we were back home," sobbed Carrie, throwing down her books. The valentines fluttered to the floor.

"But this is the best home we've ever had," said her mother. "Have you forgotten the broken-down houses and dark apartments we used to live around and the ugly streets? I know you miss Grandma, but think, dear, there isn't a single dreary, sad home here for anyone. You're going to make friends from everywhere in the United States."

Carrie shook her head and groped for a handkerchief in her jumper pocket.

"You will," her mother insisted. "You can't be a stranger anywhere if you really feel friendly yourself. There's everything here, even room for a garden. And where else have the stores and library and post office and movies been all together under one roof, and even a hospital nearby, and such a fine school? The last school you went to had only two rooms for all the grades and your school in first grade was held in a church, remember? We used to drive miles to get anything most places Dad worked. Besides, you can be proud of Dad's job."

"He can't even tell us about it," said Carrie, picking up her books.

"Of course not. It's too important. Now cheer up; you just haven't been here long enough yet. I believe in you, Carrie, and so will your new friends. You'll see."

Carrie shook her head, remembering Ruby's and Myrtle's pitying glances. Tomorrow would be even worse, trying to look as if she didn't care when the others ran back and forth to get their valentines and she had to sit there in her seat. She went to her room and lay down on her bed. I can't go to school tomorrow, she thought, but Mother will make me go.

"Carrie!" her mother called from the kitchen, "hadn't you better start making valentines for school tomorrow? It's getting late."

Carrie sighed, then got up and opened the drawer of her table. She found the paste and a rag to wipe it off when she used too much. She had spent her allowance on two boxes of valentines from the dime store down at the shopping center, but so far she'd made only the few for today's party. Now she pulled out paper lace and sticker seals with doves and pairs of hearts and "Someone is thinking of you" printed in gold.

She chose the largest valentine for her home room teacher, Miss Pratt. When she had selected one for each new friend and pasted on lace and printed their names on the envelopes and hidden her initials, "C.D.," upside down, she stopped to think. No one else would send her one. Then she remembered Allen Tod, who never played ball with the boys at recess but stayed alone drawing pictures of airplanes. She could send him two. He was sure to be forgotten. Just like her. Only maybe he didn't care.

Carrie tried to think of others like Allen, but he was the only one. Beside herself. Maybe she could get sick. She prodded her bad tooth with one finger, but she couldn't make it hurt. "I've got to do something; I've *got* to!" said Carrie out loud, gripping her pencil so hard it began to crack. She bent her head and her curls slid over her shoulders and into her eyes.

Suddenly Carrie started up out of her chair, clutching a small blue valentine. There was a way! There was if she dared to do it!

She glanced toward the window as if she were afraid some winter bird might see what she was about to do. Three boys were chasing a puppy down the street, and next door the neighbor's Airedale raced around his yard.

Nobody was looking. Nobody could ever find out. Not possibly, if she were careful. Besides, people always printed what they wrote on valentines.

Carrie snapped on her lamp and pulled down the shade. Then, seizing the blue valentine, she thrust it into its envelope, and turning it over, held it down firmly with her left hand as if she feared it might wriggle out of her grasp. She picked up the cracked pencil and printed quickly on the envelope her own name, "Carrie Duncan— from guess who?" She chose five other valentines, then nine more, and started printing "Carrie Duncan" on them, trying to print each one in a different hand.

It wouldn't be any fun to get them tomorrow, but at least when Ruby and Myrtle asked how many she had, she could pile them up carelessly and say, "Too many to count." They wouldn't feel sorry for her like today.

When all the valentines were sealed in their envelopes, Carrie felt very queer and weak. She was going to walk fifteen times up to the front of the class tomorrow to act a lie and carry back to her desk the valentines she'd sent herself.

A knock on the door made her jump and drop the pencil.

In came her mother and set a tray with milk and cookies on the table. "They're still warm," she said. "What's the matter, dear, do you feel sick?"

Carrie shook her head. "Thank you, Mother." She bent blindly above the heart-shaped cookies, longing to push the envelopes on the floor. "Why, Mother, the cookies are valentines!" she said at last, staring down at the spicy, pink-iced hearts. But the stack of envelopes on the table accused her, and she was ashamed to meet her mother's eyes.

"Carrie!" cried her mother. "Look at that pile of valentines!"

"What do you mean, Mother?" Carrie's cheeks flamed, and she reached out to cover up the heap of envelopes with one hand.

"Look how many you're sending! It's grand there are lots of new friends you want to remember. You must be giving half the class."

"Oh," breathed Carrie, not looking up.

"That's the right way, dear," said her mother. "It's the ones we give that count; that's where the fun is."

Still blushing, Carrie nodded silently. When her mother went out, closing the door, Carrie picked up one of the heart-shaped cookies in a trembling hand and bit off the point. But she choked when she tried to swallow it. The cookie was a little valentine, one of countless tokens of her mother's love. So were the valentines she was sending to her new friends and to the lonely boy. But the ones she was sending to herself were just pieces of paper.

Carrie jerked up the shade and sat a long time staring out the window at the friendly houses, each one as gay as the next, like valentines themselves. A shower began, and they looked as if their icing-pale colors might melt in the slow falling rain.

Abruptly she opened the table drawer and hunted frantically for an eraser. Then she erased the "Carrie Duncan" on the first envelope, almost rubbing a hole through the paper. She hesitated a moment, then wrote instead, "Adele Adams." Then, erasing again, she wrote on the second one, "Tom Cash," and on the third, "Barbara Crane," and on the fourth, "Bert Crane." She printed the names of her classmates as they came in the roll call, skipping Ruby and Myrtle and others for whom she had already made valentines. With eight more she would have one for everybody in the class!

Quickly she cut out hearts and colored them and pasted on lace. She drew horses and painted them. She drew birds flying. When the envelopes were addressed, she ran out back to help her mother fix supper. It was just as if she had taken off an iron coat that had weighted her down. Through the closed windows she heard the call of a white-throated sparrow singing in the rain. He sounded so gay that Carrie copied him, whistling his clear notes the best she could. She felt as if she were floating and forgot to worry about the party.

That night Carrie dreamed that the valentine box at school had snow birds perched on it pecking off red candy hearts. But the flapping of their wings turned out to be her father's tapping on the door to tell her it was late.

Instead of snow outside, Carrie found three small blue violets by the door. Violets in February! That had never happened anywhere else she'd lived. When she walked into the new school building with its many windows, she felt as if she were going to an exam for which she had studied hard. Somehow, she was not so nervous as she might have been. She found everyone crowded around the valentine box.

The great round hat box covered with silver foil had a red chimney painted with heart-shaped bricks to receive the valentines. As Carrie pushed hers inside, she was glad she needn't sneak them in as she would have had to if they were addressed to herself.

It was hard for anyone to work that morning. Ruby kept saying "Valentine" by mistake when she translated French, and Myrtle and Carrie lost their places in the book by staring at the valentine box. After recess the party was to begin.

When the box was opened, Miss Pratt chose Rose Hobart from Montana to call out the names on the valentines. It wasn't long till Rose called, "Carrie Duncan." Carrie skipped to the desk and back, but before she could open the envelope, her name was called again. She traveled to the desk so many times she lost count. And every time she was glad there wasn't a single valentine she had sent to herself. When all of them were given out, every desk was covered with gay hearts.

Carrie counted her valentines and found thirty-four. "I've a valentine from everybody in class except one person," she said.

"How many did you get?" asked Sue.

"Thirty-four."

"Of course," said Ruby. "In this school we all send one to everybody. Didn't you?"

"Yes, I did," said Carrie. "Only I didn't know we were supposed to. I wonder who it was that didn't send me one?"

Tom chuckled. "Goofie! The thirty-fifth would be yourself!"

Carrie's face was on fire. "Then I'm glad I didn't get another." But no one could guess how glad she really was.

Going home she admitted to Myrtle, "I didn't mean what I said about Oak Ridge yesterday. It's a grand place."

"It sure is," said Myrtle. "My pa says Oak Ridge changed the face of the world."

"That's it," cried Carrie. It changed me too, she thought. Proudly she carried her valentines home. She was going to keep them as long as she lived and never feel like a stranger anywhere again, now that Oak Ridge had suddenly become home.

—MAVIS GAREY MOORE

The Magic Feather

Growing Peaches in Ohio

"Make haste slowly," Abel always said in his big, booming voice. "Great oaks from little acorns grow."

Janey preferred to make haste in a big hurry, especially now that spring was coming on the beautiful Lake Erie Island where Janey and Mama and Daddy and Abel, the hired man, grew peaches for a living.

"And I'm tired of being a little acorn, anyway," declared Janey, who was almost ten years old and felt like at least a medium sized oak.

She had a hundred things that she wanted to do right

now, most of them things that she wasn't let do because
of the oak-and-acorn business, but most of all she wanted
to help Daddy and Abel spray the peach orchard. That,
she thought, was the biggest, most important job of all—
but much too big for her, said Daddy and Abel.

She sat down on the back steps out of the way of the
cold March wind and got out the little box with her magic
feather in it.

> "Feather, feather,
> Bring good weather,"

she chanted, making only a small wish the first time to see
if the feather was in a good mood.

"I plan on working up little by little," she told
Augustus, the six-toed cat, who was rubbing sociably
against her ankles. See, the sun's shining a little brighter
already."

Out behind the barn the tractor let out a roar, and in a
minute the tractor and the big yellow sprayer lurched
into view. Daddy climbed down off the tractor seat and
beckoned to Abel, who came hurrying out of the tool
shed. The red beard which helped make Abel more
fascinating than anybody else's hired man shone in the
sun like Mama's old copper kettle from up in the attic.

Janey smoothed her feather and put it carefully back in
its box. Wishing, said Abel, was all right but not as good
as being on the spot in case something might happen. Still,
Janey couldn't help a second look before she rushed out
to the barn. The feather was a real peacock feather from
Dr. Hannibal's peacock, although not from the bird's

handsome tail. To everybody else it looked like a plain brown feather that might even have come off of a hen, but Janey knew it was magic because when she turned it just one certain way into the sun a thin film of peacock blue covered the plain brown surface—all very unexpected, like Cinderella going to the ball.

"Should I make the big wish now?" Janey asked Augustus, but she immediately decided it was too soon, with the feather hardly warmed up yet.

There was no use pushing her luck, although Abel said that all sorts of things were apt to happen on Floating Island. Fletcher Island was the real name for the island where Janey lived, but Abel said the island deserved a more exciting name than that. When Mama had first heard about Floating Island, she had laughed and said that floating island was a kind of old-fashioned dessert, and that real islands didn't float, anyway.

"It's nice to pretend they do," Abel argued, and Janey had pretended so long that she could almost feel the island lurching up and down when the lake around it was especially wavy.

Janey hurried over to the sprayer, which Abel was touching up here and there with yellow paint.

"Have to get this thing spruced up some," he said. "It's going to be warm enough to spray one of these days." He picked a paint-brush hair off the freshly painted metal. "We ought to buy us a camel, seeing I need a new camel's-hair brush. There's nothing handier around the house than a camel."

"I could ride him to school," said Janey.

Usually Daddy liked to make jokes right along with

Abel and Janey, but now there was a worried little frown between his eyes and he acted as though he didn't see Janey at all.

"All we can do is the best we can," he told Abel, "but I did hope we could get that spray on first."

"First before what?" Janey wondered, but already Daddy was striding off toward the house.

Because of having tried so long to be a great oak, Janey had learned how important it was to get the first spray on at just the right time—not too early, not too late, not too warm, not too cold.

"If it isn't just right, it's all wrong, like the old lady's wig," said Abel. "No peaches next summer and no new dresses for Janey."

Janey couldn't imagine there really not being any peaches, after all the work everybody did all year, even Janey with her little-acorn jobs. She loved to make a calendar of peach-growing in her mind, just from the chores that she helped with, herself. Trimming trees in January and February, burning brush in March, thinning out the hard little green peaches in June, sorting fruit for the stand in August, spooning mothball-smelling crystals around the tree trunks in September—Janey could help with every single job, although of course like a little acorn, not a great oak.

"If I can help with all those things, I can help spray, too," Janey thought stubbornly. "Abel, tell me again how it's going to be."

Abel stopped peering into the depths of the spray tank and rubbed the back of his neck.

"I'm too big to fit into a spray tank very well," he observed. "I need a reducing pill, like what's-her-name."

"Alice in Wonderland," said Janey, "only it wasn't a pill. Abel, please tell me."

"Oh, yes, spraying. Well, you'll stand on the sprayer platform with the spray gun in your hand, ready for anything, somewhat as though shooting lions in Africa. Then you will turn the handle of the spray gun, which will immediately twist out of your hand like an elephant's trunk and give everybody within ten feet a faceful of lime sulphur."

Janey loved to hear Abel tell about the calamities which would occur when she helped with the spraying, but she knew that wasn't the way it would be at all. She would hang tight to the spray gun, just like Abel and Daddy, and douse each tree carefully with a cloud of greenish lime sulphur as the tractor pulled the sprayer through the orchard.

"Abel," said Janey, "did Daddy say anything about letting me spray this year?"

"Never a word," said Abel. "The spray guns are still too heavy for you."

"I don't think they are," Janey insisted. "I'm much bigger than I was last year. Maybe I'll just ask him."

"A good way to find out things," Abel agreed, "if you can't wait."

From the look on Abel's face, she knew that he was going to say something about making haste slowly, so she wandered around back of the barn and looked at her feather again. Augustus came back from a mouse hunt and looked too.

"The sun's still shining from my first wish," said Janey. "I wonder—"

She saw Daddy coming back from the house to help Abel.

"I can do it," she decided. "I know I can."

She took the feather out of its box, turned it until it was bright blue in the sun, and chanted the verse she had thought up especially for this biggest, most important wish.

> "Oh, feather, however
> You magicked before,
> This wish needs more magic—
> Yes, twice as much more."

She said it three times, to make sure, and marched up to Daddy, still clutching the feather in one hand. Augustus stalked along behind her.

"Daddy," Janey began, hoping that her voice wouldn't shake too much, "may I help you spray this year? Please, double please?"

"Why, Baby," said Daddy, "I don't think you're— Or are you?" He looked doubtfully down at her. "I'll tell you what! You may if you can handle the spray gun. Abel, run some water in the tank, and we'll let her try right now."

"Oh, Daddy! Now?"

Janey patted her feather gratefully and was about to lay it in its box when Augustus reached up and batted the feather out of her hand. A sudden gust of wind whirled it far away across the orchard. Janey gulped.

"I—I guess I don't need it any more, anyway," she said wistfully.

She had no time to feel sad, though, because Abel was putting water into the spray tank, and Daddy was running the tractor motor to work up the pressure that made the spray come out of the nozzles.

"It'll be easy," Janey assured herself cheerfully. "Easy as pie."

The spray gun on its long hose looked a good deal like the rug nozzle on Mama's vacuum cleaner and so could not be nearly as hard to handle as Daddy and Abel always said. Janey stood on the back platform, just as she had always imagined, and held the spray gun firmly in both hands.

"Ready?" asked Daddy.

Janey nodded. The spray gun was bigger and heavier than it looked when Abel was holding it in his big fists. It wobbled a little, and Janey took a firmer grip.

"All right!" said Daddy. "The pressure's up. All you have to do is turn the handle—and hang on!"

Janey turned the handle and felt as though she had a wildcat by the tail. The spray gun leaped in her hand, and water sprayed in all directions—over Daddy and Abel and Janey and even Augustus. Finally the gun got away from her entirely, and Abel had to capture it where it lay flopping at the end of its hose and turn it off again.

"Too bad, Baby," said Daddy, wiping water out of his eyes. "Next year we'll try again."

"I won't cry!" thought Janey. "I won't! Or they'll think I'm an even littler acorn than I am." She managed an extremely wobbly smile. "Oh, dear, why do oaks have to be such very slow growers?"

Janey woke up early the next morning and felt under her pillow as usual for the box with her magic feather. Then she remembered with an empty feeling that it was gone—and so was her chance to help spray. Even Mama and Daddy were gone when she went down to breakfast.

"Had to go to the mainland on business," said Abel. "Here, have a few fried eggs. Best I can do until Mrs. Haskins comes to look after us."

Janey thought that before breakfast was an odd time to go to the mainland, and she did wish that Mama and Daddy had wakened her up so she could have gone, too. She loved the bouncy winter ferryboat, which was much more exciting than the big summer one that glided so smoothly over the water.

Abel pushed back his chair and studied the thermometer, which was fastened in plain view outside the kitchen window.

"Just what I thought," he said. "I'll have to spray, no matter what. Do you still think you can help me?"

Janey looked at him doubtfully. Before yesterday, she would have declared that of course she could help spray, but now she knew better.

"Most people never learn anything except the hard way," Abel often said, "and lots of them are so hen-headed they don't catch on even then."

"Anyway," thought Janey, "I'm not all *that* hen-headed."

She looked Abel in the eye and said the words she had thought she never would say.

"No," she said, "I can't help spray. I'm not big enough."

Abel stroked his beard and looked at her approvingly.

"That's where I'm bound to differ with you," he said finally. "I think you're anyway twice as big as you were yesterday. Get on your things and come out to the barn. You'll have to skip school just for today."

The air felt warmer than it had yesterday, and Janey unbuttoned her jacket in the bright sunshine. She remembered that in only a few weeks now the peach blossoms would be bursting into bloom. Dark pink, light pink, and all the shades in between would make the orchard look like rows and rows of fluffy ballet dancers swaying in the wind. But now—

"Abel," she protested, "I'll try again, but I truly don't think I can hold that spray gun, any more than I could yesterday."

Abel placidly cranked up the tractor, hauled out the sprayer, filled it with water from the big overhead tank, dumped in the powdery lime sulphur, and turned on the agitator which stirred the whole mess up like Mama's egg beater. He looked at the pressure gauge and nodded in satisfaction.

"All set, now," he announced. "I'll steer the tractor with my knees and spray the trees with my hands, like the man that played the violin, mouth organ and drums all at once. That'll take care of the trees on one side of the row. You will stand on the back platform and spray the trees on the other side. All perfectly simple." He glanced down at Augustus. "And you, my six-toed friend, had better keep out of the way."

"Abel," Janey began again, "I don't think—"

"Bless my stars!" said Abel. "Some days I don't think, either, and this seems to be one of them. I forgot my Alice-in-Wonderland spray gun—and after I stayed up half the night fixing it, too!"

He dived back into the tool shed and immediately emerged carrying a spray gun that looked exactly like the regular ones, except that it was only about half as big. The handle was shorter, the crosspiece where the spray came out was thinner, "and," said Abel, "the whole thing should be a lot lighter."

"It is!" said Janey in surprise. "Light as a feather. A biggish feather, of course."

"Alice got shrunk down to fit the place where she was," said Abel, "and I figured I could shrink a spray gun down to fit you. Used an aluminum tube I had around." He grinned down at Janey and climbed up on the tractor. "Some days you have to make haste a little faster than others. Get on the sprayer platform, now, and hang on. This vehicle jolts the least bit."

Janey didn't care how much the sprayer jolted or how much it lurched in the spring mud. She was exactly where she had dreamed of being—on the platform of the sprayer behaving like a great oak instead of a little acorn. The spray gun still tried to get away from her, but after accidentally spraying Abel in the back of the neck just one time, she managed to hit what she aimed at. The spray billowed out just as it was supposed to do, enveloping the trees in misty lime sulphur.

"No bugs will eat them now," thought Janey. "Oh, my, won't Daddy and Mama be surprised?"

At noon, Abel helped her down from the sprayer. Her arms ached, her neck was stiff, and her cheeks stung from the lime sulphur which the wind had blown in her face. She staggered up to the house and eased herself carefully down in a chair. Mrs. Haskins set a bowl of hot potato soup in front of her.

"It's still fun," said Janey.

"Telephone," said Abel from the kitchen. "Your Daddy has a surprise for you."

Daddy was calling from the mainland on the long-distance line that made everybody sound as though they were talking under water. Janey could almost hear bubbles as Daddy talked.

"Twins!" he said in a great hurry. "We've got twin boys! Mama sends her love, and I'll be home on the boat tonight."

Janey wanted to tell him that she had been a great oak all morning and was going to keep on being one all afternoon, but Daddy, sounding bubblier than ever, had said goodby and hung up.

"Abel," said Janey, I'll have to go over to Dr. Hannibal's tonight for sure."

"Caught cold out in that wind, I've no doubt," said Mrs. Haskins. "Where's the camphorated oil?"

But Janey only laughed and leaned over to scratch Augustus's chin.

"I just want to get two magic feathers off the doctor's peacock," she said. "Not for me, of course. Great oaks don't need magic feathers, but little acorns always do!"

—Mildred Lawrence

Buttons

Fishing for Mussels in Arkansas

The green and white rowboat *Boranders* drifted down the White River with the current so slowly that it made scarcely a ripple on the waves. Donie Lee, with her jeans rolled high above her knees, kicked aside a pile of mussels to make room for her feet, and settled herself more comfortably at the stern.

Tom Lee, her father, sat at the prow, with his face half-turned from her, guiding the boat now and then with an oar. He was a man of few words, but there was a contentment even in his silence. They had had an unusually good day, with the mussels grabbing at the hooks almost as fast as they could let down the lines. Now the boat was so full it could hold no more and they were heading home, with the lines dangling in rows from the iron bars which hung suspended high on each side.

Donie looked idly at the familiar landmarks she passed. There was the tall sweetgum tree growing so close to the river banks that its roots could be seen, like giant black fingers clutching the earth to hold on. The leaves had already turned scarlet and the little starry balls had fallen, bobbing up and down on the waves. A tall blue crane stood on one leg beside it, but he ran awkwardly away at their approach. But two mallards, the first of the season to come down from the north, floated undisturbed in a quiet cove, knowing full well they were safe until the hunting season started.

September had always been the month that Donie liked best of the whole year. The days were just right, neither too hot nor too cold. All of nature seemed to be waking up from the drowsiness of summer, with squirrels burying pecans and hickory nuts as fast as they could find them, and rabbits patching up their burrows. Summer birds were fluttering about, getting ready to fly south as the winter birds began coming in. Even the fish seemed to know the seasons were changing, for their runs in the river were as crowded as the flyways of the air.

But now September meant something else, and the thought kept coming back to Donie's mind to nag her. There was a new consolidated school at St. Charles, and it took in the settlement of Indian Head. And the little one-room school where she had been going had been torn down.

It was said of Donie's mother and her people that they

never knew a stranger, which meant they could make friends as soon as they met a newcomer, talking and laughing with them as if they'd known each other all their lives. But Donie was like her father. She was more at ease alone on the river than with people, unless she knew them very well. And there wasn't a one in the consolidated school that she knew. She could feel their stares and sometimes she wondered if they would not be laughing behind her back.

At a clearing around the bend, where a rice field came down to meet the river, two girls were playing. They had taken off their shoes and socks and were holding their crisp starched dresses high, to wade cautiously in the water. They stared at Donie and her father floating past in the *Boranders* and Donie lowered her eyes shyly. She had recognized one as a girl named Ella, to be in her class at the new school. Suddenly a loud scream caused her to look up quickly.

"An alligator!" one of the girls exclaimed.

"Oh! He's coming after us!" the other cried.

Donie could see nothing but a gar, with its long, pointed face showing through the muddy water. But the girls were already scurrying away as fast as they could, with their shoes and socks dangling in their hands.

Now it was Donie who stared as they ran through the field of ripe rice to a house high on a hill. How could anybody be afraid of a garfish! Many a time, when she was swimming in deep water, she had come across even larger ones than that, but she hadn't given them a second thought. There was nothing about the river to be afraid of, Donie mused. Even in flood time, with the water rising high over

the banks, or when a strong wind blew, shaking and rocking their houseboat as a terrier shakes a rat, she was never
frightened.

There was only one fear that Donie had. The very
thought of the room full of strangers she must face again
on Monday morning, filled her with dread. All week she
had looked forward to Saturday when she could go out
on the river with her father. And now that Saturday was
here, she could not get that dread out of her mind. It had
been different at the old school where she had always gone
before. There were only the few children that she knew
so well, who lived on the river as she did. And they were
all in one room, from the first grade to the last.

"Seems like I hear somebody playing a mouth harp,"
Donie's father spoke at last, when they came within sight
of the houseboat where they lived.

"Uncle Allan!" Donie exclaimed, forgetting her fear
for the moment. No one else could play such gay, lively
tunes as her mother's brother. "It couldn't be anybody
but Uncle Allan!"

He was a sailor, and once a year he came back on a
furlough to visit them, with his songs and music, and his
wild tales of adventure.

He came out on the porch of the houseboat when he
heard the splash of the oars, and he caught the rope
Donie's father threw to him to make fast the *Boranders*.

"Well, Tom, I see you've got yourself a helper," he
said, pretending not to recognize Donie in her jeans.
"Who is this young fellow anyway?"

"She's about as good a fisherman as there is on the river,
I reckon," Tom Lee answered with a slow smile.

"And she's so much a part of the river, I vow I believe the fish all know her," Donie's mother laughed as she came out to greet them. "And the mussels too, I'm bound," she added when she saw how full the boat was.

A tin-bottomed wooden tub, filled with water, was already simmering over an open fire on the river bank. Uncle Allan joined them as they worked in the shade of a drooping willow. His sailor collar and wide-bottom trousers flapped with each step he took. The mussels were thrown in the hot water to make them open easily, then they were cleaned and put in piles.

"Look, I found a pearl!" Uncle Allan called out.

"That's not a pearl," Donie teased. "It's nothing but a slug. A pearl is round and smooth and full of pretty colors."

"You call that a slug? Why that's as fine a pearl as ever I saw," he answered, holding it up between his fingers. "That is, except that black pearl I found off the coast of old Mexico."

Uncle Allan had a way of spinning yarns with such a straight face that Donie found herself half-believing them, even though she knew they couldn't possibly be true. She could almost see the man-eating octopus guarding the bed of giant oysters, each with a priceless pearl inside, as she listened while she worked.

The mussels were assorted into separate piles, and on Monday the shell boat was coming to take them up the river to the button factory. The pile of small yellow sand shells was larger than usual this time. They were used to make the dainty, pearl-like buttons on fine blouses and babies' dresses. The elephant ears, big and black with purple inside, were the cheapest, for they made buttons for underwear and playsuits. But they were the easiest to catch on the hooks that dragged the river bottom. All the grandma shells and creepers were put in a pile together to be thrown back into the river, for they were of no use in making buttons.

They finished just as the sun went down, with a splash of color on the tree tops across the river, and Donie's mother started up the stage board of the houseboat to prepare their supper.

"What will it be?" she asked. "Venison, bear meat, pork, fish or chicken?"

It was a game they played whenever they had fried turtle, for each part of a turtle has the flavor of some kind of meat.

"Chicken," Donie replied.

"The wishbone for me," Uncle Allan joined in.

It meant they would have meat from the turtle neck, for that was the part that tasted like white meat of a chicken.

Donie took a bath from the back side of the boat, and put on a clean shirt and jeans. Cool and refreshed, she sat down on the bank, with her knees drawn up, and looked out on the river. The sky was gray, with the first star of the evening appearing above a tall sycamore across on the other shore. There was that silence that comes in the pause between the bird songs of the day and the cry of the tree toads and crickets and the whippoor-wills. Now and then a river swallow, flying back to its nest in the banks, skimmed the water slatwise, tipping it with a wing. Or a snake passed silently by, with its head held high, like the prow of a toy boat.

"I wish it could be like this always and always," Donie sighed as her uncle came to sit down beside her.

"It seems to me like it is," he said, taking a pipe out of one of the funny little pockets of his sailor suit. "It was like this last year when I came, and the year before—the houseboats tied to trees on the bank, the mussels in piles and the old muddy river running by. I don't see anything that's changed except the way you've been growing like all get-out. Why you sprout up another six inches every time I see you."

"If I just didn't have to go to school," Donie answered.

"Oh, so that's what's bothering you," Uncle Allan laughed. "You've had enough learning you think."

It wasn't because she had had enough of learning. There were still so many things Donie wanted to know besides how to read and write and add. How far was it from here to the evening star, and what went into the making of the boulder on the opposite shore, and what it was like in all the places where the river ran, from the first little spring up north to the ocean it emptied into. But Uncle Allan would never understand what it was to be shy with strangers and to stumble over a lesson just because it had to be recited aloud.

"I knew everybody in the school here at Horseshoe Bend," Donie said. "But there's not a soul in my class at St. Charles that's my friend."

She half-expected her uncle to laugh at her, but instead he quietly knocked the ashes from his pipe and put it back into his pocket and he answered, slowly, "Yes, I know how it is."

Donie looked up quickly to see if he was teasing, but his face was never more serious.

"There wasn't a more bashful boy in the whole school than I was," he went on. "And it was even worse in the Navy when I first went in. Why I'd sit off in a corner by myself while all the other fellows were having fun, singing and talking and pranking, and none of them paying any attention to me. That is, not until I found the lynx eye. Of course everything changed after that."

"The lynx eye? What is that?" Donie wanted to know.

"It's something that came from some heathen idol, I was told. It was at a strange port with a name I don't remember, where we'd put in after a long voyage."

All of Uncle Allan's yarns began that way, and Donie found herself listening, as she always did, half-believing though she knew it could not possibly be true. She tried to picture her uncle, lonely and shy, with all the other sailors leaving him to go ashore. And the wizened old medicine man rowing out to the ship, trading a magic lynx eye for a pouch of tobacco.

"Where is it?" Donie asked, when her uncle had finished his tale.

He hesitated, then shook his head.

"I'm not sure I ought to let you see it," he said. "I can see right now you don't believe me. Why you might even call it a plain old button, for it does look something like one. And could you imagine a lynx eye working magic after that!"

Donie coaxed, and at last he went back to the houseboat where he kept his duffel bag. He brought something back in his hand, and when he gave it to Donie, she laughed aloud. It was nothing but a plain old button.

"I knew that's what you'd think of it," he said with a frown as he took it back. "Of course those holes make it look like a button, but they're to put the string through so it can be worn, like this."

He took a string from his pocket and threaded it through one of the holes, then he tied it around Donie's neck.

"I'll bet a silver dollar it would work the magic if you'd wear it to school on Monday," he said. "All you have to do is look straight at the first girl you see in the classroom and smile at her like this," he smiled down at Donie in such a warm, friendly way that she could almost believe what he said was true. "And you say 'hello,' like this. Then watch them come swarming around you like bees after clover. Why you should have seen how it was when the fellows came back from shore leave, right after I'd got it from the medicine man. It was 'Hi, there, Allan.' 'Why didn't you come with us, boy.' You'd think I'd been their pal all my life."

"Supper's ready," Donie's mother called. "And whatever tall tale that is you're telling now will have to wait, Allan."

But Uncle Allan said nothing more about the magic lynx eye until Monday morning when Donie was ready to go to school.

"Now don't forget to wear the magic eye," he whispered. And when he saw it tied around Donie's neck, he added, "And mind you, you've got to believe it, or it won't work for you. Remember, just smile, like this."

His smile followed Donie to the road where she waited

for the school bus. When she got on, the first person she saw was Ella, the girl who lived on the rice farm. Donie's cheeks burned at first, and she started to turn shyly away. But she felt the lynx eye, cool and firm beneath the neck of her dress, and she turned back to Ella, smiling the way Uncle Allan had told her, and she said "hello" as he had said it.

Ella looked surprised, then she smiled back and made room on the seat beside her.

"You live on a houseboat, don't you," she said. "That must be lots of fun."

"It is," Donie answered.

She found herself talking about fishing and swimming and rowing on the river as easily as if they had been friends all their lives. They walked into the classroom arm in arm, and when the others in the class turned to look at her, Donie smiled at them. She felt the warmth of friendship all around her, drawing her in as a part of them. Even the teacher was not stern as Donie had once thought her to be. And when it was time to recite her lesson aloud, Donie did not once stumble. Could it really be that this button around her neck was a magic eye after all? She must tell Uncle Allan about it as soon as she reached home.

"Mercy, child, what's come over you?" her mother said, looking up from her sewing when Donie came rushing up the stage plank late that afternoon.

"Where's Uncle Allan? I've something to tell him."

"Well I've something to tell him too," the mother answered as she rolled up a pair of socks she had mended.

It was she who spoke first when Uncle Allan came out on the porch, fresh from a swim in the river.

"I thought you had to learn something about keeping socks darned and buttons sewed on in the Navy," she said. "Here, I've finished all your socks, and they were peppered with holes, all right. But your pea jacket, there's a button missing and I can't find it high or low in that duffel bag of yours."

She held up the jacket, and Donie gave a little gasp. There were the remaining buttons, exactly like the magic lynx eye her uncle had given her, and one of them was missing. An embarrassed grin came over Uncle Allan's face and he caught her eye and winked. Donie winked back.

"Here it is," she said, as she untied the string and took it off.

She didn't need it now, for she knew that the friends she had made that day would still be her friends tomorrow and all the days after.

—CHARLIE MAY SIMON

Rosina's Chickens

An Arkansas Tornado

With her yellow curls sparkling in the early morning sun, Rosina Siori sat in the doorway of her very own broiler house in the village of Tontitown in the Arkansas Ozarks. Carefully, she counted her White Wyandotte chickens as they ate hungrily from the feeding-trays she had just filled with wet mash.

"Eighty-two . . . eighty-three . . ." she murmured. "But where is eighty-four?"

Worried, Rosina looked into the dimness of the broiler house.

"Here, chick, chick, chick," she called. "Please come and get your breakfast. It's almost time for me to go to school."

Rosina often talked that way to her chickens—when her big brothers who went to high school in Springdale five miles away weren't around to laugh at her.

And why shouldn't she? She had fed and watered her chickens and kept them warm and dry from the time they were pale-yellow balls of fluff only two days old.

Now, three months later, they were ready to be sold. In fact, Rosina's father was to take them tomorrow to the wholesalers in Springdale with his own broilers.

Again Rosina called. This time, number eighty-four ran from behind the broiler house and began to eat with the others.

Rosina sighed sadly, remembering that in exactly one day, she would have to say good-by to them all.

"But, anyway, they'll sell for enough money for my Easter trip," she told herself. "And when I get back, I can start another batch."

The Easter trip to the wonderful St. Louis zoo! That had been Rosina's fondest dream ever since January when the teacher had told the fifth and sixth grades about it.

At last she would be able to see all the animals she had read about so often—the pandas, the lions, the boa constrictors!

"Rosie! It's 8:30!" came a call from the white farmhouse where she lived.

Rosina hurried back across the fields scarcely giving a glance to her father's and brothers' hundreds of White Wyandotte broilers. It wouldn't do to be late for school today, the last day before the Monday that meant St. Louis and the zoo.

In the cozy kitchen, Rosina picked up her lunch, and kissed her mother good-by. Then she banged down the porch steps and pedaled away on her blue bicycle.

In a few minutes, Rosina came to the tiny farm where Mrs. Fontagni lived all alone. Mrs. Fontagni was working in her chicken-yard.

Rosina and Mrs. Fontagni were great friends. Even though Rosina was now ten, she still loved to play with the lovely *bambolina* which Mrs. Fontagni had brought with her from northern Italy way back in 1898 when Tontitown was first settled. The doll had real hair and was dressed exactly as a little blonde Italian girl should be dressed.

"Good morning, Mrs. Fontagni!" called Rosina, slowing down.

"*Buon giomo,* Rosina!" Mrs. Fontagni answered. "Today I go to Springdale to grapejuice factory—I find work for summer maybe."

"I hope so," Rosina called back.

Soon, Rosina was in front of the Tonteretti farm, this one a big grape and chicken farm like her own.

In a moment, Mary Tonteretti dashed out and so did her brother Julio. Pell-mell, they wheeled down the front lawn on their bicycles. Even Julio didn't want to be late so near the St. Louis zoo trip.

"Hey, Rosie, did you hear what the radio said this morning?" asked Julio. "There was a tornado down in Oklahoma last night—a bad one."

"I hope we never have one here," Mary said with a shiver.

"Me, too," said Rosina. "It might kill my chickens."

"You and your chickens!" laughed Julio. "Think they were made of gold or something. I'd *like* to be in a tornado—wow! And wouldn't one of your broilers look funny with all the feathers blown off of it?"

Still laughing, Julio sped down the road ahead of them.

"Don't mind him, Rosie," said Mary. "He's always teasing me, too."

The two girls rode on down the dirt road between the neat farms with their rows of trellised Concord grape-vines, now just starting to bud out. And past the long chicken-houses where hundreds of young chickens scratched about—some White Wyandottes like Rosina's and some New Hampshire Reds like Mrs. Fontagni's. Everybody in Tontitown raised broilers and grapes, it seemed.

A few minutes later, Mary and Rosina turned cautiously on to Highway 68, riding close to the edge as they had been taught to do.

The last bell was ringing and boys and girls from the first grade to the eighth were running or riding toward the little white schoolhouse next to the church buildings.

Classes that day went slowly for Rosina. Twice the teacher had to speak to her for dreaming instead of studying.

Finally at three o'clock when the teacher gave the last instructions for the trip on Monday, Rosina thought she had never been so happy.

As soon as she could, she dashed out to her bicycle, not even waiting for Mary. What if something had happened to her eighty-four broilers while she'd been in school? What if a dog had broken into their yard? She pedaled hard toward home.

Without warning, something cold and brittle hit her on the nose as she turned off the highway. Then, whatever it was bounced off. Rosina looked up at the sky. Tiny hailstones were falling from dark puffy clouds. Then, more hailstones hit her face—bigger ones.

"Oh, my poor chickens!" she gasped. "I closed their door—they can't get in!"

She passed the Tonteretti farm. She could see Mr. and Mrs. Tonteretti and the hired man running about closing up all their broiler houses. They must think there was going to be a bad storm. Did they expect a tornado like the one in Oklahoma?

She searched the clouds for the huge funnel like the picture she'd seen in the weather book. One enormous cloud off to the west did look ugly and purple, and it curved and moved around like boiling sirup, but there was no long funnel.

Now Rosina was in front of Mrs. Fontagni's little farm. Mrs. Fontagni's red chickens were huddled together against their house. Their door was closed, too.

Rosina thought, "Why doesn't she let them in?" Then she remembered. Mrs. Fontagni had gone to Springdale.

Rosina got off her bicycle and started to run toward the broiler house. There was a peculiar quiet everywhere and a queer yellow light. She looked again at the sky. The purple cloud was closer and it had something long like an elephant's trunk hanging from it.

Rosina stopped running. "If that *is* a tornado cloud," she said aloud, "I'd better get home to my own chickens."

Her father and mother wouldn't know she had left the door closed. And they wouldn't notice it when they closed in their own chickens because her broiler house was almost hidden behind the old barn.

Rosina ran back to her bicycle. At top speed, she headed toward her precious chickens. The elephant trunk was bigger now. It *must* be a tornado cloud!

Rosina's heart beat faster. Her chickens might get blown away or hit with something. And then how could she go to St. Louis? But Mrs. Fontagni had only those broilers to pay for her living until the grapes were ready to be harvested in July. What would *she* do if they were killed?

Rosina's feet lagged on the pedals. Then she turned back. She just couldn't let Mrs. Fontagni lose her chickens.

The dark funnel seemed almost above Rosina as she opened the door of the chicken house. Frantically, the chickens scurried in.

Now a heavy rain began to fall and the wind blew hard. It was too late for Rosina to go home. It was even too late for her to run to Mrs. Fontagni's "cyclone cave" near the house. So she went inside with the chickens and closed the door.

Timidly, she watched the storm through the windows. "Oh, my poor little chickens," she thought. "They'll think I've forgotten them."

Rosina had heard what strange things a tornado can do. It can lift up a whole house and set it down.

She knew that a tornado wind can drive pieces of straw right into a tree-trunk. And once down in Texas, her father had told her, a tornado picked up a corncob and hit a cow on the head with it, and stunned it.

Think what such a wind could do to a soft little chicken! Rosina's eyes filled with tears, she just couldn't help it.

Outside the wind and rain still beat against the chicken house. Then suddenly, all was quiet. The sun came out. Rosina opened the door cautiously. To the west, the sky was blue. To the east, the dark clouds hurried away.

Rosina ran to her bicycle. The dirt road was muddy and the going was hard. And here and there, trees were lying on the road. But soon she was in her own driveway.

Then her mother hurried out of the kitchen. "Rosie, my *bambino*," she cried, hugging her tightly. "Where have you been? Julio and Mary were home long ago . . . I phoned."

Rosina pulled away. "I've got to see my chickens!" she said. "I left their door shut . . . they couldn't get out of the storm!"

"Rosie, *carissima,* wait!" said her mother. "Your chickens are safe. The whole town's safe. The foot of the funnel went through the woods."

Rosina was so happy that she took her mother by both hands and whirled her round and round in an Italian dance-step.

"Rosie, stop!" said her mother. "Tell me—where were you during the storm?"

Rosina giggled. "I was in Mrs. Fontagni's broiler house! She left the door closed and I was afraid the tornado would carry her chickens away—and she needs them."

"Well done, my brave one," said her mother. "Mrs. Fontagni will be grateful. Now come into the house and try on your new Easter dress."

"It will be my St. Louis zoo dress, too," Rosina said with a gay little skip up the steps.

—GLADYS M. RELYEA

Down from the Hills

*From the Hills of Tennessee, to
Arkansas and Back*

"Where we goin', Ma?"

A little girl sat on top of the wagon. It was piled high with bedding, bundles, and boxes.

"We're goin' to Arkansas to pick cotton," said her mother.

"Is *this* Arkansas, Ma?" asked the girl.

"Yes, but there's no cotton here," said Ma. "We got to go farther south. Is that wheel near-about fixed, Big Joe?"

Trixie's big brother was kneeling on the ground. He

pounded boards on a wobbly wheel of the second wagon.

"Yes, *ma'm,*" said the boy. "I got her fixed. Let's go, Pa."

He spoke to a man who came out from the yard of a near-by house, followed by a younger boy. They brought water in buckets, which they poured into a milk-can. Big Joe put the cover on tight and lifted the can up.

"Let's go!" said the man, climbing on the first wagon and taking the reins.

Pa Medley was a lanky, unshaven man dressed in overalls. He whistled sharply and three hound dogs came running. Little Jeff jumped on the rear end, leading a small pony by a rope. Big Joe took his place beside Old Granny and drove the second wagon. Trixie and her mother dangled their bare legs over the side. The wagons began to move, with the dogs trotting underneath.

"I was a-scared on that ferry," said Trixie. "River so big and wide and all. I was a-scared we'd fall in."

"Biggest, widest river in the world—the Mississippi," said Big Joe. "Never seen it so low before. We coulda waded over."

"Waded over and got drownded," said Trixie.

"Can't git from Tennessee to Arkansas without crossin' that big ole river," said Ma. She took a pinch of snuff from the can in her pocket and tucked it inside her lower lip.

"I wisht I was back home again, back in the hills where we come from," said Trixie sadly. "Don't like no river, don't like Arkansas, don't like cotton-pickin'."

"You hush up, Trixie," said Ma. "You can pick cotton jest like the rest of us. You not a baby no more."

"I ain't homesick, Ma," called Little Jeff. "I'll pick cotton for you."

The little caravan moved slowly on. Cars and trucks passed it by. People put out their heads and looked. People in houses along the road came out and stared. Old Granny shook out her pipe and began to sing *Rock of Ages* in a quavering voice.

"Why's all the folks lookin' at us?" asked Trixie.

"They ain't never seen a hoss before, I reckon," laughed Big Joe. "Hosses gone clean outa style over here in Arkansas."

The rolling hills flattened out and the cotton fields looked larger. Some were filled with pickers. But there were no signs saying: *Pickers Needed.* Pa Medley stopped his horses and hailed a man walking.

"Know where there's any cotton to pick?" he asked.

"No, I don't," said the man, staring.

They kept on going. They did not know whom to ask about cotton-picking jobs. They felt like strangers in a strange land. It was near nightfall when they pulled up at a corner. A small country church stood across the road opposite a country store. A few houses were just beyond.

"Oh, look at the purty little church-house," said Ma.

"And there's a store," said Pa. "See all them cotton-pickers goin' in. There's bound to be plenty cotton to pick around here."

"Not much grass for the hosses," said Big Joe.

"All the fields are growed to cotton," said Pa. "Plumb out to the road."

"That grass in the churchyard looks good," said Ma.

"Sure does," said Pa. "Best we've seen since we left the hills."

"We'll camp in the churchyard," said Ma. "A church-house belongs to everybody. Nobody'll bother us there."

"Good!" said Granny. "Let's sleep in the churchyard."

They drove slowly in. They stopped at the back, as far from the road as possible. Trixie and Little Jeff jumped down to stretch their legs. The youngest hound-puppy scampered about with them. Trixie ran to the door of the church-house and opened it a crack. She and Little Jeff peeked in. Ma came up behind them.

"See! The door's open," she said. "They keep it open so people can come in and rest—and say their prayers." She looked inside. "It sure is purty. So nice and clean. Such purty cushions on them benches—the color o' wild roses."

"We gonna sleep in the church-house?" asked Trixie.

"We could each have a bench to ourself," said Little Jeff.

Ma closed the door quickly. "No, we ain't," she said. "It'll be a sight cooler sleepin' outdoors." They walked back to the wagon. "I'd sure like to come to meetin' here jest once, to hear the preachin' and singin'." She began to unpack and get ready for supper.

"Trixie," called Ma, handing her a quarter. "Go over to that store and buy us a quarter's worth o' coffee."

"Ask if anybody needs cotton pickers," said Pa.

"Ask if it's all right for us to sleep in the churchyard," said Ma.

"I'm a-scared to go," said the little girl.

"Go on, nothin' ain't gonna bite you, honey."

The little girl ran across the road.

Trixie slipped into the store and looked around.

A truckload of Mexican cotton-pickers came up and stopped. Men, women, and children crowded into the store. They made gestures and talked loudly in a strange language. They pointed to bologna, crackers, bread, and canned goods. The storekeepers filled up many paper bags with groceries.

Trixie was hemmed in. She stared through the dirty glass of the candy case at the back. She kept her eyes fixed on the candy. After the cotton-pickers went out, a boy came in.

"Hi, George!" called the storekeeper.

"Hi, Jim!" said George. "There's a bunch of gypsies campin' in the churchyard. Betcha they're gonna steal things tonight. Better lock your store up tight."

The storekeeper laughed. "I seen 'em come a while ago, but I don't guess they're thieves. They couldn't git away fast enough in them rickety ole wagons. Thieves have cars nowadays."

"Horse-thieves, maybe," said George. "They got so many horses. Or maybe they're horse-traders."

"How do you get such big ideas, boy?" asked Jim Harter.

"I bet they stole that bicycle they got up on that front wagon," said George.

"Likely they're jest country folks goin' on a journey to visit their kinfolk," said Jim.

George looked back and saw the little girl by the candy case. He pointed with his thumb. "There's one of 'em, Jim," he said. "Better watch her. She'll snitch a cracker or somethin'."

"I'm not worried," said Jim.

The boy went out and a well-dressed man came in. He had parked his large black car out front.

"Howdy, Mr. Bryce," nodded Jim Harter. "What can I do for you?"

"My son Edward came home from school today," said the man, "and reported that gypsies were camping in the churchyard. So I came right over."

"There they are." Jim pointed out the window. "Take a look."

"Where are they from?" asked Mr. Bryce. "What do they want?"

"Dunno, Mr. Bryce," said Jim. "I ain't asked 'em. It ain't none of my business."

"Well, as President of the Board of Trustees of the Promised Land Church," said Mr. Bryce, "I think it *is my* business . . ."

Mrs. Bryce hurried in.

"I went over close and looked, Randolph," she said in an agitated tone. "They're terrible people. The Ladies' Aid has just put those new rose-colored cushions on the pews. If they go in, they'll sleep on them sure, and likely they've all got . . . you-know-what. They're not clean, anybody can see that. They're all in their bare feet. It took six pie-suppers to buy that upholstery cloth. We paid $4.98 a yard for it."

Several other cars drove up and people hurried in. "You seen 'em?" The heads nodded, and a confusion of talk filled the store.

"They'll go right in and sleep soon as it's dark," said Mrs. Bryce. "The door's unlocked, you know."

"Remember the time those picnickers got in and tore up all the hymn-books?" asked Mrs. Hollis.

"Why do you leave the door unlocked then?" Jim Harter, who never went to church, sounded angry.

"Well . . ." Mrs. Bryce began, "it's the House of God . . . and it's kept open for prayer and meditation."

"Let 'em go in!" said Jim Harter. "They need to pray and meditate." A smile passed over his angry face.

Mr. Bryce had been talking to the men. "We'll be legal about this," he said. "We'll call the State Police." He went to the telephone behind the counter and had a short conversation. Then he told the crowd, "They'll be right out. They'll take care of it."

"Well, I'll be dog-goned!" exclaimed Jim Harter.

The store was quiet after the people left. It was dark too, so Jim turned on a light. Then he saw that the little girl was still there. He went back to her.

"What you want, sister?" he asked softly.

Trixie put the quarter in his hand and whispered the word *coffee*. The man poured some ground coffee in a paper sack and handed it to her. "Anything else?" he asked.

The girl kept on staring into the candy case. Quickly Jim Harter reached in and picked up a stick of candy. "Here!" he said, handing it out. "Here's some candy for you."

The man's kind words had the effect of the shot of a gun on a frightened rabbit. One minute the girl was there, the next minute she was gone. Her thin figure like a fleeting shadow leaped across the road. The storekeeper was left standing with the candy in his hand.

"Well, I'll be dog-goned!" he said.

The campfire was burning nicely. The pot of coffee was boiling and its fragrance filled the air. Big Joe chopped more sticks and put them on. There was just enough wind to make the sparks fly. Trixie loved a fire. She squatted down and watched it. Old Granny sat on a box near by singing *Jesus Lover of My Soul*. Trixie went over, leaned against her, and the two sang together. They stopped abruptly when they saw they were not alone.

A crowd of people had come into the churchyard. The boy George was right in front. A buzz of conversation began. Trixie ran to her mother, who was setting out food for supper.

"I'm a-scared, Ma," she cried. "What's all them people come here for? Why can't they go away and leave us alone?"

A State Police car drove up and a man stepped out. After talking to Mr. Bryce, the policeman came over. "I'm sorry," he said to Pa Medley, "but you folks can't camp here."

Medley bristled. "What right you got to order us off? You're not the preacher, be you?"

The policeman opened his coat and showed his badge.

"*Po*-lice, be you?" gasped Medley.

"Oh Ma, it's the *Po*-lice!" cried Trixie. "They takin' us to the jail-house, all for me and Granny singin'? Can't we sing hymns, not even in the churchyard?"

"Hush up," said Ma. "You hush up, Trixie."

Pa Medley never liked to be bossed around by somebody else.

"Well, we'll study about it," he told the policeman.

Ma felt suddenly brave. "We'll go when we git good and ready," she said.

"Oh Ma, don't let 'em take us to the jail-house!" cried Little Jeff. *"We ain't done nothin' bad."*

"No camping allowed in the churchyard," repeated the policeman. "The trustees of the Promised Land Church don't like it. You'd better be moving along."

Suddenly Jim Harter was there. "Hey, officer," he cried. "These folks are all right. They're honest, they won't steal a thing." But no one listened. "They're just goin' to visit their kinfolk," cried Jim. But nobody listened.

When Pa Medley saw that the officer meant what he said, he gave in. "We was jest goin'," he said weakly. "We'll move on like you say."

The policeman went into the church, where he saw that everything was in order. "They haven't hurt a thing," he reported to Mr. Bryce. "Haven't even set a foot inside the door."

Old Granny roused up and exclaimed: "What's this? They won't let us sleep in the churchyard? Why not? Why not?" She began to sing:

> "Sleepin' in the churchyard,
>   There I'll rest my head;
> Gittin' my eternal rest,
>   As cosy as in bed . . ."

Pa Medley and the boys began putting mattress,

buckets, bicycle, boxes, and bundles back on the wagons. Big Joe hitched up the horses.

"They'll move on now," repeated the policeman to Mr. Bryce. "Call me again if they give you any further trouble." He hopped in the police car and drove off.

Mr. Bryce and the others went home. No one was left to watch as the two wagons pulled slowly out of the churchyard. No one but Jim Harter, staring out through his darkened store window.

"What we done, Ma?" asked Trixie, her eyes full of fear.

"Nothin'," said Ma. "They don't want us to sleep there, that's all."

"What did the *Po*-lice come for? To put us in the jail-house?" Little Jeff was crying noisily.

"You better hush up," said Ma, "or that *Po*-lice will hear you and come back and ketch you."

Little Jeff hushed up promptly, a look of terror in his eyes.

The wagons creaked along the road. The setting sun had sunk behind a fringe of trees beyond the cotton fields. Darkness fell.

"Wisht we could find grass for the hosses," said Big Joe.

"They don't use horses here no more," said Pa, "only tractors. Them machines don't eat no grass."

"Grass and trees would make nice shade on a hot summer day," said Ma.

"Shade don't fill their pockets with money like cotton does," said Pa. "Every inch is planted to cotton."

The family spoke sadly in low voices. They were not angry or resentful. They accepted what came. When you are far from home, you never know what to expect. They were strangers in a strange land.

"That boy's name was George," said Trixie. "He was in the store, and he come over to see the *Po*-lice too. He called the storekeeper Jim. He told Jim we was gypsies and thieves. What's *gypsies,* Ma?"

"I dunno," said Ma. "Hush up now, Trixie. You talk too much."

Pa Medley pulled the horses up at the side of the road.

"Might as well stop here," he called back to Big Joe on the second wagon. "It's night already. We got to sleep somewheres."

The paved highway had a bank at one side covered with weeds. It sloped down to a ditch of stagnant water below.

"They can't run us off the public highway," said Ma. "Highway belongs to everybody, I reckon."

"No grass for the hosses," said Big Joe.

"Stake 'em up yonder," said Pa. "Looks a mite better there. Little Jeff, you and me's goin' over to that thicket and hunt us up some wood."

"*Po*-lice can't run us off if we're sleepin', can they, Ma?" asked Trixie.

"I'd like to see 'em try it," said Ma.

Soon a campfire was burning, throwing sparks up in the night sky. Ma put a skillet on the fire, mixed some dough and threw in some grease. In a few minutes large round cakes of dough were sizzling. Pa and Big Joe ate first. Then they left to walk down to the gas station at the next corner. "I'll ask about cotton to pick," said Pa.

Trixie and Little Jeff crouched down by the fire. The light shone on their faces and threw big shadows across the road. Granny on her box began to sing her made-up tune:

"Sleepin' in the churchyard,
 Underneath the trees,
I'll listen to the birdies sing
 And feel the gentle breeze . . ."

Suddenly Trixie screamed: "PO-LICE!" Her scream faded away, and her mouth remained open, as she pointed.

"Who is it?" asked Ma, turning quickly. "Mr. Bryce again?"

Trixie ran to her mother. "It's that boy, George, and Jim, the storekeeper," she said.

Ma stepped forward boldly. "*Now* what? We gotta move on again?"

"How you folks doin'?" asked Jim Harter. "All right?"

Ma Medley gulped. The man's voice was friendly. "Sure," she said.

"I brought you some stuff," said Jim. He leaned over to put down some cans of beans and milk and three loaves of bread.

"We've got rations," said Ma stiffly. "We brung stuff from home."

"I know," said Jim Harter, "but I thought . . ."

"We got money, we'll pay you . . ."

"Better keep it till . . ."

"But why should *you* . . ." began Ma.

Ma and Jim were groping toward an understanding.

"They was so afraid you'd mess up their purty church-house," said Jim Harter.

"But that's no reason . . . why you should give us . . ." said Ma. "It's the purtiest church-house ever I did see. I don't blame 'em for not wantin' it messed up. I took one look in at the door . . ." then hastily, "but I didn't touch nary a thing."

Granny's head was nodding. Her chin sank down on her breast, as she fell asleep.

The boy George walked up to Ma Medley. "I thought you was dirty people," he said.

"It's hard to keep clean without plenty of water," said Ma.

"I told 'em you-all was goin' to visit your kinfolk," said Jim Harter, "but they wouldn't listen."

A scuffle broke out. Ma turned to see Trixie and Little Jeff fighting. "What you doin'?" she called out. "Stop it!"

"This-here George called us gypsies and thieves!" shouted Trixie.

"We're a-beatin' him up," shouted Little Jeff.

It was a fierce fight while it lasted. Jim Harter tore the children apart.

"I'll learn him to call us names," said Little Jeff.

George wiped a bloody nose. Whimpering, he ran behind the storekeeper for protection.

"Can I do anything for you-all?" Jim Harter asked.

"Jest tell us where we can git water," said Ma. "We don't like to bother the folks in this town. Some folks won't even give you water. We always stop at the poorest houses. Poor people are bigger-hearted."

"There's a pump right by my store," said Jim. "I'll send George back with a bucketful." The two disappeared in the darkness. A little later, George brought the water, set it down, and left without a word.

When Pa and Big Joe returned from the gas station, Pa said, "No use. We gotta go farther south tomorrow. Man said they got too many pickers here, with all them Mexicans. No grass neither."

"Let's go to bed then," said Ma, "so we can git up early and leave at sunrise."

Pa and Big Joe spread the mattresses under the wagons. They all stretched out and pulled up their quilts. Cars passed and people stared. Curious people walked by on the highway, but did not speak. They all slept but Ma. She watched the stars for a long time. Then, worn out with weariness, she too dropped off to sleep.

The next morning when George and the school children passed on their way to school, the camping place was empty. A blackened spot showed where the campfire had been. Bent weeds showed where the horses had been tethered. That was all. No tin cans or torn paper littered the roadside. There was nothing to tell that a lonely family had slept there on cornshuck mattresses, with two wagon-beds over them for shelter.

It was a week later when the Medleys came back, driving northward. When the little caravan passed the school-yard, all the children lined up, staring.

"There's them gypsies!" cried George. "They're mean fighters. That boy gave me a bloody nose."

But the people on the wagons did not look or hear. Big

Joe slapped the lines on the gray horse's back and Pa Medley called *giddap* to the team. Old Granny hummed her hymn-tunes contentedly. Little Jeff pulled gently on the rope to keep the pony moving.

"There's that purty church-house," said Ma. "*Promised Land,* they call it."

"We don't want to stop here," said Pa.

" 'Promised Land?' Be this the place they call 'Promised Land?' " asked Granny. "The land of milk and honey?"

"It would be nice to see inside that church-house again," said Ma, "but I wouldn't go near it now. Not even if they asked me to. Let's keep goin' . . ."

But they had to stop, for there was Jim Harter running out of his store and hailing them.

"You folks all right?" he asked.

"Sure," said Ma. It was good to see his friendly face.

"We didn't find no steady cotton-pickin'," said Pa. "Most of 'em said they had plenty pickers and didn't need us."

"Did you want to pick cotton?" asked Jim Harter in astonishment.

"We sure did," said Ma. "We heard over the radio back home, that they needed hundreds of cotton pickers in this county in Arkansas. So we thought we'd come down from the hills and pick a while. We aimed to camp out if we couldn't git us a house—the nights is so warm."

"One man give us a job and told us to sleep in his storm-cellar," said Pa. "But we ruther sleep up top o' the ground."

"There was snakes in that-'ere cellar," piped up Trixie. "I was a-scared."

"That man, he hired everybody that come along," said Ma. "He hired so many pickers, they got his cotton picked in one day. So our job was soon over." It was good to talk over troubles with a friend.

"I picked twenty pounds," announced Trixie.

"I done picked eleven," said Little Jeff.

"If I'd a known you wanted to pick cotton," Jim Harter said, "I coulda got you a job right here. My brother-in-law was lookin' for cotton-pickers. I didn't like to ask you what you was after. I figgered it wasn't none o' my business."

"They wouldn't a hired us after . . . what happened in the churchyard," said Pa. "They thought we was bums . . . bad people . . . but the Lord knows . . ."

"If I'd a known, I coulda spoke to . . ." began Jim again. He turned to Ma. "You folks needin' anything? Bread or milk or any other stuff?"

Ma smiled. "Thank you," she said. "We got enough to git us back home. We'll go back to the hills and stay there."

Jim Harter stood by awkwardly, then he looked down at Trixie. "Come over to the store a minute," he said. She put her hand in his and walked with him.

When Trixie came back, she was sucking hard on a stick of candy. She took another stick out of a paper sack and handed it to Little Jeff. They climbed up on the wagon with Ma. Big Joe and Pa slapped the lines on the horses' backs. Little Jeff pulled gently on the pony's rope.

They all waved good-by to Jim Harter.

The little caravan passed the country church, but no one looked at it. It went slowly up the road and disappeared in the distance.

—LOIS LENSKI

The Meaning of the Word

In Iowa's Corn Belt

"Re-spon-si-bil-i-ty," Peter spelled slowly, his blue eyes tight closed so he wouldn't see the dictionary page before him. It was a mouthful of a word all right, and there wasn't much chance the teacher would get up to anything that size. Still you never could tell; when there were only two or three left in a spelling-match, she was apt to jump clean out of the sixth-grade book into words stout enough to knock you down.

"Petey!" Mrs. Vanderberg called. "Your supper's getting cold."

Peter's brows drew together in a frown as black as he

could manage. "Ma, for cryin' out loud, will ya quit callin' me that? You got all the fellows doin' it now. Peee-teeee! My gosh!"

"Ah, now, you're still my little boy yet awhile!" his mother laughed, ruffling the straight fair hair that fell over his eyes. "Come, so many words you know now you'll spell down the teacher herself."

"Well, I better," Peter muttered. Only by some amazing feat like that could he hope to erase the laughter that followed him now around the schoolyard. "Oh, Peeteee, you mowed down any haystacks today?"

It had happened way back in early Fall, but though now it was mid-November nobody had forgotten. Not the kids, nor his brother, Dirk, nor his father.

Ever since Peter's tenth birthday, he had teased to drive the tractor. Jeepers, when a boy wrote his age in two figures, he was practically grown-up, wasn't he? Why, there wasn't another farm-boy his size in the whole county who couldn't run every piece of equipment on his place!

"Too young yet, Petey," his father kept saying. And even when Peter's eleventh birthday came and went, "Being grown-up is not something you measure with years."

It just didn't make sense to Peter. He kept pestering and pouting till at last this Fall Pa showed him the workings of the tractor, and let him make his first trial run. Boy, that was a day! Peter felt like a king up there on the high tractor seat. He couldn't keep still about it. All over the house, and all over school next day, he bragged about the way he'd handled that little old machine.

Still, he wasn't so crazy about tractor-driving that he

let it add to his chores. He stayed on at school afternoons, playing ball when he knew Pa and Dirk were starting Fall plowing and would have given him a turn at it. But he always got out to the fields by dusk to beg to drive a tractor back to the farmyard. Usually either Pa or Dirk was so saddle-sore by that time that he welcomed the chance to walk and let Peter take the tractor in.

It was one of such evenings when a half-dozen boys from Peter's school came bicycling past the Vanderberg farm just as Peter was driving the tractor down the lane inside the fence. Peter was drifting along in low gear, keeping well behind the cows that were moseying toward the barn, when he heard the whistles and yells from the road.

"Hey-yay, lookit Roy Rogers there! Ride 'em, cowboy! Rope that there steer!"

Peter had yelled and waved in return. Sitting up a bit straighter, he'd shifted to a higher gear and closed in on the cows. A frisky heifer near the rear got nervous about the buzzing on her tail and pranced out of line. Peter just couldn't resist the opportunity to show off. In a fine sweeping arc, he swung out of the lane to herd the heifer back into line. The startled cows broke into a clumsy trot and came mooing and bellowing into the farmyard like a movie stampede. Nimbly, Peter circled them, swinging the tractor this way and that as though it was Trigger himself.

And then—he made the mistake of taking a peek out at the road to see how it was going over with the boys. Just five seconds of not watching where he was going, and— pow! Something hit him like a bale of mattresses falling off a hundred beds. He'd run smack into the old haystack! Bundles of hay came rolling down on his head and shoulders. Hay got in his mouth and up his nose. Hay packed so solidly around his arms he couldn't reach the tractor controls and shift into reverse. He couldn't yell; he couldn't breathe. He just kept on grinding deeper and deeper into the dusty, scratchy, solid heap until—

Whoof! In a cloud of dust and floating hay, he burst out the other side! Ma was pounding the big triangle in the yard, and Pa and Dirk were coming on the run, and the boys in the road were laughing so hard they had to lean against each other for support.

That was the last tractor-driving Peter had done. He guessed it was the last he'd ever get to do till he was an old man with a white beard. Pa had made him fork the hay back into its pile all himself. But that wasn't half as bad as going to school the next day. Peter's ears burned, just remembering what the kids had said. He'd never live that business down till he did something to make headlines a different way.

Like winning this spelling-match, maybe . . . beating Arie Huibregste who'd been to the state spelling contest in Des Moines last year, and was nearly always last one up.

Well, he couldn't be any more ready for him, Peter guessed, closing the dictionary with a big sigh. Words floated in the air around him. When he closed his eyes, words bombarded his eyelids.

In the twilight outside the window, he could see Pa coming slowly up from the cornfield. Corn was the Vanderberg money crop. Pa had planted eighty acres of it this year, and then everything had held it back . . . a wet spring, cold summer, the slow-drying bottom land on which it grew. Not until late August had there been real corn weather with bright sunshiny days, and nights so hot and still you could fairly hear the leaves rustle as the corn grew higher. Now Pa was worried that it wouldn't dry enough before winter storms struck. The neighbors had all finished harvesting last week, but Pa's corn was slower. It looked plenty dry to Peter, its long rows golden and rustling, its dry leaves whispering, whispering, like waves washing against a shore. But Pa wasn't quite yet satisfied. Harvest corn when it was too moist and it would spoil in the crib; they couldn't have that happen.

Peter staggered to his numb feet and went out to the big warm kitchen where supper was spread. Dirk was already putting away his second helping of sauerkraut and wienies while his eyes ran down the open book beside his plate.

"Books! Books! I never thought to raise such a pair of bookworms!" Ma scolded, but with pride in her voice. Dirk was in his second year of the town high-school and already captain of a debate team. Peter knew he had a debate coming tomorrow from the pile of library books on the chair beside him. Dirk tackled school like he tackled farm-work, slow and steady and thorough.

"Hi, Petey," he said absently.

Peter opened his mouth to protest and then shut it hastily. Next to Pa, Dirk was top man around here; even Ma treated him with respect. How did he get that way, Peter wondered enviously? With only a four-year head-start on Peter himself?

"Pa is out looking at the clouds again," Ma said worriedly. "All day it's either the sky or the weather-map or the forecast on the radio."

"There's a blizzard up in Minnesota," said Dirk. "We're sure to get it."

"Ah, not with the corn still in the field!" Ma gave a little anxious sigh and turned back to the stove.

Both boys knew what she was thinking. The big, heavy ears of corn were good as gold to meet the bills, to make the payment on the mortgage, to buy the new furnace . . . but not while they hung in the field. If a blizzard came before they could be picked, the stalks would be blanketed with new moisture, and it might well be spring before the field was again ready to pick.

Pa came in the back door, shutting it with firm decision. "Tomorrow we harvest," he said flatly. "The corn is ready, and it is foolish to take any more chance on the weather. We will start with daylight."

"Tomorrow?" yelped Peter, bouncing upright in his chair. "I can't miss school tomorrow. There's the spelling-match!"

Pa looked at him with stern disapproval. "Dirk is all the man I need."

"But Dirk's got a de—" Peter broke off, silenced by the anger in his brother's cold glare. Well, all right, he was just trying to help Dirk out! A debate team wasn't much good without its captain, but if Dirk just didn't care—

Why was everybody down on him all at once? . . . Pa frowning, Dirk glaring, even Ma looking kind of sad. Peter gobbled his supper and hiked up to his room. Families sure could be funny sometimes.

When Peter reappeared for breakfast the next morn-

ing, Pa and Dirk were already in the field. The air was
frosty cold and crisp, the sky clear. Huh, thought Peter,
no sign of the blizzard that had caused such a commotion;
Dirk could just as well not have missed his debate.

Peter ate steadily through his usual breakfast of pan-
cakes and sausage and homemade preserves and milk and
applesauce, skipped as many chores as he dared, and was
ready for the two-mile walk to country-school by eight
o'clock. Might as well get started, Peter figured; there
was a bigger dictionary at school, maybe he could brush
up on a few more words before the match.

"Responsibility," he tried out his memory on one of
yesterday's mouth-fillers. "Re-spon-si-bil-i-ty." Yep, he
still remembered it.

Peter lingered on the doorstep looking toward the field
where the cornpicker had just come to a stop. Dirk was
waiting to unhitch the loaded wagon of corn from the
picker and couple it onto the other tractor. Now he
started off, rumbledy-bounce, to tow it to the crib. He'd
have twenty-five minutes to back it between the tall legs
of the derrick, upend the wagon-box, start the elevator
running to carry the corn to the crib, empty the wagon,
and have it back at the field before Pa filled another one.

But Pa hadn't started down the next row of corn. He
was driving his tractor lickity-bump up to the barnyard.
Low on gas, Peter guessed. Now he'd leaped off, and was
dragging out the hose from the gas-storage tank.

"Hey, Pa!" called Peter, recollecting the first lesson he
himself had been taught about the tractor. "Pa, you didn't
turn off your engine!"

Faster than the words, it happened. One second there

was Pa holding the nozzle over the funnel, and the next second there was flame raring up in a red curtain, shutting him off. Gas had sloshed over the hot machine and exploded into instant fire.

Peter's legs weighed a ton apiece; took him seven years to move a step. He had confused glimpses of Dirk running, running from the crib . . . of Pa's hand coming through the flames, shutting off the ignition . . . of Ma passing him like a tornado wind with a bucket of washwater snatched up from the back step.

Then, as suddenly, it was over. The last sparks hissed and sizzled down the trail of gasoline drops from the hose Pa had flung far behind him. Dirk was off to the house for oil and soft cloths, and Ma was gently ripping the shirt-sleeves from Pa's burned arms.

Peter couldn't look. He felt shriveled and small with the pain that was hurting Pa. And he couldn't do anything, not anything. Quiet, soft-spoken Ma had become a commanding general, taking prompt, efficient charge. Now she had backed the old sedan from the garage . . . why, Peter hadn't even known she could drive! . . . and was helping Pa to the seat beside her.

"Best to run you right in to the hospital," she said firmly. And to the boys, "He'll be all right. Don't fret."

Dirk stepped close to the car. "We'll stick by the corn, Pa," he said, his voice very steady and confident. "We'll get it in okay. Won't we, Pete?"

Peter gulped. Warmth crept back into the tight ball of his stomach. He looked at Dirk with gratitude. Pete! And something he could do for Pa after all.

"Sure," Peter said shakily. "Sure, we'll make out fine, Pa."

He saw Pa's eyes shining back at them, warmly, proudly, as Ma swished down the drive.

"Let's get going, Pete," Dirk said briskly. "I'll take the cornpicker. You handle the tractor. Okay?"

The tractor? Dirk was giving him the tractor without even a crack about keeping the straw out of his hair? Say, he was a *good* guy! And Peter would show him he was to be trusted.

Driving as carefully as if it was a baby-buggy he handled, Peter chugged back to the cornfield. Dirk was still filling the second wagon, the picker stripping off the heavy ears, and flinging them onto the moving belt of the elevator that swooshed them upward into the high-sided wagon.

"Ought to run ninety bushels an acre," Dirk said, unhooking the wagon and putting the empty in its place. He sounded just as though he was talking to Pa.

"Yeh," agreed Peter, striving to be equally man-to-man. "Sure looks good."

He towed the wagon to the derrick, backed it between the legs without even a bump. Proudly he fastened the derrick hook to the wagon-bed, cranked it up, started the golden flow up the elevator and raining into the crib. Why, this was man's work he was doing, Peter thought, his chest expanding. This was grown-upness. This was what went with the name of Pete.

Far off, the school-bell tinkled. It jerked Peter back to remembrance of the spelling-match for which he'd prepared so hard. Disappointment hit him so keenly it hurt. Then he shrugged it off. Shucks, a spelling-match was kid stuff beside this!

As the morning hours dragged on, Peter's glow wore off, and plain aching tiredness took its place. The sun climbed higher and burned the back of his neck. The derrick handle turned harder and harder. Never were hooks so cantankerous to handle as those connecting wagon and tractor. Peter's rumbling stomach reminded him lunch-hour had come and brought nothing but continued work. Why hadn't Ma come back from the hospital? Was Pa worse? On the cornpicker, Dirk was more and more silent, smiling briefly as he unhooked a loaded wagon, saying nothing.

Occasionally, Dirk glanced at the sky. Peter looked, too, but there was nothing to see but a dab of cloud on the north horizon that he could cover with his hand.

Back and forth. Hitch on, unload, bounce back to the field. One load every twenty-five minutes. How small a square of corn lay stripped compared to all that waited. Peter gave a big tired sigh and looked at the cloud again. He put his hand against it, and the cloud mushroomed all around it.

"Hey, Dirk!" Peter called uneasily. "It's getting bigger!"

Dirk didn't ask him what he meant. He'd been watching, too. "Be here by dark," he said briefly.

Peter looked at the untouched acres of corn. "Dirk, we can't finish it!" he cried.

"Nope," Dirk answered, not stopping. "But we'll get all we can."

Doggedly, Peter settled down to help, bending his sore shoulders over the derrick handle, cranking faster, hustling between elevator and tractor, jouncing, jolting between field and crib. It was a losing battle, and he was ready to cry with weariness, but he couldn't quit. Every extra ear of corn garnered in counted a lot.

Suddenly, he straightened and stared unbelievingly at the road that ran past their farm. What crazy kind of parade was that coming along? It was a long, crawling worm with giraffe heads shooting up every few feet! It bobbled and swayed and curved right up to the Vanderberg gate!

At the edge of the field, Dirk gave a great shout and halted the picker. "Pete, they're coming to help us—all the neighbors! Look at 'em! Seven, eight, nine cornpickers! More than two dozen tractors and wagons!" Dirk's voice choked up. He dropped off the picker and gave Peter a big hug. "We got it licked, Pete! We'll beat the blizzard. We got it licked!"

There were tears in his eyes, and tears rolling down Peter's cheeks, and neither boy cared who saw them.

The parade came churning up around them. Mr. Huibregste rode the lead picker, and Mr. Vellinga the second, and all the other neighbors for miles around followed behind them.

"Heard about your Pa's bad luck," Mr. Huibregste said kindly. "The boys here thought we'd better give you a hand; sky don't look too good." He gazed out over the harvested acres. "You kids already do this much? You really been a-humping!"

"Pete here helped fine," Dirk said. "Good as a man."

"Yeh, I can see that," Mr. Huibregste nodded. He gave Peter a keen glance. "Guess there's enough of us to handle the unloading now. Why don't you knock off and get yourself a breath, Pete? You've done a man's job today."

Gratefully, Peter staggered toward the back steps while nine cornpickers, and Dirk's the tenth, slashed into the waiting rows of corn with a mighty roar. Peter felt a big lump welling in his throat at the sight. Let the cloud grow now, let the blizzard come . . . the corn would be harvested before dark!

A man's job. That's what he'd done. For six mortally weary hours, he'd been grown-up, and he'd found out what it meant. Not a thing more or less than that long word he'd mastered yesterday . . . re-spon-si-bil-i-ty. He'd missed the spelling-match, and Dirk his debate, because they felt responsible for their family. All these men had left their own work because they felt responsible for their neighbors. Why, Pa was right! Grown-upness wasn't measured by years; it was measured by the number of people you felt obligated to help!

The old sedan bumbled into the driveway, and Ma hopped out, her face tired but shining.

"Pa's fine!" she called happily to Peter. "I stayed till he was over the shock and resting easy. They'll let him come home in no time. And oh, Petey, the neighbors came, didn't they? Bless them, they'll want coffee and such; I'll go fix it."

She bustled off, and Peter was left with his mouth open, his protest at the baby name unspoken. Because suddenly he didn't mind it; he even liked it a little. It proved he still had time to work up gradually on this big and sobering business of grown-upness.

Cautiously, he stretched his aching back and flexed his arms. Hey, why didn't he head for the parlor couch, with a couple of apples to crunch on, and a good book to read? Nobody could say he hadn't earned a rest.

But his eyes went from Dirk still in the field to his mother hurrying to the kitchen and her neglected tasks, and he sighed a little. It was plain to Peter that once you let a big word like "responsibility" get into your veins, you couldn't ever quite shake it loose again.

"Ma," Peter called plaintively, trailing her into the kitchen. "You want any chores done?"

—NAN GILBERT

Kip and the Red Tractor

On a Texas Ranch

Kip Hunter stepped out of the school bus and into another world.

At least that's the way he always thought of it Friday afternoon when he had the whole long week end on the ranch ahead of him. And this Saturday was extra special, for Dad was going to teach him to drive the tractor.

Kip stood watching the bus until the "Texas" on the license plate got too small to read. Then he turned and crossed the cattle guard into the lane that ran along the barbed wire fence and led to home.

It was a different world. There were entirely different

230

things to do here on the ranch—hunting, fishing, training his cow pony, working cattle, tagging after his big brother, Paul. No more sitting in rows bent over lessons! No more standing in line before you could eat lunch! No more keeping quiet when you felt like shouting!

"Ye-ow!" he yelled just to prove it. Satan, the vicious steer grazing near by, turned to stare at him, then started toward him belligerently.

Laughing, Kip raced to the oak tree with the hollow limb where he always parked his gun, took it and left his books instead. He slid his Benjamin Pump under the fence carefully and crawled after it into the Brushy Pasture. He liked the names of their pastures. The one he had just left was the Highway Pasture. It had only a few scattered oak trees and was full of grass, except that now in October after the long months without rain, all the pastures were so brown and dry the cattle had almost nothing to graze on and had to be fed every day.

The Brushy Pasture was green with bushes and small trees, mesquite and chaparral and agarita. But except for the mesquite beans they didn't do the cattle any good. All they were good for, it seemed to Kip, hurrying through on his way to trap lines, was to reach out long thorny branches to snag his shirt and blue jeans.

He had set his traps in what he and Paul had named Sherwood Forest. Here wide-spreading oaks grew, swinging with Spanish moss or covered with grape vines, and along the river great tall pecan trees were shedding their leaves and showing their clusters of nuts. It was cool and shady here after the heat and glare of the sunlight.

Kip slipped along, making no more noise than a lizard

rattling among the dry leaves. He had his gun ready to shoot as soon as he saw the frisk of a squirrel's tail. In a minute he sighted three squirrels chasing along the limb after pecans, and fired. One of the squirrels fell, but before he could shoot again the others had whisked out of sight.

He had shot the squirrel cleanly through the head, and he was glad, for he wanted the skin. He was tanning skins to sell. That's why he was trapping, too. You never could tell what you might find in your trap. Only a little while ago he had found a little animal none of the boys had ever seen before. He looked it up in an animal book at school and decided it must be a mink. When he sent it off, the company said it really was, and paid him fifteen dollars for just that one little fur.

Today there was only a rabbit in one small trap. Something had gotten the bait out of the big trap without springing it, and there was nothing at the other three except some coyote tracks.

Well, that was all the time he had this evening. Now during football season he was doing Paul's work as well as his own, so Paul, who quarterbacked the high school team, could stay for practice. He hurried along through the long shadows of early evening, enjoying the clean, dry smell of the sun-baked land. As he came in sight of the barns, he heard his father calling him. When Daddy shouted like that, you'd better come running. Yelling an answer, he climbed the fence and cut across the pens where cattle and horses were drifting in for feed and water, and turkeys were flying to roost in the oaks.

"Kip," Daddy said impatiently, "where have you been? Have you forgotten I wanted you to close the water trap

in the North Pasture? I want to sell those cattle tomorrow."

"Oh, Dad, I'm sorry!" Kip said. "But I'll go right
away."

He gave his shrill whistle for his horse, Lightning.
When the pony came trotting up, he had the bridle ready
to slip on. "I won't wait to saddle up," he said. Dad helped
him straddle Lightning. "I'll do my work when I get
back," he called as he rode off.

How could he have forgotten that Dad had asked him
to close the gate in the North Pasture? The cattle must be
penned there when they came to the tank for water.

He raced across the pasture as fast as he dared in the
fading light of sunset. He must reach the Frozen North—
as he and Paul called it—before the cattle had finished
drinking and wandered out of the pen. The first cows were
leaving just as he got there, but Lightning made quick
work of rounding them up. Kip closed the gate and
fastened it, and the cattle were rounded up in the water
trap, ready to be loaded on the cattle truck in the morning.

It was dark before Kip reached home. High in the sky
a crescent moon shone golden, and below it the lights on
the oil derrick on the Braun farm twinkled like a Christmas tree. "Pretty," thought Kip. Then suddenly he began
to worry. Would Dad be so angry because he forgot about
the water trap that he wouldn't let him drive the tractor
tomorrow after all?

Paul drove up in his rattling jalopy.

"What's the matter, son?" he asked. "How come you're
so late?"

Kip explained, as Paul helped him shuck corn for the

squealing pigs and bawling cows. "And now I'm afraid he won't let me drive the tractor tomorrow," he finished.

"Oh, it probably isn't as bad as that," Paul consoled him. "Maybe I can help you out."

"Oh, Paul, would you?" Paul was swell!

"But you'll be sorry you ever asked to drive a tractor," Paul warned. "That runs into work, son, and don't you forget it."

"I'll like it," Kip said stoutly.

At breakfast next morning even before the sun was up Dad was so full of jokes that Kip knew he wasn't angry, and his heart sang. But when Dad pushed his chair back from the table, "Kip, I'm sorry to disappoint you about the tractor," he said, "but it'll have to wait till next Saturday—"

"Oh, Dad, why?"

"Because Mr. Lennox can't go to San Antonio with the cattle today and I'll have to go."

"But couldn't Paul teach me?"

"I have other work for Paul. Paul, with the grass burned up and our feed running low, I've decided to have you burn pear today."

"Yes, sir," agreed Paul easily. "But couldn't I teach young squirt to drive the tractor too? I could start him off in the south forty. I could burn pear in the Brushy Pasture right next to it and keep an eye on the kid at the same time."

"Sounds reasonable," Dad agreed. "If you think you can manage it, I reckon it's all right."

"Oh, thank you, Dad," Kip said, smiling at Paul and

trying not to show how excited he was. It was all he could do to keep both feet on the ground; he really wanted to jump with joy.

Paul got the pear-burner and drove the tractor out of the garage. "Now show me just what you think you should do to drive this thing," he commanded.

Kip knew. He had watched so carefully and sat on the tractor seat in the garage pretending to drive it so often that he really did know.

"Well, how about that?" Paul exclaimed in surprise. "All you need is practice!"

He fastened the pear-burner and his .22 to the hood. "Might have a good chance to shoot a few doves," he explained. "Now you drive slow, and I'll hang on back here to take over if things get out of control. But they won't. Just take it easy and everything will be all right."

Kip climbed onto the tractor seat, turned the key in the lock, put the tractor into gear, fed it gas, and started slowly off. He felt scared and triumphant and solemn all at the same time.

The tractor rolled along steadily, turning when he turned it, stopping when he stopped it, starting when he started it. It was like a mechanical monster, a giant slave.

It gave him a wonderful feeling of power. He could feel himself grinning from ear to ear with the thrill of it. This red tractor could do only what he wanted it to do. He was its complete and lordly master.

"Now stop," Paul ordered, "and I'll plow a row along the edge of the field that you can use as a guide row to keep your rows straight."

"Just keep the wheel in this furrow," Paul said, bringing the tractor back to Kip, "and your rows will be straight."

Kip plowed, slowly and carefully, and his rows were straight. Not as straight as Paul's or Dad's, but straight enough. The third time around he even managed to watch Paul burning pear. From his seat on the tractor he felt like a king looking down on a poor toiling subject.

Paul was moving from one clump of prickly pear to the next, burning the thorns off with his gasoline torch so that the cattle could eat the cactus. A few cows had already discovered what he was doing and had started eating the prickly pear. "After the burnt pastures and dry food they've been getting," Kip thought, "the cactus must taste like a nice green salad to them."

He began to feel so much at home driving the tractor that he made up games to make it more exciting. He played that he was in a tank leading an assault. He forgot all about Paul, and his rows weren't always quite as straight as before.

Suddenly he heard Paul shout and looked to see why.

"Hi!" Paul yelled. "Hi-yah!" the way you did at cattle.

Kip saw that he was waving his hat to drive away Satan. Satan, the trouble-making steer, had found out about the cactus and was coming for his share.

But he wasn't waiting patiently like the other cattle. He was bellowing and pawing and snorting.

When Paul waved and shouted, the other cattle went away, some with frightened jumps, others with sad slowness. But Satan just circled around and came back. Paul turned the pear-burner toward him. "He's trying to scare Satan away with the flame," Kip knew.

But instead of being scared, Satan was angered by the flame and its intense heat. Bellowing, he charged straight at Paul.

Paul dodged, stumbling and dropping the pear-burner, but Satan missed him. While the steer was turning to attack again, Paul scrambled to his feet and ran for a little mesquite tree a few yards away. He pulled himself up on a forked limb, but one of Satan's horns caught the leg of his blue jeans and slashed it open.

"Kip!" Paul shouted. "Come and help me! Satan's gone plumb loco!"

Kip started to jump down from the tractor. "But I can get there much quicker in the tractor," he decided and careened and jolted across the field at full speed.

When he reached the fence, Satan was still dashing at Paul in the tree, only maddened that much more each time he bumped his head on a limb. The small branch where Paul perched was sagging perilously.

"Son," Paul ordered, "you've got to shoot Satan. My gun's in the fence corner over yonder. Get it— And hurry! This limb sways like it's about to break."

Kip raced to the fence for the .22, pulled it under the barbed wire, and loaded it.

He walked to the fence opposite Paul's mesquite to shoot so that the bullets would not go in Paul's direction.

But how could he possibly kill Satan? The steer was pawing and kicking and charging so furiously, how could he aim?

He raised the gun and sighted. Then he shouted as loud

as he could. Satan stopped short, wheeled to investigate this new enemy, and started toward Kip. But the instant he turned, Kip pulled the trigger. He shot again and again, until the steer's front knees crumpled and he fell to the ground and lay still.

"My hero!" Paul joked, pretending to throw a kiss. He started to jump down. But as he did, the branch snapped and Paul hurtled to the ground.

He looked so funny and awkward as he fell, trying to fight free of the branches, that Kip laughed, now that the danger from Satan was ended.

But Paul didn't laugh back. He just sprawled there motionless, almost touching Satan.

"Paul," Kip cried, "are you hurt?"

Paul didn't answer. Kip skinned under the fence and rushed to Paul, afraid to his soul.

Paul's eyes were closed. He lay on his back with the broken mesquite limb under him and the little branches and leaves sticking up around him. From under his head a little red line of blood was staining the grass.

"Paul, oh, Paul!" moaned Kip.

He wanted to pull him free of the thorny limb, to stretch him out more comfortably than the awful twisted way he was lying, to hold him close in his arms.

But he remembered his First Aid. He must not move Paul.

The best thing he could do was to go for help. But then Paul would be there all alone!

Suddenly he smelled smoke.

He turned and saw a circle of fire creeping through the dry grass. When Paul had dropped the pear-burner, he had turned it off, but not before the flame had touched the grass. It must have been just a tiny smoldering patch at first, but now the flames were beginning to crackle and race. Luckily the little wind was fanning them away from the pear-burner. If it should explode, the whole Brushy Pasture would soon be blazing.

But the fire was getting closer to Paul.

Kip ran around it and pulled the pear-burner toward him, carefully, for he was afraid it might still explode. He dragged it a safe distance away from the fire. His knees felt like water and there was a sick swirling at the pit of his stomach.

He took off his shirt and began stamping and beating out the flames nearest Paul. The fire was gaining headway, the drought-parched grass feeding it like tinder. Unless Kip could beat it out quickly, it would soon be roaring out of control through the whole pasture.

His shirt was not heavy enough. It only made the flames flicker and jump to a new clump of grass. He took off his blue jeans and, holding them by the legs, whacked them down on the fire. They were heavy enough. Wherever they hit, they smothered the flames.

Kip beat the blaze frantically, as if each little tongue of flame had been a loathsome snake. He stamped and pounded until his legs were weak and his arms ached and his throat burned from the smoke. But at last all the flames were dead.

He turned again to Paul.

Paul was sitting up, the mesquite limbs all around him. "Good work, son," he said weakly.

"Paul, oh Paul," Kip cried. "I thought you were dead!"

"Me too," Paul said.

"Are you hurt bad?"

"I don't know. Help me out of this thorny forest."

Kip ran over to him. If Paul could joke, maybe things weren't so bad.

"I don't think I have any broken bones," Paul said. "Just the wind knocked out of me, and this cut on my head." He felt it and his hand came away bloody.

"Is there anything I can do, Paul?"

"No. Nothing clean to put on it."

"Can you get up if I help you?"

"Let's see." Kip braced himself and Paul pulled on his hand hard. He stood up, then sank back with a little moan.

"It's my knee," he said. "I must have twisted it."

"Oh, Paul, your football!"

"Yes," said Paul. "I'm thinking of that."

They were both silent a minute, Paul fighting pain and dizziness, Kip miserable with helpless sympathy.

Then, "We'd better get me home," Paul said.

"Can you drive the tractor?"

"No—I feel sort of sick and dizzy," Paul admitted. "But I think I can hang on if you drive."

"Wonder what Dad will say when he finds out I killed Satan," Paul said, crawling toward the fence.

Paul didn't say "You killed Satan." Instead he said "I." Paul was swell!

Kip held the wires up while Paul rolled under the fence. Paul's forehead was beaded with sweat, more from pain than from heat, Kip could tell from the white look around his lips.

"Help me get my blue jeans off," Paul said. "We'll use them to sort of tie me on if I should get dizzy or anything."

"Paul!"

"It's all right, son. This is just in case. But what will Mom say when we both come riding home in our shorts?"

They both laughed a little, shakily.

With Kip helping, Paul managed to brace himself against the seat of the tractor and Kip drove off, slowly so that he wouldn't jar Paul too much. Twice Paul asked him to stop till a dizzy spell passed. Neither boy talked much. Kip was concentrating on driving the tractor; Paul was using all his strength just to hang on.

But at last they were home and Kip untied the blue jeans and helped Paul hop to the house.

Mother saw them coming and met them at the gate. "What happened, Kip?" she asked quietly, taking Kip's place and putting Paul's arm around her shoulders. "Just lean on me," she said.

Kip told about the fall, his words tumbling over each other, finishing as they reached the screened porch.

"Well, that shouldn't be too bad," she said. "Paul, you lie here on the glider. Kip, you get Dr. Carson on the phone for me. Then bring me the gauze and alcohol from the medicine cabinet."

She eased Paul to a comfortable position with her best porch pillow under his bloody head.

Everything was going to be all right now. Mother had taken command. Even Paul, big as he was, had sort of let go and turned things over to her, Kip thought as he waited for the doctor to answer.

"But what if Paul had been alone in the pasture when Satan attacked?" Kip wondered. "What if Paul hadn't taught me how to drive the tractor?"

—CAROL HOFF

Unto the Hills

In Colorado

FIRED!

Mrs. Smith dropped her tissue-paper pattern with a soft rustle and sat staring. Penny went on washing the cooking dishes. Penny had met the Smiths when she ran away from the Home. She had permission to stay with them "If they could keep her." After her first glance at Mrs. Smith's face, she kept her eyes turned away; but her hands moved slowly, softly, and her ears listened.

"Dad! Oh Dad!" wailed Virginia. "Oh, Dad—maybe it'll mean you'll get something better. Maybe it was time

"Unto the Hills" is from *Penny for Luck* by Florence Crannell Means; copyright, 1935, by Florence Crannell Means; reprinted by permission of Houghton Mifflin Company, publishers, and Florence Crannell Means.

you cut loose from such a poor job. It *was* a poor job."

"Something better." Mr. Smith laughed. "This isn't 1929, Virginia. I guess you've forgotten what year it is."

Grandpa shuffled his feet helplessly, and Penny stood with her hands in the cooling dishwater, staring at the wall. For it needed no words to make it clear that without any income at all the Smiths could not afford to keep a chance orphan any longer—a chance orphan and her dog.

Grandpa and Penny went to church next morning. Grandpa missed the homely friendliness and warmth of the little churches he had always known, where everyone was acquainted with everyone else; but a Sunday without any church at all he could scarcely have imagined. The old man and the young girl had sat side by side in the cushioned pew these Sunday mornings. This experience, too, Penny had liked.

Her mind soon wandered from the sermon, for she was unused to giving continued attention. It came back today, when the minister repeated the words: "I will lift up mine eyes unto the hills."

The hills. Penny listened to hear what this man had to say about them.

He went on to explain the question and answer that followed the stately sentence. "From whence cometh my help? Not from the hills," he said, "splendid and strengthening as they are; but from the God Who made them and Who can aid His children when nothing else can. From whence cometh my help? My help cometh from the Lord, Who made heaven and earth."

Penny was not well acquainted with God. A'nt Sally

and Unc' Jeff, with whom she had lived until she was sent to the Home, had used His name only as a handle for hard words. But the hills she did know, and her mind fled away into their fastnesses.

Longing swept up through her like waves of sickness. She had never thought about loving the hills. But suddenly she was feeling as if they were a part of her, as if she was a part of them. Or as if she were a brook trout tossed up out of their cool water to die in the underbrush. And as if she would stifle if she could not fill her lungs with piny air. Unconsciously she nodded her decision.

"If they send me back to the Home, I'll run off. I'll run off to the mountains. I could make out myself in the mountains."

Suddenly her hands gripped each other in her blue silk lap, and her breath quickened. She had a new thought.

When they came home from church and settled down to dinner, the family, all but Virginia, were resolutely cheerful.

"Good preaching, Paw?" asked Mr. Smith. "Won't you have another little slice of meat? Here's some of the brown part you're so keen about."

Grandpa passed his plate, peering in pleased anticipation at the crusty brown slice on his son's raised fork. "I'm afraid I wa'n't paying such good attention as I'd ought to," he confessed.

Penny moistened her lips. "They was one part about lifting your eyes," she mumbled. "Lifting your eyes to the hills, he said."

They looked at her in surprise. Penny usually froze into

complete silence when they were all present. Flustered by their regard, she picked up her fork backward and set it down quickly.

"It don't cost hardly nothing at all to live up yonder in the hills a summer," she said desperately. "You-uns could take your otto. I can catch fish. They's even a heap of old houses a body can live in for nothing."

This was the new thought that had blazed upon her in church that morning.

The Smiths looked at each other. "Why, we couldn't very well do that, Penny," Mrs. Smith deprecated. "Just pick up and leave. We never could afford a summer's vacation like that."

"It don't cost hardly nothing at all," Penny repeated.

"If I couldn't find a job," Mr. Smith observed, "why then it might be something to tide us over the summer, Mamma. Of course I've got to find a job; but if—well, by next fall things ought to be looking up. Good gosh, they've *got* to be looking up by that time."

Penny went on chewing.

Grandpa was sitting with his knife and fork gripped hard and looking at his daughter-in-law over his spectacles, his kind old eyes bright.

"I do believe that I could tinker up that old automobile so't she could carry us up there all right. Seems like it would make a fellow over new, being out in the mount'ins all summer. Cooped up like this—" He waved a knife at the crowded room— "And it's going to be as hot as tunket here this summer."

"Jones, down at the office, he made a trailer that works

as good as a made one. Got some wheels off a junked car, see, and—" Mr. Smith narrowed meditative eyes.

Later, Virginia looked sharply, suspiciously, at the pencil sketches her father was making on old envelopes.

"Dad, you surely aren't thinking seriously of any wild plan like that?" she flamed at him.

Mr. Smith dropped his ruler with a self-conscious clatter. "I should think a person could figure out a trailer if he wanted to," he said defensively, "without having everybody jump on him."

Mr. Smith continued to look for a job, but during only a part of each day. The rest of the time he was toiling away in a friend's back yard (no room in an apartment house) building a trailer. In spite of worry about his job, he looked more contented than Penny had ever seen him. His evenings he spent poring over books on the internal arrangements of automobiles.

And through the varied activities of all the family ran the phrase, "If we should spend the summer in the hills." That phrase changed little by little to "If we spend the summer in the hills," and at length, "Since we're going to spend the summer in the hills."

It was the middle of June when the Smith caravan set out: a sultry day for Denver, with the wall of mountains half hidden by clouds. Mr. and Mrs. Smith and Virginia filled the front seat, Grandpa and Penny, Junior and Napoleum, Penny's dog, crowded the back, and the trailer bobbed along behind, well packed and covered with a tarpaulin.

Junior wriggled round and knelt on the seat to watch the trailer, for it carried those of his treasures that he had been allowed to bring: his box of tiny cars, red, yellow, blue and green; roadsters, coupes, sedans. This summer his whole interest was divided between his cars and Napoleum.

Penny had a special interest in the trailer, too. A certain canvas-wrapped parcel rammed into one end held a secret that belonged to her and Grandpa. But Penny did not look around at it.

Virginia sat sulkily silent, Mrs. Smith wearily relaxed, Grandpa eagerly straining forward. But Penny was still as an image. She was afraid to breathe or to shift her eyes, lest something should change the scheme of things and take from her this summer. Summer was a piece of heaven which might be hers to live fully. "When I'm an old, old woman," she was telling herself, "I can look back and recollect it. The hills and a family. If only nothing don't happen to spile it."

Mr. Smith had tinkered the car with loving care; he had greased it; he had oiled it; he had consulted his many booklets, propping them up so that he should not soil them. The car responded by spinning along cheerfully through the town and onto a highway that bent back and forth across the mountain side, each loop laid above the last—something like rickrack braid, Mrs. Smith said.

For an hour the car clucked along contentedly, letting out its own cracked bleat at every turn in that crooked road. Then it began to protest with loud smackings.

Mrs. Smith jumped. Grandpa leaned forward, hand

cupped behind ear, and mutely inquired of the engine. Mr. Smith drove doggedly. The smack continued.

"And it's settin' in to rain!" said Grandpa.

"Oh, it's raining already!" shouted Junior. And it was!

The windshield was hastily closed. The windows were screwed shut, rebelling noisily, for they had been warped out of line by a past wreck. And still drops splashed plumply on heads and spattered off. Mr. Smith peered upward.

"I kind of hoped that top would last out the summer, after I painted it. It claimed on the label that the stuff was waterproof."

The sky emptied upon the world, as it can do in a canyon, in blinding sheets of rain that hissed on the pavement and rebounded in spray. Large spots darkened on the ceiling and small streams trickled from the centers. Gleefully Junior drew his sweater over his head. Grimly Virginia turned up her collar and took off her brand-new hat. Anxiously Mrs. Smith craned backward.

"I hope to goodness you tucked in the tarpaulin tight enough so our bedding won't get wet, Henry."

Mr. Smith could spare no answer. The car labored, it crept, it halted.

"It's getting dark, Dad, do you realize that?" fretted Virginia as a new stream smote her on the nose. Behind her Penny wrapped her coat around Junior and smiled down at him palely. He sparkled up at her, the only one of the six who was entirely happy.

Mr. Smith pressed the starter, jiggled the choke, and coaxed the car to limp on through the hissing rain.

Dusk had fallen, hastened by the storm clouds that over-hung them in a low, wet roof, when they coughed and smacked and snorted into a village.

"We can't possibly camp out such a night as this, with everything we've got wet," Mrs. Smith said. "But I don't see a sign of an auto camp."

"They's a row of them little houses," said Penny, pointing.

"Sure enough," Grandpa crowed. "There's your auto camp all hunky dory, Son. Down between the road and the creek."

Thankfully they crawled to the nearest cabin, its logs dark with rain and its roof streaming. A face appeared at the window; a man stood in the doorway. "Want a cabin? Well, drive in under this next shelter, pardner, and I'll be right over with the key."

"My heavens!—" Virginia got out and made a dash for the door as soon as it was open—"What did I tell you? Oh, heavens!" In its frightened haste a chipmunk had run over her foot.

Penny scurried with Junior through the downpour. Mrs. Smith and Grandpa followed stiffly. Mr. Smith buttoned his coat tight and turned up his collar and attacked the knotted rope that crisscrossed the tarpaulin on the trailer. It was a wet job and he came in presently, his patient arms piled high with bedding, water streaming from his old hat.

"It's wet," groaned Mrs. Smith, pouncing on the bedding.

"Oh, not hardly more than damp, Mamma! Not hardly more than damp."

"Wet!" she contradicted firmly.

"I'll build a fire," he promised, "and we'll have it dried out in a jiffy."

Penny could not persuade even herself that the first night of their adventure was a comfortable one. Valiantly as the little stove roared and crackled, it succeeded better in bringing out damp smells of wood and wool than in driving out the chill.

Penny, sharing a cottage with Virginia and Junior, fell asleep at once. She woke with her heart in her mouth when Napoleum padded round the room on clicking toe-nails and stood growling by the door. All night she slept and woke, slept and woke; woke finally in the grayish dawn with a furry feeling mouth and heavy eyes. The clothes that they had hung on chairs when they went to bed were chilly and damp.

By the time smells of coffee and bacon were issuing from the other cabin, Grandpa called them to breakfast. The scene was more cheerful than it had been the night before. Mr. Smith came in after they had started eating, holding grease-blackened hands away from his clothes.

"Well, Son, find anything?"

"Vacuum tank!" said Mr. Smith. "Line's pulled right loose, see? I just this minute made it out!"

"That ought to be easy fixed," Grandpa cogitated. "Mebbe with adhesive tape."

"That's what I thought," Mr. Smith agreed, inter-rupting himself with a large bit of bacon. "That's just precisely what I tried, Paw."

When breakfast was finished, the Smith car started on.

The sky had cleared to a deep, rich blue. The fresh washed trees and bushes sparkled in the sun. The spirits of the adventurers soared high—all but Virginia's. Even the blue car seemed to feel the tingle of the mountain morning. It climbed an endless hill steadily, if noisily.

"The old girl isn't doing so bad today," Mr. Smith said. "Not for her. But listen to her boil."

They not only listened but they felt. She rumbled and gurgled and shook.

"I jiggle like I was the lid of a tea-kettle," Junior said, giggling.

Mr. Smith stopped the car, clambered down to the stream, far below the road, and brought back a battered tin filled with water, unscrewed the radiator cap and stood back to avoid the geyser of oily water.

"Can't blame her for boiling on a hill like this," he excused the blue car, and they went on.

"Jest where we bound for, Son?"

"The little old town I'm aiming at was a placer mining camp, name of Jane."

"You mean the town's named Jane?" Mrs. Smith asked incredulously.

"Placer mining?" Grandpa was sitting forward, waiting for a chance to speak. "Crick through the town, mebbe, Son? Man told me sumpn funny about this stretch along Clear Crick not so fur from here. White men worked at it long as gold came easy. When they got done with it, bunch of Chinamen went after it. Took out seven million dollars' worth in one mile."

"Lots of gold around this district," Mr. Smith assented, "if it didn't cost so darned much to get it out. Now you-all be watching for a road that leads off to the right. Partly overgrown now—hasn't been used for so long."

"Son," Grandpa called presently, pointing a knobby finger ahead. "That looks likely, that road amongst the quakin' asps. You reckon that's the one?"

It looked like a wood-hauler's road. Mr. Smith, craning forward over the wheel, coaxed the car up the jolting ascent. It jerked and sidled between and under raking branches. It came out upon a small hillside clearing, where cabins slept in the sun.

The clearing was a saucer, tilted at an angle among the evergreens and aspens that pushed in, pushed in to take back the open space. A mountain brook bordered its higher edge. Across it straggled a few log cabins. A few larger buildings, whose flat fronts, extending above their roofs like cap visors, turned straight up, showed that they had been stores or saloons. Evidently a broad road had run between them, but grass and weeds had taken the road as the trees had taken the clearing. Squarish holes in the earth were all that was left of some of the houses.

Penny was out as soon as the car had found a level stopping place. She walked sedately when she could remember. One cabin after another she surveyed with care, and at length she approached Mr. and Mrs. Smith.

"I found one we could fix up awful easy," she said.

By night the cabin had changed. It would take more scrubbings to rid it of mousy odors, and Grandpa and the Mister had only begun the work of repairs. Penny found some ancient can lids, scoured them fairly bright with sand, and used them in pairs for candle holders. She bent one at right angles and nailed it up for a tiny shelf with three nails through the bottom to hold a candle. Each one held its gleaming light. And over the springy spruce bough mattresses in the bunks the neatly spread bedding added its suggestion of comfort.

"Seems kind of like the little old shack must be happy tonight," mused Grandpa, "holding a regular fam'ly again, after goodness knows how many years."

"Ain't it about time me and you showed the rest of 'em what we brought up here, Penny?" asked Grandpa, the next morning.

Penny darted away to the old blue car. She staggered back with a large, canvas-wrapped parcel. Breathlessly she squatted down on the grass beside it to unknot the cord. The family gathered close.

"Rusty old pans!" Virginia protested. "Why would you make such a fuss over rusty old pans?"

Mr. Smith lifted one, tilted it thoughtfully. "Gold pans, Paw?"

"Gold pans?" echoed Mrs. Smith. "What for, Father?"

"Are they the kind that old miners used to get gold out of the streams?" asked Virginia, coming closer.

"Yeah, but we wouldn't make much of a go of it. There's a trick to it," Mr. Smith said reluctantly.

"Sure there is." Grandpa hooked his thumbs into the armholes of his vest and chuckled. "That's where me and Penny comes in. First we went to the liberry and learnt all we could about placer minin' and pannin' the streams. And then we went down to the Platte and watched the men pannin' there.

"And then," Grandpa went on, "we found us a free

class, under the employment bureau, and we learnt some more. Penny did. I vum if it didn't run in one ear and out of the other, as fur's I was concerned."

"You mean you get *gold* with one of the dishpan effects?" Virginia asked, eyeing them with new respect.

"When can we try it?" asked Mrs. Smith. "And where?"

"Now," said Grandpa. "And we might as well try it in our little crick." Crouching at its edge, Penny scooped out some earth from the overhang of the bank, carefully dipped in water, and then cradled and sloshed, cradled and sloshed, while the others bent over her, scarcely drawing breath.

She sent the floating sand and gravel out over the edge of the pan, dipped in more water, cradled it again, and drained off the water with care. The Smiths crowded so close that their heads bumped above the pan.

"Gosh," said Virginia, "there isn't any gold, is there?"

Penny nodded. "Yes, mom!" she said proudly. "Got color first whack. Looky!" She nodded toward the edge of the fine, dark sand in the bottom of the pan. Palely bright gleamed the thinnest hair-edge of flour gold.

"And looky," Penny urged again. She set down the pan, took out a pin that was run through the shoulder strap of her overalls, and with it picked out a round grain of gold. "Nugget," she explained.

"How much is it worth?" Virginia demanded.

"Oh, a dime, mebbe?" Grandpa guessed.

"Why, I thought a nugget— Why, *that's* nothing!"

"Well, look, Virginia," her father remonstrated, "these

days it's something when you can pick even pennies out of the water. And there may be enough of 'em in this crick to count up to dollars."

"Pennies!" Junior said with a gurgle of delight. "First we get Penny and then we get pennies—a bushel of 'em, likely."

And that was what really happened.

—Florence Crannell Means

A Battle for Mastery

Busting an Outlaw Horse in Wyoming

When the men came in to dinner, they were arguing fiercely. At first Bob could not make out what it was about. He could see that Montana was defending himself and that the other men all seemed to have taken sides against him.

"You're so doggoned sure of yourself," Crowbait was saying sarcastically. "You're supposed to be a top hand. You have quite a reputation for hoss sense. I reckon then that you're willing to back up your reputation in this matter by something worth-while."

"You can be sure of that," Montana said positively. "I'll give you my silver-mounted rodeo saddle if I don't ride that hoss."

Bob gasped, then held his breath. He knew that, next to his favorite horse Silver, Montana treasured above all his possessions the handsome saddle he had won as prize in the rodeo the year before. It was a finer saddle than any of the other men owned.

The conversation continued, growing louder and more serious. Still Bob did not discover what it was all about until Montana burst out hotly, "I'll not only ride Dynamite but I'll bust him, too."

At this all the other cowboys broke into loud and jeering laughter.

Shorty, who had seemed to be partly on Montana's side, shook his head at this statement. This was evidently going too far in his opinion.

"Success has gone to his head," Bob heard Shorty say to Uncle John. "He's plumb loco. Thinks there isn't any animal he can't get the best of. Too bad. When a top hand gets that notion, he's headed for the dust. Dynamite will throw him so high the birds'll build nests in his hair before he lights."

"I'm so sure I can bust Dynamite," Montana said calmly, "that I'll throw in Silver along with my saddle if I don't do it." The cowhands gasped. "But this whole thing is pretty one-sided," Montana went on evenly. "I ought to have some sort of prize if I succeed."

"If you break Dynamite," John Benton promised, "I'll give him to you."

"And the rest of us will pitch in," Shorty cried, "and

buy you the best pair of cowboy boots Ted Russel can make." The others cheerfully backed up Shorty's offer.

"I'm glad you fellows are making the ride worth my while," Montana drawled. "I'd do it anyway, just for the fun of it, but such fine prizes make it more interesting."

Everyone broke into excited talk. They all agreed that Dynamite was an outlaw horse. One that could never be ridden, much less broken. They also agreed that probably he was a killer.

Bob felt shivers run up and down his spine. He knew that the other men were experienced in the ways of horse nature, too. It did seem that Montana was being pretty reckless to risk his life this way. He felt all tied up in knots of tension. He looked inquiringly toward the head of the table, wondering if his uncle would allow him to go to the corral.

"Go ahead," John Benton nodded, and relief flooded Bob's heart. Evidently nothing more was going to be said about his misadventure of the previous day.

Bob followed the men outside and climbed to the top rail, his heart beating hard.

Montana said nothing as he walked toward the corral. But he strode ahead of the other Circle K hands with the air of self-confidence that Bob admired. Three of the cowboys went to the large corral to cut out Dynamite and force him into the chute that led into the smaller corral where the horses were gentled.

The commotion in the big corral was terrific. It was evident that the other horses there considered Dynamite a killer, for they squealed with terror and scattered in all directions every time he came their way. And when the maddened animal threw himself, pawing and wild eyed, against the side of the corral, Bob wondered if the poles would hold.

Montana was saving his energy for the great contest ahead. He sat on the top rail and laughed at the perspiring cowboys who were trying to get Dynamite into the small corral.

"I reckon I'll have to come and help you," he drawled.

"Save your steam," Crowbait puffed. "You're going to need every ounce of it or I'm a spavined hunk o' hoss meat."

"I reckon you are," Montana grinned. "But do get a move on. I'm getting bored with this inaction."

"You won't be that way long," Shorty called to him, as Dynamite was finally cornered in the narrow chute between the corrals and the gate dropped behind him.

When the horse found himself imprisoned, he went crazier than ever. He squealed and battered the poles with his forefeet until Bob could feel the corral tremble. Then Shorty swung the gate leading from the chute into the small corral, and Dynamite came into it like a ton of his namesake.

Bob involuntarily drew up his legs as the enraged animal came his way. But Montana only continued to gaze at the horse with quiet amusement.

"A hoss with that much spirit will be a good animal after I take the spook out of him," he drawled.

"Huh!" grunted Crowbait, who was now sitting on the top rail beside Bob. "You're as crazy as popcorn on a hot stove. Ice will melt at the North Pole before you get the spook out of that boy. He's a killer or I never saw one."

Bob glanced quickly up at Montana and was surprised to see a look of tenseness on the foreman's face in spite of the grin. In a flood of understanding it came to him how much this contest meant to his friend. It meant not only his most prized possessions—his fine horse (and Bob knew that a cowboy's horses were like members of his family) and his saddle, the finest in the whole range country—but he was also staking his reputation as the best horse-breaker in the country. And perhaps, Bob thought with a sudden start, he was even staking his life.

"What are you waiting for?" Crowbait called, a jeering grin on his face. "Ain't scared, are you?"

"Scared of that amiable creature?" Montana drawled. "Naw. I've just got to give my dinner a little time to digest before I let him begin tossing it around."

"Huh, you're hoping he'll get himself all worn out," Crowbait scoffed.

Bob didn't like the tone of Crowbait's remarks. The cowboys, although they teased each other constantly, were usually good-natured about it. But there was always an undercurrent of meanness in Crowbait's teasing remarks to Montana. Bob wondered again if Crowbait envied Montana's top ranking in the Circle K.

But Montana paid no attention to Crowbait. Deliberately, he untangled his long legs from the top rail, jumped down into the corral, and commenced to twirl his rope.

At sight of this hated, two-legged enemy, Dynamite stopped his wild prancings. Then, with a squeal of fury, he threw himself at the man, rearing high into the air, forelegs pawing. At the same time Montana's rope snaked out.

Bob almost stopped breathing. Would his friend waste his loop and not have time to form another before those sharp hoofs would be upon him?

But miraculously the loop settled neatly around Dynamite's neck. Quick as a thought, Montana wrapped the other end around the snubbing post. His high heels plowed the dirt as he tightened the noose that was choking the meanness out of the horse. Then he yelled for someone to bring a blindfold and for someone else to hold the end of the rope while he lifted the saddle to throw on Dynamite's back.

"Well, I'm a spavined hunk o' hoss meat," cried Crowbait. "If he don't aim to ride that ornery animal without trying to gentle it first!"

And that did seem to be Montana's aim—to get along without any of the usual preliminary motions of letting the animal become accustomed to the man smell or to the feel of first the blanket, then the saddle, on his back. Swiftly Montana threw the saddle blanket on, then the saddle. Then, while Shorty and Crowbait twisted the animal's ears and held the blindfold in place, he leaped into the saddle. Crowbait jerked the blindfold and along with Shorty clambered to the top of the fence.

For a moment the horse stood still as though unable to believe that the weight on his back was real. Then he exploded all over the corral.

"Jumping Jimminy!" Shorty exclaimed. "He has all the mean tricks of all the mean hosses I ever saw rolled into that ornery carcass of his. He can wrinkle his spine, highroll, weave, sunfish, swap ends, jackknife, and everything else."

Bob did not see how any human being could remain seated on the leaping, twisting animal. Most of the time Dynamite's back formed a peak in the middle and his head was between his forelegs. Time and again he swapped ends, as Shorty called it, so suddenly that it seemed a miracle that Montana stuck in the saddle. He had a dozen different motions of the terrific, jerky sort that make a talented bucker.

"I'm beginning to wish we hadn't started this," Shorty gasped. "I'm too fond of Montana for this sort of thing."

"But Montana's riding him!" Bob cried. His hands gripped the top pole of the corral until his knuckles showed white. He ached all over, outside and in, with his concern for his friend and the intensity of his desire to have him triumph.

Shorty shook his head soberly. "That ornery devil hasn't used up all of his tricks yet," he said. "If he does throw Montana, he'll likely paw him to death before the fellow can get up. Or he's likely to start rolling if he can't get rid of him any other way." The cowhand drew a long sigh. "As for me," he concluded, "I'm willing to call it a day. But it's too late now. Montana's got to ride, or else . . ."

Bob gripped the rail and breathed a silent prayer. "Oh, stick on, Montana! Stick on!"

Around and around the corral they went. The spectators were silent now, lost in admiration for both horse and rider. They had been witnessing daring and skillful riding for most of their lives, but never had they seen anything like this. And never had they seen so tireless a horse.

Long before this time an ordinary horse would have collapsed. Dynamite was covered with foam and at every leap his breath was forced from him with an agonized grunt, yet he would not give up. But finally the leaps became less wild and at last the horse's head came up. This, Shorty explained to Bob, was sign that the bucking was over, for a horse cannot buck unless its head is between its legs.

Montana slid to the ground. Instantly Crowbait snatched the saddle and bridle from the horse, before it could find energy for more tricks.

Everyone slapped Montana on the back as he walked toward the bunkhouse. Even Crowbait seemed sincere in his admiration over the ride. And that night at supper no one could talk of anything else.

"You won your prize with interest," John Benton said. "That ride was worth a lot. What do you say, men? Has Montana earned the right to keep his saddle and his cow pony?"

The men gladly agreed with Mr. Benton's generous suggestion. Bob heaved a sigh of relief. Montana certainly should not be required to do any more, to risk his life again after such a wonderful ride. Perhaps luck would not be with him another time. Besides everyone believed that it was impossible to break Dynamite.

Montana looked up from his plate. "What's the matter?" he asked coolly. "Are you men trying to back out of your offers?"

"No," said Shorty. "It isn't that, and you know it. We're only trying to do the square thing by you. We know and you know that you can't break Dynamite. We don't hanker to have you risk your hide, trying a fool stunt like that."

"You've never known me to back out of anything, have you?" Montana asked.

"No," cried Shorty in exasperation. "And you aren't backing out now. We're asking you as a favor to us not to risk your fool neck again. We're shorthanded on the Circle K as it is. We can't spare any top hands."

"I made a proposition and I'll stick to it," said Montana quietly. "Either I'll break Dynamite in a week's time or you fellows get my saddle and my cow pony."

The men shrugged and went on with their eating. Bob wished that Montana would not be so stubborn. Oh, why wouldn't he quit now!

"You'll have to break Dynamite on your own time, Montana," Bob's uncle said. "I'm inclined to agree with Shorty and the other boys that there's an unbreakable horse. I don't think he's worth taking time to work with. I planned to save him for a rodeo horse. But if you want to work with him in your spare time that's your business."

"I reckon he'll be the top hoss in my string one of these days," said Montana with a broad grin.

"Don't go countin' your hosses until they are broke," Crowbait warned.

That night Bob took his flashlight and wandered out to the breaking corral. Dynamite was to stay there until the end of the week, because the cowboys had refused to risk their necks cutting him out from the cavy and getting him into the chute again.

At the sound of Bob's footsteps Dynamite let out a fierce whinny. Bob heard his hoofs hit the poles. "Steady, boy, steady," he said soothingly. "Steady, boy, yourself," he heard, and jumped at the sound.

"What do you think you're doing out here all by your lonesome?"

Bob recognized Montana's familiar voice. "Oh," he laughed, "you scared me more than the horse did! I just came out to talk to Dynamite a little. I thought it might help you if I talked to him a bit and sort of got him used to people."

"Thanks, pal." Montana chuckled. "You have the makings of a real cowboy. You and I had the same idea. Climb up here to the 'opery rail' and we'll have a little powwow and let Dynamite in on it."

Bob perched beside his friend contentedly.

"You know," Montana went on, "I believe he is beginning to understand already that we're meant to be friends."

But if Dynamite had such an understanding, he was very backward about showing it. For two days the men watched Montana each time he gave Dynamite his workout, then they tired of it. By now the horse was able to throw his rider once in a while. He had the advantage of not getting worn out in the battle of changing corrals and he was bursting with energy. But Montana was as agile as a panther. Almost as soon as he hit the ground he was on his feet and back in the saddle again, letting Dynamite feel the bite of the spurs after each victory. Finally the horse began to understand that the short triumph was hardly worth the punishment.

Only Bob knew that Montana went out every night and worked with Dynamite. Talking to him soothingly. Roping and tying him to the snubbing post. Rubbing his neck. Letting him wear the saddle for an hour at a time.

When the night before the end of the week came, Montana said to Bob, "S'pose you can get up before daylight tomorrow?"

"I reckon I can," said Bob, who would have slept standing on his head if Montana had requested it. "Why?"

"Well, I aim to get up before the birdies myself," Montana drawled. "Tomorrow is the day for me to collect my prize. So I want to give friend Dynamite here a bit of a workout before the sun rises. Take some of the spook out of him before the boys are up. When they come out, I want you to open the gate so I can come riding out on a hoss with his head up."

"I'll sure do that," Bob told him with delight.

That night Bob set his alarm for three o'clock, the time when Montana said he was going to begin the workout. Dynamite had never given up bucking whenever Montana first got into the saddle. But now it was more like the game of a mischievous child than the determined meanness of a killer horse.

Bob had seen Montana ride Dynamite around the corral after several of his bucking sprees. The horse acted promising enough then, but Montana had not yet attempted to ride him out in the open. After all, that would be the test. Dynamite might have learned the uselessness of fighting his heart out in the prison of the corral, but when he saw the wide open spaces the urge for freedom might prove to be stronger than the brief mastery Montana had managed to attain.

It was with considerable uneasiness the next morning that Bob called down to his friend, from his lookout on the top of the corral, that the men were coming from the bunkhouse.

"Open the gate then," Montana called, "and keep your fingers crossed, pal."

Dynamite stepped between the poles of the gate with head high and ears perked up.

"Steady, boy, steady!" Montana said quietly, his hand firm on the rein. Dynamite jerked his head as though in an attempt to get the bit between strong teeth, but Montana was prepared for just such a trick.

"No you don't, boy," he said. "Just remember that I'm boss, and we'll get along fine."

The spirited animal made two more attempts to bolt for the beckoning freedom of green meadows and blue hills. But the grip on the reins remained firm and the suggestion of spur against flank reminded him that the two-legged creature astride him was still determined to be master.

Bob held his breath. Would Dynamite bog his head and use his tremendous energy to rid himself of the burden on his back? There was plenty of room for the horse to put his strength to the test if he happened to take the notion.

But the horse trotted around the buildings with beautifully arched neck and high steps.

The men stood speechless, their mouths open with amazement. Cookie came out to whang the triangle and froze midway in the motion. John Benton appeared at the door, half his face clean-shaven, the rest covered with lather.

No one said a word as the handsome horse continued to high-step around the yard. Bob's heart, however, was still in his throat, for Dynamite's nostrils were dilated and he threw walleyed glances about.

Montana was the only one who seemed undisturbed. "How do you like my new hoss?" he called as he trotted by the men. "Isn't he a handsome brute? Don't you wish you had one as good?"

"Well I'll be a hornswoggled hunk o' hoss meat," Shorty cried. "If Montana didn't go and do it again. I never saw his like!"

Several times Dynamite tried to get his head down, but the alert, strong hand on the reins reminded him who was master.

After riding around the buildings for several minutes, Montana signalled Bob to open the corral gate. The foreman rode inside and removed the saddle.

As he came out, John Benton called, "That's a splendid new horse you have there, Montana."

The cowboy grinned. "I reckon he is," he drawled. "And my silver-trimmed saddle will look mighty fine on him."

"Right today," Shorty promised, "we'll get the order off for those new boots. You've really earned them."

"He sure has," the other cowboys echoed.

Bob looked down at his brown oxfords. "I wish I could do something to win a pair of cowboy boots," he thought. Then quickly forgot his desire in his joy over Montana's triumph.

—SHANNON GARST

Catching Wild Horses
Utah and a Bronco Hunt

The very next day it rained. Blessed, blessed rain. Uncle Orson smiled happily as he heard the rain pounding down on the roof of the ranch house. The irrigation ditches would be brimming over. The alfalfa fields would stay green. Perhaps he might get an extra cutting in late summer. The grama grass would grow and he would market strong healthy steers in September.

Shorty announced over his hotcakes at breakfast, "This 'ud be a good day, Martha, to clean out the 'ram pasture,' " as he called the bunk house. Aunt Martha smiled her approval. An hour later Peter pushed open the heavy door of the bunk house. He hardly recognized the place. Shorty had swept up cigarette butts and dust, old newspapers were gathered into a neat pile, even the spiderwebs were wiped from the windows. The cowboy had pulled up the army blankets and spread them neatly over the four crude bunks.

Peter always liked the smell of the bunk house. It smelled excitingly of leather, horse medicine, dust, stale cigarettes, blankets, sweat, and many other odors he did not know. Shorty was mending a broken bridle strap, whistling his favorite tune, "The Cowboy's Lament." The boy flung himself on a bunk. He glanced through one of Shorty's magazines, *Western Stories*. The cowboy only read stories of cow camp and cattle range.

After a long silence, Peter inquired, "Shorty, did you hear Jim say yesterday that he saw wild horses at Coyote Springs?"

"No, I didn't," answered Shorty, looking up from his work.

"Did you ever catch broncs when you were young, Shorty?"

"Did I ever catch broncs, Half-pint? I'd like to have a nickel for every bronc I caught in my day. I'd be rich now."

"Were you a *real* mustanger, Shorty?" queried Peter, awe in his voice.

"You bet I was a mustanger, and a bronc buster too. But gentling wild horses is bad business, Half-pint. A bronc I was gentling threw me and broke my ankle once. Never was too much good since."

"Did you *like* awfully to chase broncs?" questioned Peter, leading up to his great desire.

"Why, kid, there's no better fun in the world. More fun than stalking lions with dogs or going after bear."

"Then why don't you get yourself a bronc? They're out at Coyote Springs now," said the eager boy.

"First I heard of it," drawled Shorty thoughtfully. "Would you like to go hunting broncs, son?" he asked.

Then Peter's bottled-up hopes burst out in a torrent. He stammered, "I've been dreaming and dreaming for weeks that I had a horse of my very own. Almost every night I dream about a pinto called Checkers. I ride him to school and show him to the boys. In my dreams, that is. He's almost real."

Peter jumped from the bed and ran over to where the cowboy was working. "Shorty," he whispered, "there's a colt waiting for me on the desert with those broncs right now. I *know* there is. Danger was found out on the desert. Maybe Checkers will be too."

Shorty smiled as he laid a rough brown hand on Peter's shoulder. His eyes had a far-away look. "I know just how you feel, kid. Once when I was about your age I went with my paw to town for the first time in my life. In a store window I saw a pair of cowboy boots. On each was a white butterfly stitched in leather. Those boots were sure pretty. I wanted them bad. But my dad was just a poor cowpuncher. He couldn't buy me any fancy boots. I didn't even ask him. I just looked at them. But when we went home and for years afterward, I dreamed about those boots. Since that time I've had boots and boots and more boots. But it's funny I never had boots as pretty as those I saw in the store window when I was a kid."

Just then the door opened. Uncle Orson entered. There was a frown on his face as he asked anxiously, "Shorty, have you seen Rosie this morning?"

"Nope. Why? She was in the west forty last night."

"She isn't there now. The fence is broken. I followed her tracks south and lost them."

"Well," answered Shorty, thoughtfully scratching his head, "she always was a wild one. Maybe she's run away again. Don't suppose she's gotten wind of those broncs do you?"

"Hardly, hardly," muttered Uncle Orson as he closed the door behind him and disappeared.

When he was gone Shorty said, "He's as touchy about Rosie as a teased snake. Thinks she's the best horse he ever had. But I dropped a seed in his mind about a bronc hunt. The seed'll be sprouting. Wait and see. He'll think he thought it all up by himself."

Peter suddenly felt very happy. Shorty knew his secret. Shorty was on his side. Shorty would help him. Peter stretched out on a bunk again. He lay for a long time playing with his horny toad. Shorty was so nice. He always seemed to know just how a fellow felt.

Suddenly Peter asked, "Are you a Mormon, Shorty?"

Shorty looked up. There was a strange look on his face as he asked, "What a funny question, kid, why do you ask?"

"Oh, I just wondered. You smoke, we don't. You drink coffee, we don't. You swear sometimes when you're mad.

But you're so *good,* Shorty. You're awful good to us kids. *Are* you a real Mormon?"

Shorty hesitated. Then he said, "Well, no, I'm not exactly a Mormon. I don't go to church, that is. I guess I ain't much of anything but a cowpuncher, come to think about it. My mom died when I was born. Never had much bringing-up. But I've worked for a lot of Mormons in my day and don't have any gripes coming."

"Are other people who are not Mormons like us, Shorty?" queried Peter.

"Half-pint, people are a lot alike even if their skins are red, black, white, or yellow. I've known some of the best Indians in the world and some of the meanest. I don't hold with the saying, 'The only good Indian is a dead one.' I knew a Chinaman cook once who was a durn lot whiter than some whites I've known. I've known Mormons too, but I must say most of them have been pretty square shooters. Now and again you run into a worthless one. It don't make a lot of difference, kid, what you *say* you are. It's what's inside that counts. But I haven't known many Mormons that stole, cheated, or lied."

"Then why do people outside talk bad about us sometimes?" asked Peter, puzzled.

"Why do people talk bad about anybody? Just cause they don't know them. Maybe they got another religion. Maybe they do things different. Maybe they're afraid of them."

Peter was quiet, thinking.

The cowboy drawled on, "I figure it out this way. The Mormons came to Utah over a hundred years ago. There wasn't anything here then but just desert. Now after a hundred years what is there? Clean towns, green alfalfa fields; peaches, apples, pears, grapes, big black cherries; beef, sheep, horses, and lately mines. You got to hand it to the Mormons. They made Utah a nice place to live in. They did it by hard work too, by pulling all together, and not by shooting, killing, cheating, like it was in the mining camps in California and Nevada in the early days. Does that answer your question, Half-pint?"

"Yes, I guess it don't make any difference," sighed Peter as if he had at last found an answer to a hard problem. "I guess, as you say, folks are a lot alike inside when you know them. So-long."

Peter ran out of the bunk house to find his cousin. Shorty whistled at his work. He thought to himself, "Pete's a queer kid, has an old head on that little body of his."

The next morning Uncle Orson asked, "Shorty, think we could hunt up Rosie tomorrow if she don't show up?"

"Sure," was all that Shorty said, looking at Peter.

"I hate to lose a good horse like Rosie. She's the best cutting horse I ever had and we'll need her next fall in the roundup."

Turning to his wife, he asked, "If we should go, Martha, for a day or two, one of the Blackburn kids can come up and milk for you."

"It's alright with me, Orson," answered Martha, "though I don't like to have kids around when I'm bottling fruit. But if you say so."

"That means *we* go along," whispered Doug to his cousin.

The boys were so excited that they could hardly do the chores. They knew now that Uncle Orson was determined to go hunting broncs, though he did not exactly say so. So they caught the pack burro, Stumpy, a stubborn little beast, and helped gather the bedrolls and the grub. The following morning long before the sun rose they were awake, dressed, ready. Clouds still hung over the country. An hour later four riders, with Stumpy lagging behind loaded with camp equipment, wound their way toward the open desert.

When they reached the Blackburn ranch and still found no trace of Rosie, Blackburn suggested, "That mare might have crossed the river and headed for the badlands at night. There's a band of broncs watering at Coyote Springs, Jim tells me. You know how the stallions steal mares if they can. I've lost two."

That decided Uncle Orson. He asked Shorty, "How about it? We got grub and bedrolls."

"Fine," was all that Shorty said.

The idea planted in Uncle Orson's mind was sprouting and he thought the idea was his. Uncle Orson liked to hunt broncs as much as his cowboy did. But he was a man whose fields, family, stock, came first to him. But the rain had made him easy in his mind. The call of the chase was strong within him. He had a good excuse to spend a day or so hunting, for had not Rosie run away and was not Rosie a fine cowhorse?

Men and boys rode over the rough desert trail. The cresote bushes and the sagebrush smelled fragrant after the rain. Soon the clouds disappeared. The sun was hot. A turkey vulture sailed in the deep sky, casting a great shadow over the plain. Cacti spread everywhere, some in bloom. The flowers looked like fragile wild roses. By midday everybody was hot and tired. They came to an ironwood tree alone in the desert—shade at last. They stopped, slipped from their sweating horses, munched strips of dried venison, and gulped water from a canteen.

Uncle Orson and Shorty were anxious to reach Coyote Springs while they could still see the tracks of the animals. So the four rode on. Peter thought the trip would never end. The desert looked so much alike. There were no landmarks. Sagebrush, cacti, more sagebrush, creosote bushes, cacti. He saw a roadrunner chasing a snake, and a coyote slinking away in the distance. That was all. But in midafternoon Shorty, who had ridden ahead, raced back to announce, "I see the entrance of the canyon. Hurry up."

The horses smelled water. They hastened their steps. Soon the riders reached the mouth of the canyon. They toiled up a quarter of a mile. Peter wondered at the beautiful green of a cottonwood grove against the red hills. There was water in the pool, but it was low. Uncle Orson and Shorty at once read the tracks in the mud around the edge of the water.

"Those mustangs were here about three days ago. What do you think, Orson?" asked Shorty, studying the maze of tracks in the mud.

"That would be my guess too," muttered Peter's uncle.

The boys watered the thirsty horses and Stumpy. They took off the sweaty saddles and let the horses graze on the sparse desert. Above the pool surrounded by boulders was a level, sandy spot, a good place to camp. Ashes of old fires were there, made by shepherds, cowmen, prospectors, Indians, and perhaps bandits. The sun set in a blaze of orange. The air grew cooler. Shorty started a fire with the dry sagebrush the boys gathered. It made a sweet-smelling smoke. Doug found a stick of ironwood. That kept heat a long time.

"Gee, how good the bacon smells out here," said Peter, terribly hungry. "Even coffee smells good."

Only Shorty drank coffee. He always had to have his "Arbuckle" as he called it. He made biscuits in a Dutch oven which he called "sinkers." The boys loaded the sinkers with dandelion honey from home, and ate all the sinkers they could hold. After they had washed up the tin plates and cups in the pool, they lay on their bedrolls, listening to the men talk about hunting.

"Those broncs were here about three nights ago I figure," meditated Shorty. "So they won't be here tonight likely, though you never know for sure."

"That's what I think too," answered Uncle Orson.

"We'll likely all get a good sleep tonight. But tomorrow night, that'll be a different story."

The boys slid into their bedrolls, after looking first for tarantulas and scorpions. The last thing Peter heard was the murmur of the men's voices as they talked about the wild horse hunts of their youth. Soon the moon rose. Coyotes yelped on the rimrock above, sounding like children at play. Peter fell into a deep sleep and dreamed of Checkers. He knew nothing until his cousin pulled him from his bedroll. It was morning.

The day that followed was hot. The men sat in the shade

of the trees and talked or ate or slept. The boys were bored, so they hiked up the canyon as far as they could go and climbed out on the rim above. They sat there, scanning the desert through Uncle Orson's field glasses.

"Pete, I see a dust cloud way over there. If it goes straight up and then fades away, it's only a dust devil or a tumbleweed. But if it goes up and levels out it's a herd of sheep or horses or beef."

He handed the field glasses to his cousin. Peter watched the dust cloud. It melted slowly away. "Dust devil," he said.

The long day dragged on. Peter lost his precious horny toad. While he was looking through the field glasses, the little animal wiggled into the sand and he could not find it.

"We'll find another sometime. Don't worry, Pete," said his cousin.

"Look at that beetle!" said Peter.

They saw a black beetle standing on its head in the sand. Peter laughed. The beetle looked so funny. Then it tried to escape as the boys teased him with a stick. It tried to walk away when it was standing on its head, so it fell over, and could not get up. It wiggled frantically, its little legs waving in the air. Peter turned it over and it scurried happily away. The boys hiked slowly back to camp and gathered firewood for the supper fire. While they were eating, the men outlined the plan for the hunt.

The cousins washed the tin plates and put out the fire with sand. Then they led their horses up into the canyon above the camp and sat down behind a rock to wait. The hunters checked bridles, lariats, girths, bridles. The moon rose slowly; it looked like a big orange. Then Shorty and Uncle Orson mounted, and slowly rode down the canyon. Soon the boys could not hear them.

Peter sat on the ground, holding Whiskers' reins tightly. With the rising of the moon the coyotes sang in chorus. A desert fox slipped like a gray shadow to the pool and lapped the silvery water. The droning of insects, the yelping of the coyotes, the moaning of a little desert owl in the trees, made Peter sleepy. He whispered to Doug, "Gee, I hope I don't get sleepy and don't hear the horses come."

"You'd better not, pal."

"There must be a night-bloomer somewhere. Something sure smells sweet," said Doug.

"Maybe a Queen of the Night cactus," drawled his cousin.

Peter laid his head on his knees. A rock slipped. He did not hear it. A lizard slithered across the sand. He did not hear it. The coyote chorus kept on. He closed his eyes. He must have dozed. Suddenly his cousin nudged him.

"Pete, hear that sound like a drum, thud, thud, thud?"

Peter listened. "That's horses I bet, those mustangs a-coming."

The moon was so bright that Peter could see the leaves of the cottonwood trees shimmer and the silver reflections of the moon in the water.

"Doug, are those really horses' hoofs?"

"Couldn't hardly be anything else, I figure."

The far-off sound continued. It grew louder.

"They're coming, sure enough, they're coming," whispered Doug.

Peter felt his heart so big in his throat he could not breathe. "I'm scared," was all he said.

Then the boys saw a little cloud in the distance that grew larger as they watched. Soon heads and legs began to appear. Horses, horses, wild horses, were galloping toward the life-giving water. At the entrance to the canyon the band of mustangs stopped. The stallion slowly advanced, followed by his group of mares and colts. He sniffed the air and listened intently. He was a handsome fellow, lean and muscular, a black-and-white pinto with a long black tail that touched the ground.

The stallion gave a signal to the mares. They crowded into the pool and drank greedily. Colts slipped into the water. The pool was a torment of ripples. Then Peter, shivering with excitement, saw a mustang that was so beautiful tears came to his eyes. The mustang entered the pool and drank. He was a copy of the older stallion. He too was strong and muscular. He too had a long black tail. Peter said under his breath, "Checkers is alive, Checkers is real. It was not a dream."

The mustangs drank greedily. When they were full to bursting they played in the water. A few of them lay down in the cool mud around the pool. Peter watched the glorious young horse playing in the water and splashing the mares. Now the stallion, his brood satisfied, stepped into the water himself and drank long and greedily. Between drinks he raised his head and sniffed the air, alert for enemies. Doug leaned over to Peter and whispered so softly that Peter could hardly hear him.

"Don't get up yet. Wait until they're ready to bust."

"Yes."

The horses played for some time. The boys did not see Rosie anywhere.

"Now let's go, Pete, it's time. Yell your loudest so the men can hear us."

"Ride, cowboy, ride! Whoopee, whoopee, whoopee," yelled the excited boys as they rode their equally excited horses toward the mustangs. The frightened horses sprang away. They galloped down the canyon, the stallion herding them from behind. The boys followed. In a few moments the mustangs had disappeared in a cloud of dust. Peter heard the sound of galloping hoofs. Then the sound seemed to change and came from a different direction. "Uncle Orson has turned them toward Shorty," thought Peter to himself as he rode after the disappearing dust cloud. Soon he was alone on the silvery desert. He rode on and on, he knew not where. He let Whiskers go where he wanted to. Whiskers had a better nose and better ears than Peter, and Peter knew it. Soon he was lost. He could see nothing, he could hear nothing. He was a little afraid as Whiskers galloped on. Suddenly Peter heard a whinny. That was Kickapoo's whinny, Shorty's horse.

Whiskers stopped suddenly on the edge of the ravine. Peter looked down into the gulch. There was Kickapoo white in the moonlight. Beside him sat Shorty, smoking a cigarette. As Peter dismounted he noticed something that made him tremble. Lying as if dead among the rocks was a young bronco.

"Shorty, is he dead?"

"Come down, Peter, and I'll tell you all about it," answered the cowboy quietly. Peter stumbled down the sandy incline.

"Sit down and take it easy, Pete. He'll be alright. You can't kill a wild bronc."

The cowboy told Peter the story of the hunt.

"I picked him out right away. I knew he was your horse. I followed him for a while. Was he a fast one! Then he ran along this ravine. I figured if I could keep him there he would get worn out. When he began to slow down, he got worried. He decided to try to jump the ravine. It was narrow alright, but not as narrow as he thought. He didn't quite make it. He fell and hit his head on a rock. It knocked him out."

Then Peter noticed blood flowing from a cut over the mustang's eye.

"Oh, he'll come out of it alright after a spell," soothed Shorty. "You can't kill a mustang. They're tough."

Peter, tears in his eyes, sat on a rock and watched the injured horse. Shorty smoked. The mustang did not move. The two friends waited for a long time. Shorty smoked one cigarette after another. He seemed nervous. Finally he slipped a hackamore over the pinto's head.

"He hurt his leg too, son, but it ain't broken. I know a broken leg," said the cowboy after a long silence.

"He's not going to die is he, Shorty?" quavered Peter, as he saw the cowpuncher finger his revolver in its holster.

"No, I don't think so, but it sure takes him a long time to come to."

Shorty seemed to grow more nervous as time passed. The coyote chorus died down. The moon was getting low.

At last Peter blurted out, "Shorty, you wouldn't shoot Checkers, would you, after all this time I've dreamed about him and waited for him?"

"No, keep your shirt on, son. I never shoot an animal if he's going to get well, but sometimes I have to so I won't watch them suffer."

To keep the boy's mind from the injured mustang Shorty told him stories of animals, pack rats and their funny habits, of trapdoor spiders and the marvelous little silk doors they build to their nests. He told him of his own childhood, of the death of his father when he was only twelve years old; of life with his uncle who ran a trading post in the Navajo country. Suddenly Peter saw the bronco open an eye. The other one was swollen shut. Then the mustang shivered and tried to get up. He fell back weakly. He tried to rise again. Once more he fell back. But the third time he stood up, trembling, and Shorty and Peter led him up the sandy slope of the wash to the level desert.

The dawn had come. The sky was getting lighter as the two riders and three horses started toward Coyote Springs. Checkers limped and staggered, but he followed. He was not strong enough to fight the hackamore. When they reached camp, day had come. Doug and Orson yelled as they saw Peter leading the beautiful, wounded pinto. Uncle Orson had lassoed a handsome chestnut mare and her colt without injuring them. The mare had fought all the way back to the springs. She was very wild.

Shorty tied Checkers to a tree and said sternly, "Keep away from those horses, boys. They might kick the daylights out of you."

They camped at the springs until late afternoon. Then the hunters started home in the cool of the evening. Stumpy was necked to Checkers. It was his job to bring the wild bronco home. For a few miles Checkers went meekly along beside the burro; he was weak from loss of blood and could see with only one eye. But after a while he felt stronger and began to buck and bite and kick the patient little burro. He tried to pull Stumpy toward the desert. Stumpy would set his four litle feet down in the dust and Checkers had to drag him along. The bronco soon grew tired of pulling Stumpy and then the burro turned toward the ranch again and the bronco followed. They kept this fight up all the way home, but always it was Stumpy who was the winner.

As for the new mare, she was necked to Kickapoo. She gave him a rough time. She fought and struggled, but Kickapoo had been necked to wild broncos before and knew how to lead them home. They passed the Blackburn ranch and only the dogs greeted them. It was late. King must have heard the hunters coming, for he ran out to meet them when they were nearing Heber's Crossing.

Aunt Martha lit the lamps and welcomed them with the words, "A surprise for you. Blackburn brought Rosie up this afternoon. He found her along the river. She's in the corral."

The men put Checkers in the breaking corral by himself, and the mare and her colt alone in another corral.

Peter was so tired he fell asleep at once and did not wake up until noon of the next day.

—MARY AND CONRAD BUFF

The Hogan
Where the Navajo Lives

Home hogan was a rounded, mud-plastered house with a blanket-covered door facing eastward. There were no windows. The chimney was a hole in the middle of the rounded, mud-plastered roof. The floor was clean yellow sand. Sheepskins were the beds; boxes were the chairs, and the stove was a hollowed place in the sandy floor. A brushed-clean place beside the stove was used for table.

This was the family hogan, their house, their home, a friendly, happy place for Doli.

When Doli and her mother and her father reached

"The Hogan" is from *Little Navajo Bluebird* by Ann Nolan Clark, illustrated by Paul Lantz; reprinted by permission of The Viking Press, Inc., New York.

home hogan from the Trading Post, day had come to cool time. Red rocks were sending out their long gray shadows to the edges of the sandwash near by.

Elder Sister, Hobah, had been out all day with the flocks, but now she was home again. She had turned the sheep and the goats into the night corral among the piñons. She had carried water from the well. She had chopped wood at the woodpile and now smoke from the newly made supper fire filled the hogan door. Hobah was beautiful, tall for her age, slender, and strong. She did whatever work there was to do, quietly and well, as her mother had taught her.

Now she came out to the wagon to carry her mother's blanket bundle into the hogan. Mother went to milk the goats and Doli stumbled sleepily to sit on her sheepskin bed beside the fire. She told Hobah of the happenings of the day. She told her about Uncle's winning the game that he played with the men and about Father's selling the bracelet to the Trader. She told about the things she had done and had seen and had heard, but she did not say Big Brother's name. One said with words those things that the eyes saw, but even with Hobah one guarded the whisperings of the heart.

Father came in. He had unhitched his horses and had hobbled them for the night grazing. Hobah hastened to serve him with food. Mother's blanket had been full of good things. Tonight the family had store bread and canned peaches to eat with the mutton stew. Tonight the strong black coffee was sweetened with sugar and colored creamy brown with milk from a can.

Fiery clouds of sunset covered the sky and changed

the yellow sands of the drywash to purple and rose. Hobah moved quietly about the hogan, serving Father with food and helping Mother end the work of the day.

Doli was sleepy but not yet was she ready to let sleep come. She sat in the door of the hogan and let the little night winds wash her face with their cooling fingers. Far away, far off, in the thickening shadows, she heard singing. Some stranger singing. At first it was just a singing sound, but little by little, as the rider came nearer, the singing sound grew into words of song, into words of the hogan song. Clearly they came across the gray shadows, the words of the hogan song:

> "My hogan,
> My hogan,
> My happy hogan,
> My blessed hogan,
> Hogan.
> My hogan."

So sang the far rider as he urged his tired horse homeward. Father came to stand in the hogan doorway. He took up the chant. He sent his singing out into the coming night to meet the tired rider to sing him home. Father sang:

> "Look!
> Yonder the hogan,
> The beautiful hogan,
> The precious hogan."

Doli gathered her skirts close around her. She hugged

her knees in delight. Father's singing wrapped her in a
blanket of happiness.

> "My hogan,
> Hogan,"

sang Father, and the rider answered:

> "Hogan beautiful,
> My hogan."

Doli turned toward the fire-lighted hogan. She watched
Hobah's blue shadow moving along the wall. It made
her think of Turquoise Woman on her way to the Western
Waters.

"Uncle must tell us again of Turquoise Woman," she
said to herself; "I will ask him to tell us when next he
comes to my mother's hogan."

"Hogan, my hogan, my hogan blessed," sang the far
rider.

Darkness came swiftly into the desert. Night came upon
the people there.

The family moved their sheepskins out under the stars.
One pelt alone was left inside, not used, not needed. It
lay to one side, partly unrolled, wholly neglected. It was
Big Brother's bed waiting for him to come home.

Outside, the night was clear and the stars hung low.
Mother moved quietly, unrolling the sheepskins, tucking
in the blankets. Doli lay upon her pelt in the soft, warm
sand, in the warm, still night. Mother's hand found her

hand in the darkness, softly, lightly, swiftly brushing it, like a raindrop, almost. Doli slept.

The next morning, after sunup, after breakfast, after Hobah had taken the flocks to graze, Uncle came riding around the red rocks and up through the sandwash. Uncle came riding, his arms held stiffly, elbows pointing outward, and jerking up and down with the pony's trotting. Doli stood by her mother's loom under the juniper tree, watching him coming. She stood still, waiting, feeling happy to see him. Uncle was young, almost as young as Big Brother. He was gay-acting and gay-looking. He wore tight blue jeans and a bright red shirt and a big black hat. His hair was long like Father's and he wore it tied in a fat queue wrapped with long white cord.

Mother was beginning a new blanket. She was stringing her loom. She was letting Doli help her. Mother's yarn that she had sheared from her sheep, had spun and dyed, was rolled neatly into balls and was piled on the sheepskin beside them. Mother saw Uncle trotting his pony through the sandwash. She smiled at Doli. She was pleased to see her younger brother coming.

Father was making a silver ring. His workbench was a cottonwood stump. His tools were a hammer, a sandstone mold, and leather bellows. He sat cross-legged on the ground with his head bent low over his work, but he heard Uncle come riding around the red rocks.

Work stopped. They waited for Uncle.

Uncle lifted his pony into a run until they were just beyond the clearing of the juniper tree. Then Uncle made him stop with stiffened legs in a cloud of flying sand. It made Doli laugh to see Uncle's pony stop so quickly that it almost sat down.

Now that he had arrived in a dashing way, Uncle felt that he could take his time. So he sat there, looking at the waiting family. Then he got off slowly, throwing his pony's reins to the ground so it would not stray. He walked slowly to the shade of the hogan wall. He sat down slowly, saying not a word. His pony, reins dragging, began to graze on the sparse clumps of green.

Now all was stillness where but a time before was swift-moving action. Father came over to the hogan shade. He sat down by Uncle. He rolled himself a cigarette. He gave Uncle a little brown paper and his bag of tobacco and a match. He nodded to Uncle, meaning, "You may smoke." Uncle rolled a cigarette. He lit it, using the match that Father used and putting his own match carefully in the pocket of his bright red shirt. Now both men puffed their tobacco. Smoke came. Two blue lines curled upward.

Then Father spoke gravely to Uncle. "Greetings, Younger Brother," he said. Uncle answered gravely, "Greetings, Elder Brother."

Doli went near them. She stood shyly by her father, looking away from the loved Uncle whom she wanted so badly to see. "Greetings, Small One," Uncle spoke softly, looking straight ahead. He did not want to frighten the little Bluebird.

Doli, still not looking, put the bag of candy down where Uncle could reach it. She said to her father, "It is a gift for him."

Uncle picked up the limp bag of squeezed and melted

candy. He looked at his pony. He said, "I, too, have a gift to offer."

Uncle took from inside his shirt a small brown bundle. He handed it to Father. Mother left her weaving and came over to look at the brown paper package. Everyone looked at it. Then Father untied the string. Two deerskin moccasins with silver buttons on the sides stood proudly in the crumpled paper. Father took Doli in his arms and put the moccasins on her small brown feet. Doli looked at them. They were beautiful. She felt them. They were soft to the touch.

Presently Mother went to the well for water. She carried a large bucket. Her yellow-brown skirts swished softly as she walked through the sand. Doli went with her. Her yellow-brown skirts swished softly. She carried a little bucket. The loose sands slid into the tiny foot-prints the moccasins made.

Mother filled her pail with water at the well. Doli filled hers. Water splashed on her foot. She saw it, but she did not feel it. She pushed her foot out from the flounces of her skirts and poured more water on it. She watched the water flashing silver on its way down, but when it touched her foot she felt neither cold nor wetness.

Doli looked up at her mother. Her eyes were big with surprise. The moccasins were shelters. They were like little houses for her feet. They were good. They must like her small brown feet!

She and Mother walked back through the sand to the hogan. They went inside. The hogan was clean and cool and quiet. Sunlight came in at the doorway and lay like a bright blanket on the sand of the floor. Mutton cooked over the coals in a big black pot. The hogan cat washed its face and shook out its whiskers to dry. Far away came the tinkle of the bell goat with the flock that Hobah herded slowly to the waterhole. Doli looked up at her mother. They smiled together, a quick little understanding smile that said, "We are glad to be together in this hogan because it is beautiful and good."

—ANN NOLAN CLARK

The Bottle

On Oregon's Columbia River

One morning when Davy went to throw out the scraps, he met Helen and Ellen Llewellen coming along the Avenue. Helen saw what he was doing, and cried, "Wait! Don't! Don't throw it in yet!"

Davy waited. Helen looked in his newspaper package and pulled out a bottle. It was a fat, round bottle of a very nice shape. "Don't throw it in!" begged Ellen. "Can we have it?"

"Sure, I guess so," agreed Davy. "What do you want it for? It's empty. Sis told me to throw it away."

Ellen explained, "We don't throw bottles away. That's

no fun. We put notes in them and let 'em float down the river."

"Who do you write notes to?"

"Oh, anybody," Helen said, "I write down all the big words I can think of."

"I'd like to write a letter, too," said Davy. "Only it ought to make sense. Not just big words."

"Let's all write one together."

Davy ran in the house and came back with some paper and a pencil. Then he and the twins sat down to write a letter. Before they had written much, Rancid Weeks came along the Avenue, whistling.

"Hello, Rancid," Helen and Ellen said sweetly.

Rancid made a horrible face. "What do you think you're doing with that pencil and paper?"

"We're writing a letter."

"Who're you writing a letter to?"

"We don't know. We're going to put it in this bottle and throw it in the river. Maybe it'll float all the way to the ocean!"

Rancid laughed. "Oh, sure! Maybe it'll float across the ocean clear to China!"

He was making fun of them, but Davy said, "Well, why not? China is on the other side of the Pacific Ocean, isn't it? Maybe it *will* float all the way to China."

Rancid laughed some more. "And I suppose some Chinese person will take it out of the water and read it!"

Davy argued, "Well, why not? It *could* happen, couldn't it?"

Rancid laughed loudly. "And how is a Chinese person going to read it if it isn't written in Chinese?" He put his hands in his pockets and walked off, taking very long steps and whistling.

Helen and Ellen Llewellen stuck their tongues out after him. Their cheeks were bright red and their black eyes snapped with anger. "He thinks he's so smart!" Ellen said.

Davy was thinking. "He's right, though," he told them. "The bottle *could* float all the way to China, and a Chinese person *could* find it, and he *couldn't* read the note unless it was written in Chinese."

Helen and Ellen thought, too. Then Helen bounced up on her knees. "I know somebody who can write Chinese!"

"Who?" asked Ellen and Davy.

"You know, Ellen! Herbert Wing's uncle."

"Who's he?" Davy asked.

"Herbert is in our class at school," Ellen said. "He can't write Chinese, but his uncle can. Oh, Helen, I know he would write us a letter if Herbert asked him to!"

"Sure he would. Look, Davy, will your sister let you go to town?"

"Sis has gone to work, and Pop's asleep," said Davy. "I take care of myself."

"Mother will let us go if you go along. Let's go to town right now and get Herbert's uncle to write us a letter."

It was a long way to town, but the street car went very fast. Helen and Ellen and Davy all sat on one seat and looked out of the windows at the river. The street car followed the river all the way to town. Then it crossed on a tall bridge. When they looked out, the water was far below them. The river was full of logs and tugs and dredges and ships. Some real ocean-going ships were anchored right in the middle of the city.

Davy looked at them longingly, for they were the ships that took loads of freight down the Columbia River to the ocean, and out across the ocean to the Pacific islands and to Russia and China. Some of them even went through the Panama Canal and up into the Atlantic Ocean. Davy tried to remember all the places he had read about in Geography class.

Helen and Ellen knew just where to get off of the street car. They stood on a corner of one of the streets near the water front. All the other streets were grey. The buildings were grey, and they looked old. But this street was different. The buildings were painted in bright colors. Nearly every shop had signs in both English and Chinese.

Helen pointed to a sign on a building across the street. "WING HOW, IMPORTER," it said. Upstairs there was a sign outlined in neon lights in the shape of a lotus flower.

"That's the place," Helen said. "Herbert lives behind the shop."

It did not look like a shop. There was nothing in the window downstairs except an old ginger-jar and an American flag. But they opened the door and went in. A bell jingled.

A boy came out of the back room. He saw who his visitors were and smiled. "Hello!"

"Hello, Herbert!" Helen introduced Davy. "He'll be in our school next year," she explained. "He lives at the moorage now. He has a bottle and we want to write a letter to put in it. But if it floats all the way to China and a

Chinese person finds it, he won't be able to read it if it's not written in Chinese."

"So we want your uncle to write us a letter," Ellen finished.

Davy added, "If it's not too much trouble."

Herbert said, "I'll go ask him." He went into the back room.

While he was gone Davy looked around the shop. It was dark and dusty. There were bales and boxes piled in the corners. On a counter at one end of the room there were trays full of strange-looking dried roots and dried fish. The place smelled of straw and ginger and incense.

In a few minutes Herbert came back. "He says he will write you a letter," he told them. "Come on." He led them into the back room.

How different this room was from the shop! There was a big window in the back wall. Davy could see a sort of garden outside. It was squeezed in between the buildings, and was just big enough for one tree and some grass and some potted plants. Inside the room there were a table and some chairs made of black, polished wood. A pale gold-colored carpet covered the floor. On the wall hung long pictures on silk. Davy was so busy looking that he forgot to speak politely to Herbert's uncle.

Helen gave him a sharp poke in the ribs with her elbow, and he remembered in time to say, "How do you do?"

"How do you do," answered Mr. Wing. "My nephew tells me you wish me to write a letter in Chinese."

"To put in our bottle," Ellen explained.

Mr. Wing smiled. "It is a fine idea," he told them. "I will write the letter, and you shall watch me do it."

They all gathered around him at the table. Mr. Wing laid a long piece of thin paper before him. Then he took a small square of ink, which looked something like a domino. He rubbed it back and forth on a black slate dish with a few drops of water. In a moment he had made his ink. Next he picked up his brush. It had a bamboo handle and a fat bunch of hairs on the end. He dipped it into the ink, and the bunchy hairs gathered into a smooth, fine point.

"Oh!" cried Davy.

Mr. Wing smiled at him. "Since this is such an unusual letter, I am writing it in the old Chinese way," he told them. "Fountain-pens are good enough for everyday business, but it isn't every day that I write a letter to send to China in a bottle."

They watched him write. He held his brush straight up and down, making beautiful black strokes on the paper. He wrote the characters up and down the page. Some of the characters looked like butterflies. Some of them looked like the branches of trees against the sky in winter.

When he had finished, Ellen asked, "What does it say?"

"It is a poem," said Mr. Wing. "If your bottle should float all the way to China, it will take a long time. There is nothing that lasts as long as poetry."

"Read it! Read it!" begged Helen.

"It says, 'May this far-travelled bottle carry a small portion of the air of peace from our calm river to China's war-torn shores!'"

"Oh!" said Davy. "It sounds just as beautiful as it looks."

They thanked Mr. Wing. "Why don't you go home with us and help us throw the bottle in the river?" they asked Herbert.

"All right," said Herbert.

So all four of them threw the bottle in the river. Helen and Ellen rolled the paper and tied it with a blue ribbon. They knew how to tie a special bow-knot. Then Herbert put the stopper in the bottle and sealed it with some red sealing-wax he brought from home. And Davy threw the bottle as far as he could out into the river.

It went up in a curve and fell with a "plop!" They all watched anxiously until it bobbed up above the splash.

They ran down the Avenue to the end of the moorage. Pretty soon they could see the bottle floating toward them. It bobbed past them, the red sealing-wax shining in the sun. They could see it for a long time as it bobbed on down the river. Then for a while they thought they could still see it, but they weren't sure. And then it was out of sight.

—CHARLOTTE BAKER

"As Long As We Can"
A Migrant Family in California

When Janey returned from hanging out the washing, she found the boards of the cabin floor darkened with moisture and the smell of wet wood adding one more odor to those already filling the room. Mom was leaning a stubby broom against the wall.

"I couldn't do a proper job," she said, frowning down at the uneven boards, "the floor's too rough. But a broom and hot suds can do a lot with elbow grease mixed with them."

Janey looked at the floor without comment. It seemed

all right to her, even if Mom wasn't satisfied. Why was she always fussing about dirt? Janey wondered, irritably. As a matter of fact, Mom fussed about a good many things. Lately nothing seemed to please her. The tired look hardly ever left her face. Of course Mom would be happier if they didn't have to move about from place to place. But there wasn't anything they could do about that. Dad had to look for work wherever work happened to be and it never lasted long in any one spot. Janey could feel herself beginning to lose patience with Mom, then remembered in time that Mom had liked Lupe. Besides, she undoubtedly meant all right and maybe it was better to prefer cleanliness to dirt, although it was a lot more trouble.

"I might as well stir up some corn dodgers as long as the oven's hot," Mrs. Larkin continued. While Janey watched, she wiped off the rickety table, produced a bowl and a small sack of yellow cornmeal and set to work. Janey eyed her speculatively. Would this be a good time for begging leave to return Lupe's call? She was nearly on the point of asking when Mom turned to her.

"As soon as I have this in the oven, we can start putting the place to rights. I can't seem to get used to living in a mess. Don't suppose I ever will, or I wouldn't mind it much by this time."

"I can untie the bedding and make up the bed," offered Janey in a small voice.

"No, it's too heavy for you. Wait till I'm through here."

Janey's neighborly inclinations strengthened.

Then, as if it were an afterthought, Mom said: "Have you done your reading yet today, Janey?"

"Not yet," admitted Janey. The two words seemed to put as many miles between herself and Lupe.

"Then you'd better be at it. You know what your father'd say if you let a day pass over your head without doing your stint."

Janey knew perfectly well what Dad would say if she neglected the two pages of Scripture which she was required to read daily. Dad believed there were some things second only to food and shelter in one's life. Reading was one of them.

So now Janey slid resignedly off her chair and dug to the bottom of the suitcase that held the willow plate. She lifted out a black leather-bound book, its back and edges worn.

It didn't seem strange to her that she should be using the Bible as a text book. It was almost the only text book Janey had ever known. Following the harvests from place to place had left her little time for schooling, even in the camp schools provided for the use of children like her. Sometimes, as now, she wished a little wistfully that she might some day go to a "regular" school where there were plenty of books, even new books, enough for every child. It occurred to her suddenly that probably Lupe went to such a school. She had lived here a whole year. Surely she belonged by this time. Janey walked slowly back to her chair, wondering what it would be like to belong. To go to school every day, a "regular" school, week after week, month after month.

She had seen a school like that once. It was over on the coast; she didn't remember just where. They had had to stop to change a tire right in front of the school house.

It was a red brick school house, with white columns in front and a green lawn that stretched nearly to the road. Janey, feeling unusually daring that day, had crept up the walk until she could reach out and touch the smooth white columns. Glancing back at the car, she had made sure that her father and mother were still busy with the tire. And then she had edged along the building, her clothes brushing against the rough bricks until she was able to peep into a window. Inside was a room full of boys and girls. Some were sitting at desks, others were writing at the blackboard, and all of them looked as if they belonged. For a long time Janey stood there watching, until a shout from the car sent her speeding back along the way she had come. It is doubtful if any in the school room had known they were being spied upon.

Yes, it would be nice to go to such a school. She wished she were there now. It would be lots more fun than sitting here in a stifling room, poring over tiny print full of "thee's" and "thou's" and words her tongue stumbled over when she asked their meaning. Still, she had learned to read by this strange method, and she supposed it would be a very good thing to know how to read if she should suddenly find herself in a district school, though goodness only knew how that would ever come about. And then, besides that, there were undoubtedly good stories in the Bible. Very good stories indeed. Daniel in the lions' den, and Noah's Ark, for instance.

She decided she would read about the Ark and the Flood today. It was a good time to read about a rain that lasted forty days and forty nights. It might help as much as the blue plate to lift the weight of the heat.

Perching herself on the chair and hooking her bare heels over its rungs, she opened the worn, black book and began to read. Now and then she would put her fingers on a word to fasten it to the page until she had sounded it out. No matter how many times she read the chapter, those queer names always caused her to hesitate a little.

The oven door had slammed shut on the corn bread and Mrs. Larkin had gone outside for a breath of what might be considered cooler air before Janey came to the last verse

> While the earth remaineth, seedtime and
> harvest, and cold and heat, and summer
> and winter, and day and night shall
> not cease.

She closed the Book and squeezed it between the two patches that covered her knees. Her hands stroked the soft leather in a thoughtful way. There was really nothing to be worried about, she decided, thinking of that last verse and of Mom's fussing. God had promised that there would always be harvests, so Dad would always have something to do. While the earth remaineth. And even the hot weather couldn't last forever. Winter would have to come along some day. And there was the blue plate. Now, if only Mom didn't look quite so sad, and if only she, Janey, could go to a "regular" school, the world wouldn't have much the matter with it, she thought. And as if to prove it, she heard Mom say just at that moment: "You can run over to Lupe's for a while if you want."

It was sundown before Mr. Larkin came home. The

shack had been settled for hours, the bed made, the suitcase shoved out of sight underneath it, while corn dodgers reposed in state in the middle of the table.

Once again, Janey was sitting on the top step to greet her father as soon as he should come into sight. Away off on the western edge of the world, a red and angry sun was being swallowed up in its own heat waves. It was nearly gone now, and the faintest hint of a breeze was beginning to stir a single hair here and there on Janey's tousled towhead. If only the wind would really make up its mind to blow, to blow good and hard and send this dead hot air ahead of it out of the valley, or at least to some other part of it! she thought.

And then a battered car came into sight up the road, and Janey, with a cry over her shoulder, "It's Dad!" was off the step in a bound and down to the road. She trotted along beside the car as it bumped across the uneven ground to the house—the heat, Mom's tired face, and even Lupe forgotten in this moment's joy. Dad was home again!

"Hi, young one," Mr. Larkin called as he slowly eased himself from behind the wheel. "Shouldn't run like that on a hot day. Your face's as red as a cock's comb."

Janey smiled happily and pressed close to him as he reached into the car and lifted out some parcels.

"Here," he said, "take these in to your mother while I lift out the cushion on the back seat."

Janey took the bundles into the house and presently her father appeared with the cushion to the back seat gripped awkwardly in his arms.

"Where do you want this?" he asked.

"Doesn't matter now," his wife answered. "When Janey goes to bed we'll put it across one of the doors. It'll be cooler."

For this was to be Janey's bed tonight as it had been for many, many nights before this one. In fact, Janey wouldn't have known how to sleep on anything else. It was all the bed she knew, and she found it entirely satisfactory in every way. Of course, now that she was ten, her feet stuck out over the end of it a little, but the suitcase, shoved across the end solved this difficulty.

"Will the job last very long, Dad?" Janey wanted to know.

"Can't say exactly. More than likely, though. We'll keep on irrigating for a while, and when picking starts I can't see any reason why I shouldn't get in on that too. You never come to the end of work in a cotton patch, Janey."

"What's the pay?" Mrs. Larkin asked.

"Two bits an hour, and I worked eight hours. How much is that, daughter? Quick now."

He whirled on Janey and stood grinning while she turned over in her mind this problem in mental arithmetic. She fastened her eyes on his as if she thought she could read the answer there. And just when the grin was broadening accusingly, "Two dollars!" shouted Janey, as quick as that.

"Correct," said her father, beaming. "That's a right pert child we're rearing under our roof."

"There are times when I'm glad it isn't our roof, like now," Mom returned, and walked heavily to the table where the parcels which held their supper lay alongside the corn dodgers.

"It isn't much to brag about and that's a fact," Mr. Larkin agreed, looking critically around him, "but it sure looks a sight better than it did this morning before you took it over."

Mom did smile at this, and Mr. Larkin, much encouraged, added in a teasing voice: "It must be awful to love to scrub as much as you do, Clara, and then never have a house worth scrubbing. Maybe it'll be different some day."

"Maybe," she returned briefly, the smile gone.

For a moment Mr. Larkin looked at her, his face suddenly sad and his shoulders drooping. Then he turned to Janey.

"Come on, young one. We'd better rustle up some more firewood before it gets dark."

Side by side, the two figures, one very tall, the other very short, both clad in faded blue overalls, moved slowly over the plain back of the shack. Each of them dragged a gunny-sack and into these they poked whatever pieces of greasewood branches or roots they could find. When the sacks were filled, Mr. Larkin took one in either hand and dragged them up to the back door. Then he and Janey took the water pail and went with it to the windmill in the neighboring field. It was necessary to open a gate strung with barbed wire in order to enter the field.

There were cattle in that field, large, red beasts that jogged away awkwardly and stood staring at the strangers as they opened the gate.

Janey hesitated.

"These steers won't bother us any. Not like real range cattle," Dad said, and Janey, apparently reassured, walked boldly beside him. Secretly, however, she was still a little apprehensive and regarded the cattle with suspicion.

"Lupe Romero from across the road came over today," Janey said while they waited for the bucket to fill. "She says the house we're in belongs to the man who owns this windmill and these cattle."

"Yes, I know," returned Mr. Larkin. "Her father told me this morning when I went over there."

"Does he know we're living in his house?" queried Janey.

"As far as I know he doesn't."

They were on the way back to the shack now. Janey closed the gate, then ran to catch up with her father, who had gone on ahead with the brimming bucket.

"Suppose he won't let us stay when he finds out; what will we do then?" she asked, a strange fear all at once seizing her. Suppose they should have to go away tomorrow or next day? She might never see Lupe again!

Mr. Larkin stopped and looked over her head to the west and thought a moment before replying. Janey searched his face anxiously.

"He'd probably let us stay if we paid him something every month. I'd rather do that than move to the cotton camp. We'd have to pay rent there anyway, and we're better off by ourselves, Janey, even if we have to do without some things in order to stay that way."

Janey nodded her head in quick agreement.

"The Romeros have stayed in their house for a year. Do you think he'd let us stay that long?"

"If we paid up, he probably would."

Suddenly a strange tingling began to creep all over Janey, and her chest felt all at once too small for what was going on inside of it. Perhaps they wouldn't have to move on after a month or so! Perhaps Dad was going to stay put and she and Lupe could become real friends. She might even go to school wherever Lupe did. A "regular" school, not just a camp school for roving children.

Before she could gather her wits for a proper reply, her father was speaking again. "We'll have to call a halt somewhere pretty soon, Janey. Mom isn't well, hasn't been for a long time. Maybe if she could stay long enough somewhere to get a real good rest, it would make a difference with her. It's hard to say, though."

"Then we'll stay as long as we can?" Janey asked.

"Yes, as long as we can."

Janey sighed and her bare toes dragged a little as she followed Dad to the house. It was the same old question and the same old answer. What wouldn't she give to be able to say just once: "We'll stay as long as we want to"!

When they got inside, they found supper ready for them. By moving the table over to the bed, there were seats enough for all three. After the dishes were washed, they sat on the front steps until bedtime. The little breeze had strengthened, and the moon was lighting earth and sky with a radiance that was like balm to eyes still smarting from too brilliant sunlight. From the top of a pole at the road's edge, a mocking-bird dropped three notes as silvery as the moon's own light.

" 'While the earth remaineth, seedtime and harvest, and cold and heat, and summer and winter, and day and night shall not cease,' " Janey remembered thankfully.

Across the road a light twinkled in the Romero house.

"And there's Lupe as long as we do stay," thought Janey with equal gratitude.

—DORIS GATES

Snow Is Your Friend

America's Northwest Frontier

Taku squatted before a cabin near Nome, on the Bering Sea in western Alaska. His white-haired grandfather, Karen, sat nearby on a packing case. The sun lighted Karen's wrinkled face, and made it look even browner.

Today the old man was teaching his grandson how to build an Eskimo snowhouse. This was a new thing to the twelve-year-old boy. His tribe of Eskimos no longer roamed the Arctic waste. Taku and his family and friends lived in wooden cabins clustered about a mission and a general store. The men hunted the seal no longer with harpoons, but with rifles. They had almost forgotten how to build the old-fashioned snow shelters.

Taku's grandfather had been a famous sealer. The boy listened eagerly to tales of the old man's adventures. Especially, Taku liked to hear about snowhouses; how they kept the Eskimo warm while zero weather raged outside, and how they had saved many a sealer's life.

"The bear hibernates in snow caves, the ptarmigan lives in winter under the soft snow," old Karen told the boy. "Snow is man's friend. Why doesn't he learn to use snow, and not to fear it? Gone would be his terror of cold and death in the Arctic."

Where Taku lived the snow was never deep. Now in April it had begun to melt into the brown tundra, so the construction of a snowhouse was not easy. The boy was wishing that he was old enough to go where there was real snow and ice—up to Kotzebue Sound, on the edge of the Arctic Circle. This month when the ice on the sea broke up, his father, Navook, would go there on his annual seal hunt.

Suddenly Taku straightened up, his snowhouse forgotten. His father stood at the cabin door talking with visitors —a tall man and a fair-haired boy, about Taku's age.

Karen and his grandson joined the group at the cabin door. Who were these white-skinned strangers, they wondered. It seemed that Captain John Horne had come from the United States to ask Navook, Taku's father, to take him sealing. They went into the house to talk over arrangements.

"Fine!" the Captain said, when everything was decided. He turned to Taku. "And why not take your boy with us? He would be company for my son, Dick."

The young Eskimo gasped with excitement. But Navook shook his head. "Taku is too young," the father replied. How his son hated those words, "Too young."

"Oh, please take me!" Taku begged. "I can look after the dogs. I'm not young. I'm big now, twelve years old."

"Why, I'm twelve too, and I'm going sealing!" exclaimed Dick Horne.

"At twelve I began to learn to be a sealer," old Karen added his plea. "My grandson should go."

Reluctantly Navook was won over. He could hardly refuse the white man. So it was decided that Taku should go on his first seal hunt. Pakok and Misi, skilled Eskimo hunters, agreed to go too. The next days were busy with preparations.

On a bright, sunny morning, with the ice of the Bering Sea turning mushy, they started north. Both sleds were packed high with tents, rifles, canned goods and hunting equipment. Taku helped his father hitch their dogs to his sled. The big huskies were so eager to go mushing that they leaped with impatience. They gave little yowls of pleasure.

Taku's mother, his grandfather and sister waved goodbye. "Good hunting!" they shouted, as the dog teams bounded off.

Dick Horne rode on one of the sleds. Taku ran along beside him. "How d'you like this?" he panted. The young Eskimo was proud of his mission English.

The white boy grinned. "It's swell!"

He's nice, Taku thought.

As they went north, the air became crisp and cold. Soon the snow was so deep that Taku sank in to his knees, as he helped to push through the sled. But the dogs liked the deep snow. It made easier pulling. In most places the drifts were hard, and the snow crunched under the sleds' swift-flying runners.

Without a mishap, the party reached the sealing grounds. The weather had turned mild, and ideal for sealing. The seals had dragged their sleek bodies from the water, up onto the ice which all winter had roofed them in. In every direction, they were napping in the warm sun.

Taku now learned the seal hunter's first lesson. "You must get near enough to a seal to shoot him," Navook told Captain Horne. For seals are wary animals. Every few minutes a seal wakes, and looks all about him. At the least sign of danger, he disappears through a hole in the ice.

Navook explained to the white man how the near-sighted seal can be fooled into thinking that a hunter is merely another seal. Captain Horne and the three Eskimo hunters lay down on the ice, and crawled cautiously up to the sleeping herd until they were near enough to shoot. Dick and Taku had no guns. But the boys wriggled over the ice, too. They pretended they were seals.

The hunt over, the sealing party started home. On the second day, Pakok and Misi decided to cut across Seward Peninsula and pick up some reindeer meat in a cache that they had built. The others would travel on down the coast. Navook's dogs were tired. The water-level route was the easiest.

"You'll save many miles by taking the short-cut across Imuruk Basin," Pakok told Navook, before they parted.

Next morning Navook's huskies came to the wide mouth of the river. The Eskimo hunter went ahead to test the ice.

"It's solid," he grunted with satisfaction.

At first the dogs were frightened. Their feet skidded on the ice, lightly powdered with snow. But soon they gained confidence. The sled runners fairly flew over the smooth white surface. It was the easiest traveling they had had on the trip.

"Too bad we can't go on ice all the way," said Captain Horne.

They were a half mile from land, where they would pick up the trail again, when Navook cried in terror: "Black ice, Taku! Look out!"

The young Eskimo's heart pounded at those dread words. They were on new, thin, "black ice," which is transparent, and dark because of the water close beneath it. Snow had covered the "black ice," so Navook had not recognized the danger. Now they could not turn back. Taku felt the fragile ice waver beneath the heavily-ladened sled. Even a halt would be fatal. And the shore, so near a minute ago, now seemed far away.

A crunch! The ice was breaking. Water splashed up over Taku's fur mukluks. The sled was cutting through!

"Mush! Mush!" he yelled at the dogs to pull hard.

It was too late. There was a splintering sound of ice,

as the sled lunged deeper into the water. Navok rushed back, a long knife in his hand. "Cut the dogs loose!" he cried. As the team bounded to safety, the men worked frantically to save what they could from the sinking sled. Then sadly they watched their belongings dragged down into the sea.

On the river bank, the two boys almost collapsed. The men were shaken, too.

"Travel on ice is dangerous, isn't it?" Captain Horne shuddered. "Give me good, firm ground after this!"

Navook nodded solemnly. "Ice and snow are always dangerous. They cannot be trusted. We saved time coming this way, but almost lost our lives."

Taku remembered what his grandfather had said. Snow was man's friend, if he would learn to use it, and not to fear it. The Eskimo boy wondered about that.

Well, here they were on dry land—and safe! Or were they? They had their dogs, but the sled with most of their food and equipment on it had vanished into the sea. They were far from any human habitation. And stronger and stronger came gusts of icy wind and snow. A late spring blizzard was brewing!

To make matters worse, Dick had turned his ankle in the mad scramble for shore. It was swollen and painful. They could not push on.

"We'll camp here overnight," Navook said.

Frozen willows lined the shore. With the aid of the waterproof matches that dog-mushers always carry, Navook kindled a blaze. The men and boys stretched out their wet mukluks to the fire. With feet dry, they felt better. Shelter for the night was the next need, and their tents had gone down with the sled. Navook began to dig a cave in a snowdrift, using a stick for a shovel. It was slow work.

"Why not build a snowhouse?" Taku suggested. "I know how, Grandfather taught me."

"Just the thing!" his father replied. Whipping out his long knife, he tested the snow.

Because of several changes in temperature, it had turned into granular or "corn snow," as it is called in Alaska. But on cutting a trial block, Navook decided the snow had enough "sticking power" to make a house. He set to work cutting blocks with his long knife. But Taku's father had never built an Eskimo snowhouse. Many of the squares of ice broke. Navook also made the error of placing the first tier in a circle flat on the ground.

"No, Father, like this—"

Taku showed the men what his grandfather had taught him—how the dome of a snowhouse is based on a circular, inclined plane. This slant is cut in the bottom tier. The succeeding layers rise in a spiral formation, each block supported on the bottom and on the side resting against the piece laid before. This makes it possible for the curved walls to lean inward without falling.

Navook and Taku made mistakes. In the second tier, they let the center of the blocks rest on the layer below. Several pieces fell.

"See, it's impossible! Against the law of gravity!" exclaimed the white man.

But Taku remembered now. Each square of snow as it is placed must rest only upon its two lower corners, and one of its upper corners must touch against the upper corner of the preceding piece. Taku showed his father how to make a strong wall.

Proudly, the boy stood inside the snowhouse beside Navook. Since the walls slope inward, the builder must stand within the circle of blocks, facing out. Slowly, the domed shelter took form. Each succeeding snow-square tilted farther inward until the forty-five degree angle was safely passed. The final roof blocks lay almost horizontal.

"Marvelous!" cried Captain Horne.

The white man and his son stood outside of the walls. They could not see what Taku and Navook were doing. Everyone knows that two handfuls of snow can be packed together to make one. In the same way, each piece of ice in a snowhouse sticks to the one next to it. When Navook laid a square high up in the roof, he could make it fast by a simple method—the only trick in snow building.

"See, Father, this way—"

Taku took Navook's long-bladed knife. He shaved down the far corner of each block until it melted and fused against the one underneath.

It was growing dark. They must hurry! Captain Horne and Dick were set to work gently forcing soft snow into the cracks between the squares. The joints thus filled would become solid, and stronger than the original blocks.

By dark, the "king" piece was fitted into the roof. The snowhouse was finished!

They were just in time. The blizzard was growing worse. The cold was intense. Navook fed the dogs. And they curled up in the snow to sleep. The two men and their sons crept through the long passage they had shoveled into their new home. This entrance was lower than the floor, so the cold air would flow down into the tunnel leaving the warm air in the dome. Navook made a small ventilation hole in the roof. He closed the door with a big piece of snow, and unrolled their sleeping bags. They were snug for the night.

Pulling a thermometer from his pocket, Captain Horne took a reading of the temperature in the snowhouse. It was twenty degrees below zero. Outside the wind was howling. But they could no longer hear the gale. Ten minutes later, Taku opened his parka and ripped off his fur gloves. It was getting warm! They rested and talked. Then the Captain took another temperature reading.

"Believe it or not!" He stared at the thermometer. "It's thirty-four degrees—two above freezing!"

All done in twenty minutes, by means of their body heat. Let the sub-zero storm rage outside, Taku thought. At least, they weren't going to freeze to death!

With a shelter over their heads, it was time to think about supper. Hot tea and crackers would taste mighty good! Captain Horne had managed to rescue his small gas-vaporing stove from the sinking sled. Filling a pail with snow, Navook put it over the flame on the stove to melt. In a few minutes the rise in temperature caused by the flame made fur caps and mukluks uncomfortable. It was almost too warm in the snowhouse!

Captain Horne looked at his thermometer again. "I can't believe it, it's fifty-five degrees!" He studied the instrument, in astonishment.

That night Taku slept comfortably, his sleeping bag unfastened. The others rolled up and slept well, too.

But the next morning snow was still falling. And Dick's ankle was worse. "We'll stay here," Navook said. "A boat will pass and rescue us."

His father looked worried, Taku knew why. What boat would pass at this time of year?

If they had to live in the snowhouse for several days, the shelter must be "iced." Navook did this by closing the door and turning up the gas-lamp. When the walls were melting and spongy, he removed the door block. Cold air rushed in, the hot air rose. In a few minutes the walls were coated with a thick film of ice, making the snowhouse even more wind-proof and strong.

Still, Captain Horne worried for fear that the roof might cave in.

"It can hold a weight stronger than you," Taku explained. Had not Karen, Taku's grandfather, once had such an ice shelter well tested—by a polar bear climbing over the roof!

The men and boys talked, drank tea and rested. By the second day the storm had ended. They took turns standing on a high rock to scan the sea for a boat.

On the fifth day, with food getting low, Taku heard an airplane overhead. Frantically, he waved. The plane sped away.

"Giant ptarmigan!" Taku ran to tell his father. For that is what the Eskimos call the airplane.

Had the plane seen them? The marooned men and boys kept a signal fire burning. Anxiously, they waited. But the fog closed down over them. If a ship came looking for them, it could pass close by and not see them.

Two days later, their hopes of rescue were growing dim. They were faint from hunger. Suddenly Taku's sharp ears heard a sound. "Oooooo—"

It was a foghorn, close by. Taku caught sight of a Coast Guard ice cutter coming into the bay through the fog. With a shout, the boy raced down to the shore. He jumped up onto a rock, where he could be seen. He waved and waved.

The Coast Guard boat stopped.

An hour later, the marooned men and boys were safely aboard the ice cutter, headed toward home. "It was a lucky thing that plane saw you," the skipper told them.

"But it was your snowhouse that saved our lives, Taku," Captain Horne made the young Eskimo proud by saying. The white man turned to the skipper, "Why doesn't every soldier in Alaska, every pilot and mountain climber learn to build snowhouses, instead of carrying heavy fabric tents?"

Taku wondered, too.

"And how about Boy Scouts?" asked Dick. "When I get home to St. Paul, I'm going to teach my scout troop how to build an Eskimo bungalow."

"Perhaps snow is man's friend, after all," said Navook.

Taku nodded. It might have been his grandfather speaking.

—ALICE CURTIS DESMOND

Told Under Spacious Skies

Compiled by the Literature Committee

of the

ASSOCIATION FOR CHILDHOOD EDUCATION INTERNATIONAL

MABEL ALSTETTER, Professor of English, Miami University, Oxford, Ohio

MAY HILL ARBUTHNOT, Associate Professor, Western Reserve University, Cleveland, Ohio

LELAND B. JACOBS, Assoc. Prof. of Education, The Ohio State University, Columbus, Ohio

ROSEMARY LIVSEY, Director Library Work with Children, Los Angeles Public Library, Los Angeles, Cal.

KATHERINE M. REEVES, Associate Professor of Child Development, Cornell University, Ithaca, New York

JENNIE WAHLERT, Consultant Early Childhood Education, Saint Louis Public Schools, St. Louis, Mo.

EVELYN WENZEL, Indiana State Teachers College, Terre Haute, Indiana

MARY LINCOLN MORSE, Chairman.

By Way of Explanation

Told Under Spacious Skies is the seventh collection of stories covering the work of the Association's Literature Committee over a period of a quarter of a century.

Told Under the Green Umbrella, our initial collection of folk and fairy tales, took its title from Hans Christian Andersen's story of "Olé Luköié, the Dustman." As the story goes, Olé comes nightly to the bedside of boys and girls, bringing with him a green umbrella covered with pictures. This he holds over "the good children, and then they dream the most delightful stories all night long." As all of our succeeding collections bring delightful stories to children, and in spite of the fact that only four of them carry its word in their titles, each one of the series has come to be known as an "Umbrella" book. With no determined plan for steadily venturing in the publishing field, each of our story collections has grown out of a sense of its need at the time of inception. *Told Under the Blue Umbrella,* a compilation of real or "nearly real" stories, naturally followed our folk and fairy tales, as likewise did *Sung Under the Silver Umbrella,* an anthology of verse.

At this point, both our committee and our Association members had become collection-minded. As one "Umbrella" book came from the press, others suggested themselves or were requested, and a choice of an added compilation demanded committee consideration.

Told Under the Magic Umbrella grew out of an appreciation of the many stories for children then available in the field of modern fancy. On demand, in the hope of laying a foundation for children's understanding and respect for each other's background, *Told Under the Stars and Stripes* developed. Here we gathered stories of children living under the flag of our country while still maintaining in their homes the customs and traditions inherent in the lands from which their families had come.

Again, realizing that behind both home and community life two differing festivals—Christmas of the Christians and Hanukkah, the Jewish Festival of Lights—come concurrently, and believing that children could both share and be helped to honor each festival for its own basic meanings to others, *Told Under the Christmas Tree* came into being. Here are grouped representative stories of each of the two beautiful annual festivals.

This brief résumé brings us up to date regarding the underlying purposes of our "Umbrella" books. Likewise, it brings us to our present collection, *Told Under Spacious Skies*.

That a collection of regional stories should become a committee project was decided by majority vote. This decision grew out of committee thinking that boys and girls living in widely varying localities and in different social, economic, and cultural backgrounds need to understand what, on the whole, it may mean to live in America.

How better than through a story can a country child come to know what it means to live in a city in a crowded tenement on a noisy, bustling street? Or, again, in a city's privileged home with the many cultural opportunities cities offer? How can a city child learn more easily of tilled fields and woods, of animals and nature life, than through a tale of the country? How else or more effectively than in a story read or heard can a child living in the mountains or on a prairie realize what it means to live in a mining region and to work in a mine? America is both diverse and challenging. Its spacious skies cover many differing regions, many a divergent type of activity, many a varied pattern of life.

In seeking stories of American life, it was decided, after considerable deliberation and some regrets, to limit our choice to those dealing with present-day life. Our stories attempt to interpret this period to America's mid-century child. At no time have we thought of America as so many states, each one having its own regional story or stories. We did, however, hope to find tales of typical areas with their own significant impact on children written into each selection. Committee research led us to a direct appeal to individual authors for original stories, to children's magazines, and to already published books in which we sought regional stories not otherwise available. Our contacts with individual authors, although they often were not free to write the stories we were seeking, reinforced the high regard in which we have always held the men and women now so ably writing for children.

The main activity of some of our chosen stories might easily have resulted in a story quite different in many of its aspects, had it been placed—and legitimately so—in another region. Peter's lamb, in "Mountain Born," might have come to life on a sheep ranch in Montana as well as on a farm in New Hampshire. Of her story, Elizabeth Yates wrote us: "Sheep-raising is coming back more and more in rural New England. All my information for *Mountain Born* was drawn from a local shepherd here in New Hampshire. I did not state its region in the story because I wanted to keep it universal in feeling."

The flood itself in the story of "The Isle of Que" might likewise have happened along the banks of the Ohio or Mississippi rivers. Here, too, a story having a different setting, different economic backgrounds and human characteristics, might have resulted.

In selecting the above stories, as it did with all we decided to use, it seemed important to our committee members to consider not only that we were seeking typical area stories, showing their influences on the activities and characters of the boys and girls involved, but that we were also seeking stories that were well written as such. This we thought true of both "Mountain Born" and "The Isle of Que."

Of Ann Clark's story of "The Hogan" from *Little Navajo Bluebird* she wrote us: "The Navajo reservation lies within New Mexico and also Arizona. I did my research for it largely in Arizona. A perfectionist might catch you in a local description. It might be safe to credit it to both states."

Lois Lenski wrote of her story "Down from the Hills," "This is a true story. I actually saw and talked to these people; also to a number of the townspeople who so completely misunderstood them. The whole experience was a tremendous one for me, and has many angles and reverberations. It is one of those actual incidents in real life which can be re-told from the point of view of a number of people."

Up to this point we have been emphasizing such regional stories as we have secured. There were some that we failed to find. That no characteristic story of the Pacific Northwest came through was a disappointment, or of southern Louisiana or Mississippi. Because of limited space, we regretfully removed an Hawaiian story, thinking it wise to limit our collection to continental America. At this point, the stories lacking in *Told Under Spacious Skies* we leave to later interpretation by authors living in representative regions, or to others, like Lois Lenski, our Foreword writer, who move designedly into a chosen community, breathe its atmosphere, share its life, and then, because of what is there, write into tales of children the influences brought to bear on what they become.

To the many teachers, librarians, and authors who have helped us generously with suggestions and advice, our genuine thanks. To the publishers who have contributed through the release of stories owned by them, our recognition for their helpfulness. To our Foreword writer, Lois Lenski, and our illustrator, William Moyer, our sincere appreciation for their contribution to our collection of regional tales.

Here we present *Told Under Spacious Skies*. This we do with the hope that its stories will help children everywhere to understand the varied patterns of life that exist in the United States of America and the courage and self-reliance they engender.

—MARY LINCOLN MORSE
Chairman Literature Committee

1952

SC
Ass   Ass'n. for Childhood
            Education
        Told under spacious skies

11760

Date Due

AR 13 80			
MAY 5			
SEP 23			
DEC			